Streaking At Harvard

Christopher E. Smith

Writers Club Press
San Jose New York Lincoln Shanghai

Streaking At Harvard

Writers Club Press
an imprint of iUniverse.com, Inc.

For information address:
iUniverse.com, Inc.
620 North 48th Street, Suite 201
Lincoln, NE 68504-3467
www.iuniverse.com

This is a work of fiction. Any similarities between the descriptions of people, conversations, and events and actual people, conversations, and events are purely coincidental.

ISBN: 0-595-10060-0

Printed in the United States of America

To Abe
Confidant, Adventurer, and Raconteur

Preface

The world changed when I was born. The Eisenhower era of the 1950s is seldom acknowledged as a time of dramatic transformation and radical change. But it was. A new era began at the time of my birth in 1958 and people's lives were never again the same. When I tell people this simple fact, I am sometimes accused of being immodest. But a fact is a fact. I cannot avoid the truth. The world really did change. Of course, it didn't change because of my birth. The change just happened to coincide with my birth. What happened when I was born? Explorer One, the American response to Sputnik, blasted off into space exactly three weeks before I was born. The Space Age began and we left the time of black-and-white television in order to rocket into the age of Teflon and Tang.

My life was shaped by the power of science and technology. The mere fact that humankind dared to defy gravity by sending a satellite into space at the time of my birth disrupted the heavens to such a degree that I was doomed to a life of odd events and bizarre experiences. It must have taken weeks (if not longer) for nature to restore the balance in the universe that was shattered by satellites and rockets blasting into space for the first time. Thus those of us who were born in the moments before that balance was restored were imprinted with an element of chaos that would haunt us for all of our days. I should have recognized this fact when I spent my childhood in places called Paw Paw and Kalamazoo rather than in cities with normal names like Chicago and Boston.

My life was shaped in another way by science and technology. In the year 2000, researchers discovered that babies who are breast fed have higher IQs than babies given formula in bottles. Suddenly, more than four decades after my birth, I can see a partial explanation for many events in life. Like other mothers in the 1950s, my mother put her faith in science and thereby fed me the latest commercial creation purported to be superior to mother's milk. I was handicapped for life by the illusion of scientific progress. There's no telling what those extra IQ points might have meant to me. If I had been breast fed, I might have gone to Yale Law School and ended up as a justice on the Supreme Court instead of galloping naked around Harvard Yard and ending up, well, you'll see soon enough.

This is not my life story. I'm not *that* egotistical. Besides, tracing a particular time line can be boring. Instead, these are my life's stories. Stories are the things of which memories are made. I don't think of my life in linear terms. My life is a series of events that produced memories. These memories jump back and forth in my mind without regard to chronology. They are grouped topically in my memory banks, not unlike the books in the Library of Congress. However, unlike the Library of Congress, which is brimming with books, I hope that I have plenty of shelf space left in my brain to gather and organize as many memories in my second forty-two years as I did in my first.

Because these are my life's stories, they are completely true except for the parts that I made up. I actually encountered all of the celebrities described in this book, except for Sinbad and Bill Gates. I'm pretty sure that I encountered Sinbad, but I am more uncertain about Bill Gates. Because these are "stories" and not news reports, I have taken the liberty to fill in the gray areas to complete gaps in my memories and improve events that would otherwise have been less humorous. The contexts described are mostly real, but the actual conversations are often embellished. Hey, I've been entertained by my descriptions of my life, both real and imagined, and I want my readers to be entertained, too. I have disguised the identities of most people, so any similarities between the descriptions of these people (and events) and actual people (and events) are purely coincidental. To the lawyers out there: Trust me, there is nothing defamatory here, except for all of the stories that ultimately harm *my* reputation.

I am grateful to best-selling author and NPR commentator David Sedaris for his quick, trans-Atlantic response to my request for advice. I took his words as encouragement and as an implicit invitation to invade his genre. I am also very grateful to my Harvard brother, best-selling author and comedian Al Franken. He has never heard of me, but I used his name to get some people to read the manuscript. Thanks, Al!

I also must thank many friends who encouraged me to write this book after hearing me tell my stories or reading the first written versions of these chapters. With apologies to my deserving friends who are omitted from this list (my memory banks are declining with age), I extend my gratitude to Dan Alpert, Melissa Crimp, Joyce Baugh, Mary Graham, Mike Reisig, Steve Mastrofski, Ronna Lodato, and Gregg Vandekieft. Hopefully others will share their view that there is something here worth reading.

Finally, I thank my family for permitting me to write this book. They cooperated on the condition that I keep them out of the stories. They held up their end of the bargain, despite the fact that I did not manage to hold up mine.

Contents

Chapter One

At Least I Have My Health

"At least you have your health."

Now there's a line that I've heard a million times, usually expressed with a sense of reassurance. No matter what else is going wrong in life, you still have your health. But what if your health is bad?

On one occasion, while standing at the end of my driveway and holding the remnants of my mailbox in my hands (it had just been crushed by a passing snowplow), my neighbor wandered over from shoveling his driveway and initiated his usual neighborly conversation.

"So how's it going?"

I looked down at the mailbox pieces in each hand and pondered whether to reply with the usual, "Oh, everything's fine." At this moment, however, I felt cold, wet, and annoyed. Thus I decided to follow my New Year's resolution: I was going to be honest with everyone.

"Well, actually the snowplow just ran over my mailbox. It's only 10 degrees so the ground is frozen. Thus even if I could dig through this three-foot snow drift, I could never pound the mailbox post back into the ground. How am I going to have my mail delivered without a mailbox? In addition, my grandfather just had a stroke and the entire family is distraught worrying about him. To top it off, something's wrong with my car. It absolutely refuses to start in this cold weather and they tell me it will cost over $500 to have it repaired."

My neighbor stepped back with a look of surprise. This was definitely not the usual chitchat about the weather. Thinking quickly, he said, "Oh, well, at least you have your health."

"Not exactly. I'm just recovering from the flu, a patch of psoriasis is growing on my forehead, and I have this abdominal pain that could be appendicitis, but I'm not sure which side of my body my appendix is supposed to be on. If it's not my appendix, I'm worried that I have an ulcer or some kind of tumor. I also think I'm getting some kind of wart on my foot, and the arthritis in my knee is killing me." Before I could go on about certain gastrointestinal issues, I noticed him backpedaling with a look of shock and revulsion. So I paused and waited for his response. My forthright honesty had finally challenged the time-tested slogan about health. After having endured that line about health from parents, relatives, and acquaintances for many years, I was anxious to stand up against the usual unthinking patter from people who can't accept responsibility for hearing bad news after asking a question that invites just such news. If you feign interest in someone, even if you're just trying to be polite, then you should be able to deal with the truth.

He shrugged his shoulders, obviously unsure how to respond to this torrent of gloom and doom, and started to trudge back toward his driveway. Then he stopped suddenly and turned around. "If you don't have your health, then I guess you really have nothing," he remarked.

Nothing! Now there was an unsettling thought. Suddenly I pictured myself standing naked and alone, adrift on an iceberg, staring across a patch of water and the endless, empty frozen tundra. This image of nothingness jolted me. He had handed my gloom and doom right back to me. The thought that I had nothing was too unsettling to leave as the last spoken word. So I called after him, "Wait a minute. I think you were right the first time. I do have my health. It just happens to be bad, but at least it's *my* health. It's not nothing. It's something and it's mine." He continued to trudge away without looking back. By this time, I was desperately hoping to gain some acknowledgment that I did at least possess my own health, as bad as it may be. "Thanks for asking anyway," I yelled, still unable to escape the thought that I might actually possess "nothing" if I publicly acknowledged all of my health problems.

As a result of this episode, I am a firm believer in the saying that "at least you have your own health." It's mine, good or bad, and it's a lot better than having nothing. Besides your health is always there to give you something to think about. Or in my case, worry about.

*　　　　　*　　　　　*

We all become members of various groups, some exclusive and some not. I remember the day I became a hypochondriac, or rather the night when it happened. It wasn't like other memorable membership dates, like the day I joined Boy Scouts, with welcoming comments and handshakes all around. Becoming a hypochondriac is like being drafted into permanent service by an uncontrollable superforce. You're its slave day after day, yet you're convinced that you are doing all of this to benefit yourself. You are saving your own life by vigilant (make that *hyper-vigilant*) monitoring of your health. In reality, the beneficiaries seem to be the medical professionals whose continued employment and rising incomes are dependent upon your service to the hypochondriacal cause. I think they have a course in medical school called "Cultivating Hypochondria 101." In this course, they teach aspiring doctors to say such things as, "Hmmm, keep a close watch on that pimple. I think I'll need to take a look at it on a weekly basis" and "Sometimes stomach discomfort can mean a serious case of…never mind, you just come back to see me whenever you feel a sensation there." Do you think some physician put a timed-release dependency drug in my infant vitamins so that I would suddenly emerge as a hypochondriac one day? Sort of like a "Night of the Living Dead" scenario, except we hypochondriacs are acting out a film entitled

"Lifetime of the Desperate to Live." We roam the earth in search symptoms, diagnoses, and treatments. All at a price, of course.

My induction notice to the army of hypochondriacs arrived late one night when I was in college. After an emotional conversation with my girlfriend lasting several hours and concerning some forgettable but, at that time, seemingly all-important aspect of our relationship, I suddenly heard her yell, "I never want to see you again." She slammed down the receiver. The jarring click and dial tone, which so abruptly ended a lengthy emotional experience, set my heart racing in surprise. It was about 3 a.m. and as I lay down to try to go to sleep, my heart kept racing. In fact, it seemed to beat faster and faster. As my pounding heartbeats kept me wide awake, I noticed that I was breathing faster and faster. My lungs and heart were seemingly engaged in an out-of-control race toward an unknown destination. As the racing internal organs went faster and faster, suddenly my brain got involved with a strange, dizzying sensation.

"This is odd," I thought to myself. "I don't remember ever feeling dizzy before while lying down." My mind began a quick search of available memory records to see if I could remember feeling this sensation before. As the search of my memory banks proceeded, the dizziness began to build and build, as if heading toward some significant crescendo. I felt myself approaching something. Some event. Some conclusion. Something unfamiliar that I could not identify. The dizziness kept building with the rapid breaths and racing heartbeats, and I went through a quick checklist of remembered physical events.

"I don't feel nauseous," I thought, "so I'm not headed toward being violently ill. I fainted before once on a hot day in church as a child with a too-tight collar and clip-on tie, but this doesn't feel like I'm going to faint." My mind continued rapidly with its logical analysis. "This sort of feels like I might faint, since I feel so dizzy that the room is spinning, but it's not that same fainting feeling." Hmmmm. "So if I'm not going to faint, then it must be that I'm going to…DIE!!!!!"

The exact moment that my logical analysis led me to the word "die," I leaped out of bed and ran down the hall into my roommate's room. I jumped into my roommate's bed at 3 a.m. and began shaking him violently to get him to wake up. Without opening his eyes, he grabbed me in a bearhug and mumbled, "Oh Sylvia, you know I like it rough." Oddly, Sylvia was *my* girlfriend's name, or my ex-girl friend after that phone call. His girlfriend was named Janet, but I was so panicked that I didn't have time to ponder what my girlfriend was doing in his dream. Actually, I guess I knew what my girlfriend was doing in his dream, but I never stopped to ask why she was doing it.

Pushing away from him, I slapped him across the face with my hand. "Wake up, will ya," I shouted desperately.

His eyes shot wide open and he bolted upright in bed. "What's going on?," he cried.

"I don't know. I feel so dizzy. My heart is beating out of my chest. I can't stop myself from breathing faster and faster. I thought I was going to faint. But then I figured out that I'm not going to faint, so then I thought…."

He jumped up and began pulling on a sweatshirt. "Let's go to the hospital. Can you get your shoes on?"

"I think so," I yelled as I ran down the hall. I pulled on my shoes and he grabbed my arm and helped me down the stairs.

By the time we arrived at the emergency room, I felt less dizzy although my heart was still beating too fast. Instead of feeling dizzy, my thoughts ran wildly through a list of horrible outcomes. Was I having a heart attack? Maybe it's a stroke. Perhaps some kind of attack that doctors have never seen before.

When I was lying in a bed in the emergency room, a doctor began to question me about whether I had taken any drugs. The doctor did not seem to believe my denials about the use of illicit drugs. However, his experience with shaggy-haired college students' late night visits to the emergency room during that era of the1970s may have led him to have reasonable (albeit erroneous) doubts about my denials. However, he had no choice but to move ahead and consider alternative diagnoses.

I did not realize it at the time, but I was at the threshold of a major life-altering moment, and my fate was in the hands of a suspicious physician with whom I had been acquainted for all of ninety seconds. At that moment, the rest of my life would have been entirely different if that physician had said to me, "Have you ever had an anxiety attack?" To which I would have replied, "What's an anxiety attack?" Then he could have answered, "An anxiety attack is an event in which someone's heart races, their palms sweat, and they start to breathe so rapidly and deeply that they become dizzy. Many people have these attacks as a physical component of psychological distress. This may be brought on by some emotional event, a phobia, or even unexplainable circumstances. A young person your age is typically not at risk of permanent harm from such an event, and you merely need to learn how to recognize when anxiety attack symptoms may be developing so that you can respond in a way to interrupt or diminish the physical symptoms. For example, many people breathe into a paper bag in order to reduce the dizziness that can develop from getting excessive oxygen through accelerated breathing and rapid heartbeat. Think about your life at this moment and try to identify any circumstances or events that might be emotionally or psychologically troubling and thereby served to trigger your physical symptoms." If the doctor had said all of these things, then everything would have made sense to me. The unknown would have evaporated and I would have had an understandable explanation for what I was going through. Unfortunately, I never heard this speech. Not then. Not ever.

Instead, as the doctor looked at the hospital admission papers in my file, his training led him in a different direction. I don't know if it was simply that I was obviously on the edge of believing that I had a terminal illness or if he noticed that I was a student at Harvard so that he concluded, "This guy will probably make enough money some day so that he can help pay for summer homes for a whole bunch of physicians." Whatever he was thinking, his training had accurately taught him that I was a fish just waiting to be reeled into the net of hypochondria and medical dependency. He quickly drew upon his schooling in "Cultivating Hypochondria 101." Thus he said, "Did anyone ever tell you that you might have high blood pressure?" I had never had an elevated blood pressure reading before that moment, but forever afterward I had borderline (or worse) high blood pressure readings every time someone in a white coat strapped that cuff on my arm. The hypertension seed was planted in my brain, and it was all I could think about every time my blood pressure was ever measured after that moment. The worry-mode into which my brain switched at the sight of a sphygmomanometer (you see, we hypochondriacs even learn the technical terms for diseases and medical devices, this one is the thing used to measure blood pressure) moved my blood pressure higher, kind of like magical levitation just from involuntarily chanting the mantra, "I hope my blood pressure isn't high; I hope my blood pressure isn't high; I hope my blood pressure isn't high…." Works every time, and a couple of internists, cardiologists, and pharmaceutical companies reaped the financial benefits for years afterward.

As if that wasn't enough, the doctor followed up by saying, "You need to have somebody take a look at those moles. You've got an awful lot of them and you never know when one will turn into skin cancer." On that basis alone, I began to devote nearly ten hours a week to mirror gazing. Not the kind where you admire your hair-do, clothes, or physique. No. This was the kind where you compulsively stare for hours at small brown dots on your body, hoping that you don't detect any growth or movement right before your eyes.

Thus I became a card-carrying member of the hypochondriacs' union. The union's official membership card used to say, "Blue Cross/Blue

Shield," but now the union's membership has diversified into various HMOs and other health plans. A lot of people want a piece of our action.

I was convinced that I had a terminal illness that simply had not been diagnosed yet. Hypochondriacal thoughts became a daily preoccupation. I knew now to worry about hypertension and melanoma, but once I got in the habit of worrying, it was easy to worry about everything else, too. I remember seeing an old *Life* magazine article about a woman in Alabama who was injured when a small meteor smashed through the roof of her house and struck her on the leg. As a good union member, I was obligated to lie awake every night for a week worrying about becoming the next meteor victim. I eventually solved this problem by sleeping on the floor under a steel table. It wasn't comfortable, but it had the added of benefit of giving me extra protection in case of an earthquake. Or a plane crashing into the house…or a tree falling on top of my room…or a…you get the picture. By becoming a hypochondriac, I found that I would never be bored again because I had my health, or perhaps more accurately, my health had me.

*   *   *

I went to the university health center to find a doctor whom I could visit regularly, especially to monitor my blood pressure and potentially cancerous moles (of which I have millions thanks to my genetic inheritance from my leopard-like father). When I arrived at the health center and inquired about registering as a regular patient with some specific doctor, the nurse at the desk began to think aloud about which doctor would be best for me. Before she could come to a conclusion, a voice behind her said emphatically, "Send him to Dr. Benson." The voice came from a stern-looking older woman whose forceful manner was not unlike that of the elementary school principal who struck terror into our hearts with her withering glare alone.

"Dr. Benson? Are you sure that's best?" Clearly the nurse at the desk did not think that was best. It was just as obvious, however, that she didn't want to disagree with her stern-looking colleague.

"Send him to Dr. Benson." The voice had moved beyond emphatic to sound downright threatening.

"Okay, if you say so," said the nurse with a shrug. I couldn't help noticing that she was shaking her head as she spoke. Her body language practically screamed, "*No!* Bad idea," but she put me down for an appointment with Dr. Benson anyway. Hey, it was no skin off her nose. Benson was going to be working on me, not her.

I found this episode disconcerting, but it was not nearly as disconcerting as when I met Dr. Benson. He appeared to be well into his eighties and he could barely move about the room. He squinted so intently at me through his thick glasses that I wasn't sure he could actually see me clearly. His gruff manner gave me doubts about whether or not he was actually listening to me.

When he checked my blood pressure, it was high (of course). Thus he ordered a variety of tests, nothing pleasant enough to discuss, such as collecting urine for twenty-four straight hours. Yeah, storing that container in my dorm room was a real joy. ("Hey man, is that homemade beer in that bucket?" "No, and please don't taste it!"). I also had to have dye injected into my veins and then have my kidneys X-rayed to see how long it took for the dye to travel through my system. The problem with this test was that just before injecting me with the dye the X-ray technician asked me, "Are you allergic to shellfish?"

"Shellfish? What do you mean by that?"

"You know. Lobster and stuff like that."

"No. Not that I know of. Why do you ask?"

"Because people who are allergic to shellfish are also allergic to this dye and sometimes they could have a fatal reaction to the injection." Of course she said this as she slid the needle into my vein. As it happened, after growing up on a Midwestern diet of macaroni and hot dogs, I didn't even know if I had ever eaten shellfish.

Fatal reaction! "Holy cow, what if I am allergic to shellfish and I just don't know it," I thought as my mind began racing. As the needle went into my arm, my life passed before my eyes. My heartbeat and breathing took off in a reenactment of my original anxiety attack. I thought I would faint while lying flat on the table. I managed to hold myself still and remain conscious while I waited for the end to arrive. As it turned out, the X-ray technician concluded the session by remarking, "Boy, that was odd. The dye didn't go through like it should. I wonder what that means?"

Just what I needed, another expression of uncertainty by a medical professional. For me such statements merely lifted the lid on the Pandora's Box of my brain and unleashed frightening scenarios of fatal illnesses and a slow, painful demise. Now I was absolutely convinced that I had a fatal illness. It was only a matter of time before they found out what it was.

*   *   *

I became skeptical of Dr. Benson's abilities when he directed his attention toward my potentially cancerous moles. I obeyed his command to remove my shirt and then watched him press his face against my chest as he tried to examine the moles through his thick glasses. Thank heavens he wasn't panting or it would have seemed just as if a dog was sniffing my body (which actually might have been preferable in some ways). To make matters even worse, here was a doctor who did not merely store his stethoscope in a refrigerator, he kept his hand in the icebox with it. Every time his finger pressed against a spot on my flesh, I jumped as his ice cube digits numbed my skin. I was reduced to closing my eyes and gritting my teeth as I tried to hold still during this bizarre examination. Suddenly Benson leaped back from the examining table.

"Oh my goodness," he exclaimed. "You were right after all. You do need to have a mole removed."

My eyes flew open and I saw Benson reach for the phone. He hurriedly dialed a number and barked orders, "Nurse Johnson, call Dr. Stewart right away. I think we need to schedule a skin surgery as soon as possible."

Instantly, my palms became wet, my heart began racing, and I started to feel dizzy. Oh, oh, here comes another anxiety attack.

Benson continued to talk excitedly into the phone. "I never encountered a mole like this before. It has an irregular shape, a raised texture, and it actually seems to have a small tumor or other growth emerging from the center. If Stewart even thinks he's going to publish an article about this case, then I will demand credit as co-author. This is such an extraordinary case that I think we can get this published in the *New England Journal of Medicine* or perhaps in the...."

I quickly waved my hand back and forth in Benson's direction. In a loud stage whisper, I interrupted his conversation by asking, "Dr. Benson, which mole is it?"

"...*Journal of the American Medical Association*. The biopsy slides will need to be preserved of course, and...." As Benson continued his excited chatter, he pointed a long bony finger toward my chest. "...if it turns out as I suspect, there may be a second article for a pathology journal. The slides will probably need to be photographed for inclusion in future editions of dermatology textbooks. And another thought that comes to mind...."

Benson's rambling became mere background noise as I looked down to the spot at which Benson pointed. My mind was reeling with the thought that one small spot on my skin could turn out to be the lethal implement of my life's destruction. As I fixed my gaze on the spot, I felt consumed by a sense of horrific shock. "Dr. Benson! Dr. Benson!" I yelled loudly to get his attention.

Benson stopped in mid-sentence, apparently stunned that I would be so rude as to interrupt his important conversation. "What is it?," he snapped at me.

"Dr. Benson, take a closer look. That's not a mole. That's my nipple!"

Benson froze momentarily, telephone still in hand, and then leaned over to peer intently at my chest again. He suddenly turned his face away from me, and began speaking into the phone in a quiet voice. "On second thought, don't call Stewart just yet. I think I'll get a second opinion from someone else here before proceeding further. Don't do anything about this unless I call you again. Thanks."

After that incident, I decided I should try a different doctor, hopefully one whose eyesight would still provide the necessary qualification for obtaining a driver's license.

*   *   *

My next appointment was with Dr. Davidson. I made sure that the stern senior nurse was nowhere to be seen when I got my recommendation for a new staff physician at the reservation desk. I was thrilled to see that Davidson did not even wear glasses. At my request, Dr. Davidson examined a mole that I thought looked suspicious. It was a dark red circle enclosed within a lighter red circle, or so I thought (but since I suffer from red-green color blindness I was probably not the best authority on the color of the mole). I watched while Davidson carefully measured the dark red inner circle. As she made her measurements, I did not find it reassuring when she said, "I really haven't done much with moles before, but I really enjoyed my dermatology rotation during my training so this is a great opportunity for both of us to learn more together. I firmly believe that the patient is an equal partner in the processes of preventive medicine." I would have preferred a physician who said, "I'm a leading expert and I'll know immediately if there are any problems that require treatment," but apparently such expertise and confidence were too much to hope for, especially among staff physicians at a university health center. I was pleased to see that Davidson was meticulous and scientific in recording her notes about the mole's diameter, shape, and color. So I left with a general feeling of optimism when she said, "Come back in six weeks and let's see if it has changed any."

I stared at that mole every day. I checked it in the mirror and looked at it directly. I watched it intently at least ten times each day. No matter how much I watched it, it still looked the same. The color and shape seemed odd to me, but it definitely wasn't changing. I saw Davidson six weeks later to the day and I watched while she carefully measured the light red outer circle. When she recorded her notes about its diameter, shape, and color and compared them to her prior measurements, she reflexively blurted out, "Oh, my gosh, it has doubled in size! We have to get this thing removed."

Now, for the first time, I actually had a doctor concerned that I faced an imminent demise, and one who implicitly indicated that my hypochondriacal fears were not merely imaginary. I was perfectly calm about her announcement, however, because I knew that Davidson had measured the *wrong part of the mole*. Instead of measuring the inner circle again, she measured the entire area. Kind of like looking at the population of New York City and later examining the population of the tri-state metro area of New York, New Jersey, and Connecticut and feeling surprised that the population of New York had "grown" so much. Despite my knowledge of this glaring error, I didn't say anything. I figured I might just as well get the mole removed. Then instead of constantly checking a million moles, I would only have to worry about 999,999.

When I went to see the surgeon, he started drawing on my stomach absent-mindedly with the same ballpoint pen that he was using to make notes in my file. I felt like one of those diagrams of a cow that shows where the different cuts of meat come from. The actual surgery wasn't so bad. I didn't feel anything except the pull of the needle when he put in the stitches. However, my heart did start racing a bit when I could see what appeared to be a significant amount of blood on the gauze that the nurse periodically applied as a blotter on the spot of the incision. Actually, I should say that the *first* surgery wasn't so bad. However, when the report came back from pathology that the mole showed unusual cell activity, the surgeon decided to go back and cut out a larger area. This time it hurt, since he had to stretch the skin farther to sew me back together. Worst of all, of course, the pathology report merely confirmed my fears about my impending doom.

I immediately bought a magnifying glass so that I could examine my other moles more closely. Since I carried the magnifying glass with me everywhere, people started calling me "Sherlock." However, instead of Sherlock Holmes, they called me, "Sherlock Narcissist," as if I derived some kind of perverse pleasure out of my medical self-examinations. Hey, it isn't easy to twist around in a way that will enable you to examine a mole on your backside with a magnifying glass. In the dorm bathroom, I could hear people whisper, "Why is that guy always looking at himself in the mirror? And what's with the magnifying glass?" The whispered answer was usually something along the lines of "You got me. That body ain't much to look at." At least these comments were better than the occasional, "Hey Sherlock, there's a mysterious pimple on your butt. Maybe you can get your faithful friend Watson to examine it for you." These comments were, of course, always accompanied by derisive laughter. None of this bothered me, however. I was going to have to save my own life since I knew I couldn't count on Benson's eyesight or Davidson's measurement skills.

*   *   *

By the time I was in my twenties, I had learned about anxiety attacks, not from a medical journal, but from a comedic movie in which macho Burt Reynolds has an anxiety attack and is reduced to breathing into a paperbag. Once I knew what it was, I could consciously calm myself if I ever felt my anxiety rising. Anxiety attacks became a thing of the past. (Mostly anyway. Well, I'm not required to admit that they continued, so I won't. Okay, I had those feelings a few more times, but it wasn't so bad. Really. I mean it.) Anyway, with the major anxiety attacks behind me, physicians examining me remained concerned about my skin cancer risk. Whenever they questioned me about my medical history and heard about the mole that showed unusual cell activity, they immediately instructed me to submit to periodic mole inspections.

The first internist who looked over my moles saw one that appeared odd to him. So he arranged for a plastic surgeon to remove the mole. As fate would have it, this was an extremely careful plastic surgeon who only did surgical procedures in a hospital surgery suite. Unlike the surgeon at the university health center, who did the surgery on-campus in an outpatient surgery room armed only with a hypodermic needle of anesthetic, a scalpel, and some stitches, the plastic surgeon had me hooked up to an automatic blood pressure monitor, a heart monitor, and an oxygen tank. These safeguards against major problems should have been reassuring, except that the sound of my heartbeat on the monitor and the sensation of the blood pressure cuff periodically inflating started to freak me out. As I lay there listening to the sound of my heartbeat, I thought, "Boy, I hope it doesn't start going faster, like one of those anxiety attacks," and naturally that thought would automatically make my heart beat faster. The sound of the quicker beats would make me worry more about an impending anxiety attack, and the pace of the sounds would increase even more. Strapped to the operating table and connected to all of the machines, I felt trapped and this feeling triggered my latent claustrophobia, which naturally increased my heart rate, which only made me freak out even more.

From the looks on the faces of the plastic surgeon and the nurses, I got the feeling that no one ever before had pleaded for an oxygen mask in order to avoid fainting during a ten-minute mole removal operation. As they whispered with each other, I started to get a little worried that they were going to call in a psychiatrist for a consultation. I actually heard someone say, "psych eval." But in the end, they were just glad to get rid of me. I got the distinct impression that the plastic surgeon did not invite my internist to send me back for additional incisions. I did get one benefit from the plastic surgeon, however. A beautiful suture job, or so the nurse told me. But then again, people were starting to tell me anything to get me to calm down. It's a tough job being a hypochondriac, but someone has to do it. How else can we keep the medical sector of the economy growing?

*   *   *

Next, my internist sent me to a dermatologist for regular mole inspections by someone who does such examinations for a living. I was more comfortable with the dermatologist's surgical procedures since he did mole removals in his office much the way the university surgeon had done the first one. None of the scary sounding machines and claustrophobia-inducing restraints as in the hospital operating room.

The dermatologist was very thorough and careful. He had a special magnifying glass attached to a headpiece that he could use to examine each mole closely. Finally, here was someone who shared my concerns about thorough examinations. After my second visit, the dermatologist raised a suggestion. "You know," he said in a strangely slow and deliberate fashion, "we can be more certain about whether any moles are changing if we have a solid baseline for comparison."

"Baseline for comparison?," I asked, not knowing what he was talking about.

"Yes, a baseline for comparison. If we can compare the future status of your moles with the present status of your moles, then we would know for sure if any changes have occurred."

"But how can you compare the future with the present?"

"By utilizing photography, of course."

"Of course," I said with a note of admiration, "you want to take pictures of my moles."

"Yes. That's it exactly," he said with an approving nod.

"Sounds fine with me."

"I'm glad to hear that. This will be a big help in monitoring your moles. It's really the best approach, although some people just aren't comfortable enough to do it."

"Comfortable enough? This is a life-and-death medical issue. Why wouldn't they want to have pictures taken of their moles?"

The doctor looked at me quizzically. "Because some people aren't comfortable with having full body nude photos taken of them."

I tried not to look surprised, although I'm sure my face turned red. Full body nude photos! I thought he just wanted to take pictures of my moles. I quickly realized, however, that since I had moles all over my body, the photos of the moles would necessarily cover my entire body.

"Of course," I said feigning confidence. "By the way," my voice was now starting to waver, "who exactly takes these photographs?"

"We'll send you to professional medical photographers in an office in the medical building attached to the hospital. Are you still game?"

"Sure," I replied, trying to appear confident, "if it's needed for my health, I'm happy to cooperate."

A few minutes later, as I stood at the desk while the nurse called to make an appointment with the medical photographers, the nurse held her hand over the phone momentarily and whispered to me, "I'm sure the doctor told you that there is no guarantee about whether your photographer will be male or female. It just depends on who is working that day." The doctor had not told me, but at this point I could not back out without appearing to be, well, chicken.

"No problem," I whispered. "Understood."

My wife was less understanding. "I assume that this will be some male person taking your picture," she said, setting her jaw firmly with a glare.

"Well…."

"What do you mean, 'Well'?"

"Well, they said they could not assure me that it would be a male photographer."

"I don't want some woman looking at your body. And I especially don't want some woman taking pictures of you when you have no clothes on."

"Look, these are medical professionals. They do this all the time. It's their job. Besides, my health is at issue here. I don't want to get skin cancer."

"Hmmm, I suppose. But see if you can make sure it's a male photographer."

"They said they can't promise me anything."

"It doesn't hurt to ask when you get there."

"Well…."

"Well, nothing. Promise me you'll at least ask. There's no harm in that. Promise me."

"Okay, okay." I felt as if I was violating an oral contract with the doctor's office since the nurse had already told me that they wouldn't promise me anything about the photographer.

As my photo shoot day approached, I could feel my anxiety level rising. What if it was a woman photographer? Would I even be able to take my clothes off? What if my face and neck become flushed as often happened to me in moments of embarrassment? Then, ever after, the dermatologist would examine pictures of me looking not unlike the color of a beet.

Driving to the medical photographers' office, I resigned myself to my fate. "I can do this; I can do this; I can do this," I kept telling myself over and over again. I recognized that I harbored significant doubts, otherwise I would not be making such strenuous efforts to force myself to keep the appointment.

When I turned the handle on the door marked "Medical Photography Associates," I simultaneously held my breath and closed my eyes. The door swung open and I timidly peeked through my squinting eyelids. Hallelujah!! There were two men standing behind the reception desk. I identified myself and they checked my name off the list while saying, "We'll be with you in a minute." I let out an audible sigh of relief. It was as if a huge weight was lifted off my shoulders. I felt much more relaxed as I chuckled to myself about my wife's worries. It turned out that this would be no worse than taking a shower in a locker room with other men standing around. As I wrote out my check to pay for the photographs, I tried to make small talk with the one of the men behind the desk.

"Have you been doing this for a long time?"

He smiled. "Sure. We're all very experienced."

"I bet some people are a little uncomfortable about having various body parts photographed."

"Yeah. It's usually the little old ladies. But once we get started, it's such a professional atmosphere, that people usually relax."

"Should I be going somewhere to get undressed?"

He looked at the appointment book. "Are we doing a full body for a dermatologist with you?"

"Yes. That's right."

"Yeah. We have several changing rooms attached to the photo studio. I'll send you in momentarily when the photographer finishes setting up the lighting." Then he yelled in the general direction of an open door behind the reception desk. "HEY JUDY, ARE YOU READY FOR MR. SMITH YET?"

Judy?? I froze as I heard a woman's voice respond, "Send him on back."

I now carry in my pocket a remote control device for locking and unlocking my car. It is very handy. At the time I heard Judy's voice, I had never heard of a remote control for a car. However, if I had known that such a device would later exist, I would have wished for an additional button: rewind. Wouldn't it be great if you could just pull your remote control out of your pocket, hit the rewind button, and make your life move backward just like a video in the VCR? Upon hearing a woman's voice from the photo studio, I wanted to walk backwards straight out of the office and back into my car. I wouldn't even mind if I moved in the herky jerky movements of a backward video. People could even laugh and I wouldn't have cared. I just wanted to escape. My mental preparation for the prospect of a female photographer had vanished when I saw the men at the reception desk, and now I didn't have the strength to retrieve my calm courage (if I'd had any of that to begin with).

This moment was the antithesis of an anxiety attack. My heart did not begin beating wildly. In fact, it seemed as if my heart stopped beating. I couldn't breathe at all. My heart sank. My stomach turned. My mind went blank. Every familiar description of physical manifestations of trepidation suddenly applied to me. I experienced them all at once. I felt myself shuffle back toward the open door, moving in a trance-like state in which I felt detached from reality. As I entered the doorway, I was met by a slim, attractive young woman who shook my hand warmly.

"Hi, I'm Judy. I'm the photographer who will be doing your pictures."

I nodded weakly, probably with an odd half-smile frozen on my face.

"You can use that changing room over there." She pointed toward an open door.

I nodded again and walked slowly to the room. I felt condemned. Condemned to an event of excruciating discomfort. Not like facing execution, but instead a peculiar kind of torture. At least the actors in the cast of *HAIR* on Broadway had the protection of distance and anonymity that comes from disrobing with others in front of hundreds of faceless strangers. I'm sure some of them initially were reluctant, but the context was far more palatable than the situation I faced. No distance. No anonymity. No shared embarrassment with my fellow actors. I was up close and personal for unique Kodak moments, recorded for all time on film, with my new acquaintance Judy. There would be no appreciative audience surveying a momentary tableau of naked bodies. Instead, the lens would be focused right at me, inch by inch. There was nowhere to run but I sure wanted to hide.

"Um, is there a robe or something in there that I should put on?"

"No problem. You don't need one. The doors to the studio are all locked from the inside. Just come back in when you're ready."

I momentarily watched her fiddle with the camera. I wanted to say, "What if I'm never ready?," but that didn't really seem to be an option.

In the small room, I slowly took off my clothes. No matter how slowly I moved, I knew I was still doomed to walk out the door naked to the world, or at least to Judy. When I stepped back into the studio while trying to hide my discomfort, I took note of my surroundings. The high-ceilinged room was painted black with various black curtains and lights on ceiling tracks. It reminded me of a theatrical performance space, without any chairs for an audience, of course. Judy had disappeared behind a curtain, but I could hear her moving around. As she pushed the curtain aside and turned around, the air was suddenly filled with the sound of music. The room obviously had an extensive sound system, and it was now blaring with strange-sounding jazzy synthesizer music. Mood music. Not elevator music, but mood music. Perhaps what an aspiring Lothario puts on his stereo as he dims the lights in his apartment and makes his move toward his date. The scene went beyond odd. It was surreal. Amid a blast of electronic music, I was standing naked in a black sound stage-type room while a woman walked toward me focusing her camera in my direction. I half expected Alan Funt to jump out from behind a curtain and yell, "Smile! You're on Candid Camera," except I was pretty sure that it would actually be Federico Fellini or maybe the gang from Monty Python. I stood frozen in one spot with no idea what to do in such an unfamiliar setting. Sort of like Bozo opening the wrong stage door and finding himself standing in the middle of a production of *King Lear*.

"Just stand there is front of the curtain," Judy said, motioning with one hand while she peered into the camera lens. "And lift your arms up."

And so I stood, arms upraised as if preparing to flap and fly, while she stood two feet away systematically shooting picture after picture. She leaned forward to get close-ups of each two-foot segment, including, yes, the private segments. I felt perfectly calm. It was all too strange to be real. In addition, since her face was always behind the camera, it never seemed as if she was actually looking at me (until she ran out of film anyway). When she stepped back to reload, she started to make small talk and actually look at me. The eye contact and conversation momentarily brushed aside the protective cloak of the scene's surrealism and suddenly made me feel like the emperor at the moment that he discovers that his clothes are not actually new. In fact they aren't clothes at all.

When I departed from the photo session, I knew that my wife would be eager to hear every detail. As I expected, my mention of the music led to loud and spontaneous expressions of suspicion and bewilderment. All I could say was, "At least it wasn't Bolero," but as I thought about it, maybe it was. I've never heard that played on an electronic synthesizer before.

*   *   *

It turned out that the photographer did not actually take photographs, as in color prints. My dermatologist received a set of color slides. As he explained it to me at my next appointment, each slide would be projected on a screen as I stood next to the screen so he could compare the mole's image with the actual status of the mole at the later appointment date. He instructed me to get undressed in an examining room with a slide projector and a screen. What he didn't tell me was that one of the nurses would be working the slide projector.

As I stood awkwardly in the darkened room with slide after slide flashing on the screen next to me, I quickly lost my discomfort about the nurse's presence, particularly because the poor young woman was clearly more uncomfortable than me. She averted her eyes and absolutely refused to look at my naked body. She merely pressed the appropriate button whenever the doctor said, "Next." The scene actually started to amuse me and so, with cruel intentions, I kept staring at her trying to make eye contact and thereby elevate her discomfort even farther beyond mine. The more I stared, the harder she tried to look the other way. I guess when one stands helpless and naked in front of an audience (albeit an audience of two) one looks for ways to assert some personal power. As it turned out, however, no cruel deed goes unpunished.

Several months later at my next dermatologist appointment, I was perfectly calm about the prospect of disrobing and standing next to the screen. This time, however, the projector operator was an older nurse who had no reluctance about looking right at me. Now it was my turn to wilt and avoid eye contact. In the middle of the slide show, the doctor was called away for an urgent phone call. Then it was just me and nurse facing each other in the darkened room. I wish I could say we stood in an uncomfortable silence, but unfortunately she started to talk in a friendly manner.

"Say, don't you teach at the university?"

"Yes," I managed to mumble as my eyes explored every small dot in the ceiling panels.

"I thought so. My son was one of your students. He said you're a really great teacher. I can't wait to tell him that I met you." Her comment shattered the sense of anonymity upon which I relied in order to relax. I had to use every ounce of my will power to avoid reflexively moving my hands to shield certain parts of my body from her view (not that she hadn't seen these parts already).

I shuddered involuntarily at the thought that she might actually describe the circumstances of our meeting. I could imagine the conversation.

"Well, I was just standing there looking at his naked body when it suddenly occurred to me that this was your professor from school."

"Really, what did his body look like?"

"Pretty pale and scrawny, but he seemed to have a pleasant personality."

"Scrawny, you say? I can't wait to tell everyone back at school."

I prayed for the return of uncomfortable silence, or at least the return of the doctor. Instead, I faced a continuing barrage of questions about applying to graduate school, career planning advice for students, and university grading policies. As the clocked ticked slowly forward, I had at the tip of my tongue "This really isn't a good time to talk about this," but I didn't want to seem unfriendly. I always feel tortured if strangers on a bus or train insist on talking to me, but having this conversation with an unfamiliar acquaintance while standing like a naked statue (literally) brought an entirely new dimension to the process of enduring the escalating pain of unwanted social interaction. Please bring back the rack and the thumbscrew. I'd much prefer them to this. Anything but conversing with some student's parent while standing naked in the bright headlight of a slide projector!

As the doctor reentered the room, the nurse concluded the conversation by saying, "I'm so glad that Joan asked me to handle this for her today. I just love to talk to people and I especially wanted to meet you."

"Joan?"

"She's the nurse who usually handles the slide projector."

As the doctor readjusted his magnifying glass headpiece, he remarked, "But I just saw Joan out in the hall. She's here today."

"Oh, I know," said the nurse happily. "She just said she was really busy and she knew I wanted to meet Professor Smith. Everybody knows that I just love to talk to people."

I smiled weakly, or rather grimaced, at the thought of Joan's generous act of revenge. When I passed the reception desk on the way out of the office, Joan kept trying to make eye contact with me, but now it was my turn to look at the floor. I knew that my next appointment would be a barrel of fun (not!), no matter which nurse showed up to work the projector.

*   *   *

When we decided to move from Ohio to Michigan, my wife suddenly became intensely interested in dermatology, or at least one aspect of it.

"What's going to happen to those naked slides at your doctor's office?," she asked emphatically.

"I don't know."

"Well, you're not going to let the doctor keep them, are you? There's no telling who will end up looking at them?"

" I'm sure they're locked away in some vault," I said, trying to sound reassuring, but at the same time remembering my student years working in the basement of one of Harvard's museums. For several decades in the late 1800s and early 1900s, a scientist at Harvard took nude photographs of every incoming student in order to study the purported relationship between body types and personal characteristics. After stumbling on a treasure trove of old glass slides, I had secretly spent many hours in a corner of the museum's basement trying to find pictures of Teddy Roosevelt, Franklin Roosevelt, or any other famous Harvardian of that era, just out of curiosity and for use in some future cocktail party conversation. I didn't really want to see Teddy Roosevelt naked or, heaven forbid, Helen Keller, but it just seemed fascinating to know that these photos existed and the rest of the world did not know about them. All I needed was for some former student of mine to get a job at the dermatologist's office, or maybe the mother of some former student, and then decide to take away a souvenir picture of the hopefully-someday-famous professor and author (me). I couldn't say any of this to my wife, however, since she was already overly concerned about shielding my body from others' eyes.

"You know, I think I'll ask the doctor if I can take the slides to give to whatever new dermatologist I get in Michigan."

"Just make sure it's not a woman dermatologist," she commanded sharply.

When I called the dermatologist's office to ask if I could take the slides with me, a nurse told me that they usually only send official medical records, including medical slides, directly to other doctors' offices upon the request of those doctors and the approval of the relevant patients. To me, that conjured up a vision of the slides being lost or stolen in the mail. "What if I run for president some day and then Larry Flynt gets the stolen slides?," I thought to myself. The next thing I knew, my presidential campaign would be destroyed by the appearance of my naked pictures in *Penthouse* magazine. I was starting to become obsessed with getting the slides, and I wasn't thinking realistically about the prospect (or lack thereof) of the political career that I wouldn't really want to have anyway.

"Can't you make an exception in my case?," I pleaded. "I don't even know yet who my doctor will be. But if a mole starts to change, then I'll need to be able to take the slides right over to the next dermatologist that I find."

"I'll talk to the doctor about it," was the noncommittal reply I received.

A few days later, the doctor's office called and informed that I could pick up the slides if I signed a dozen waiver forms absolving them of any responsibility if the slides ever became lost or misplaced. I rushed over to pick up the slides. When I returned home, I placed the small box of slides in the back my dresser's top drawer. The kids knew that they were forbidden from digging through those drawers. As it happened, however, my wife decided to clean out the drawers in the process of packing for the move. When I found that my drawer was empty, I immediately asked her, "What happened to the box of slides that was in there?"

"I don't know. I think I threw them into one of your boxes with all of your other slides."

"But those were the naked slides."

"What naked slides?" She looked startled.

"You know, the ones from the dermatologist's office."

"Well, I didn't know that. Why didn't you hide them someplace?"

I resisted the temptation to respond with a sarcastic, "I did," and instead asked, "Where's the big box of slides?"

"It's already sealed and stacked with the other boxes in the garage."

"Okay, but whatever you do, you've got to help me remember to get those slides out of there when we get to the new house."

"Don't worry," she said seriously, "this is one thing that I won't forget."

She was true to her word. When we moved into the new house, she reminded me three times to find the "naked slides" and put them someplace where the kids could not find them. Unfortunately, however, when I opened the box, there were hundreds of slides jumbled together everywhere. Many of the smaller slide boxes as well as the slide tray boxes had come open during transit and the slides were mixed together in the large box. Despite the prospect of digging and sorting, I breathed a sigh of relief at the recognition that I was in control of straightening out the problem and none of the kids had stumbled across the box first.

After the kids went to bed, I carefully held each slide up to the light and sorted them by subject matter. I decided to help my future dermatologist by putting all of the medical photos into one of the three slide trays that I owned so that they could immediately be placed into a projector for viewing. Because the slides were numbered, it was easy to place them in the same order in which the doctor had viewed them in Ohio. With the greatest of care, I put all of the medical slides into a single slide tray, slides of my high school tour of Europe into a second slide tray, and the slides from a ski trip in a third tray. All remaining slides went back into the small boxes. I double-checked each box and each slide tray to make sure that none of the medical slides had ended up in the wrong place. I then marked the box containing the tray of medical slides with the label "MED." I marked the Europe slide box as "TRIP" and the third box as "SKI." For once in my life, I had prevented a problem before it had a chance to occur. I stored the boxes on the highest shelf in the back of the closet so that the kids could not reach them. My wife didn't trust me, of course, so she went through and double-checked each individual slide, too. In the end, however, even she felt compelled to congratulate me, especially since I never organize and label the contents of boxes. She had one request, however. She wanted me to get the medical slides out of the house and into the dermatologist's office as soon as possible so that the kids could never stumble upon them.

A few weeks later, I had my first appointment with the primary care physician I had chosen from the HMO list. We went through my medical history and, as usual, my blood pressure was elevated when he put the cuff on my arm as I silently chanted "I hope my blood pressure isn't high; I hope my blood pressure isn't high." He did a quick visual inspection of my moles, but upon seeing the scars from prior surgeries and hearing about the unusual cell activity discovered in the initial mole removal, he agreed that I needed to be referred to a dermatologist. He called his assistant into the room and instructed the assistant to make an appointment for me with a Dr. McCool. When the doctor left the room for a moment, I quickly scanned my list of HMO dermatologists and felt relieved to see that it was Dr. *George* McCool. Now my wife could get off my back about having a woman inspect my body for cancerous moles. When the doctor and the assistant returned, I was handed an appointment slip for an examination by a Dr. Rhodes.

"I thought it was supposed to be a Dr. McCool," I said.

"He was all booked up for months," said the assistant, "but Dr. Rhodes had openings available."

It wasn't until I got into my car that I was able to check the HMO list and find the name Dr. *Darcy* Rhodes. Darcy? Is that a male person or a female person? I wasn't sure, but I knew my wife would be interested.

"So who's your new dermatologist going to be?" My wife began to interrogate me the moment I walked through the door.

"A Dr. Rhodes," I replied.

"Is this doctor a man or a woman?"

"I think it's a man."

Her brow furrowed and she glared at me. "What do you mean you *think* it's a man?"

"The name is a bit gender ambiguous. Darcy Rhodes. But I heard the doctor's assistant refer to Dr. Rhodes as 'him.'" Okay, I lied. But it wasn't worth going through a conversation that would result in her forcing me to promise to ask for a male dermatologist. Even though I didn't feel especially comfortable at the thought of a female dermatologist, I felt more uncomfortable at the thought of admitting to someone that I had a gender-specific hang-up about who would be my doctor.

"Well, good. I just don't like the thought of some other woman looking at your naked body."

"You know, there's usually a nurse present when they run through the slides and the nurse could very well be female."

"I don't mind that so much, just so the person standing next to you and actually touching various parts of your body is a man."

I felt bad about being untruthful, but now all I could do was hope that the dermatologist would, indeed, turn out to be a man. When I called the dermatologist's office to tell them that I would be bringing the slide tray, I tried to chat with the receptionist in the hope that I could elicit a telltale "he," "she," "him," or "her" in reference to the physician. Unfortunately, the receptionist consistently said, "the doctor says" and "the doctor always wants" in response to my questions. Thus I was left with uncertainty and anxiety about the potential for discomfort at my first visit to the new dermatologist.

On the day of my appointment, I climbed on top of a chair to reach the "MED" slide box. As I pulled it out of the closet, I suddenly wished that I had not told the dermatologist's office that I would be bringing the slides. What if it was a female dermatologist? Past experience indicated that the examination process was much slower when the doctor was looking at slides and making comparisons with my naked body. By contrast, when a doctor just made a visual examination of my moles, it tended to be a much quicker examination *and* I would be lying down with a hospital gown strategically placed and lifted only momentarily when necessary to minimize exposure and embarrassment. I was tempted to leave the slides and claim that I had forgotten them, but then I thought about my wife's insistence that I get the slides out of the house. I couldn't hide them at my office. I had janitors and grad students entering my office at all hours of the day and night. In the end, it seemed best to get the slides into the custody of the dermatologist.

While working at my office prior to the doctor's appointment, the phone rang. I immediately recognized my wife's voice and was startled to hear the urgency in her tone.

"Did you take the slides with you for your appointment?"

"Yes, of course. You wanted to get them out of the house and today is the day to do it."

"Whew," she said with a clear sense of relief. "I caught your daughter standing on a chair this morning trying to reach the slide tray boxes."

"What was she doing?"

"She said that they're studying Western states or mountains or something, and she wanted to take our slides from the ski trip."

"Oh. I'm sorry. I forgot to tell you that she asked about those slides the other day. I told her it was okay, but I thought she would ask one of us for help in getting them down."

"I wish you would have told me that sooner," said my wife with annoyance. "Now it looks like I overreacted in fussing at her about trying to reach the slides."

"Sorry about that. Just look at it this way. It's a good thing that she asked me about it beforehand," I said. "Otherwise she might have been rooting around in the closet on her own. Heaven forbid that she would stumble across the medical slides."

"Fortunately, your slides are out of the house now so that potential problem no longer exists," said my wife, her voice conveying her sense of relief.

I looked over at my box of medical slides and began to get the eerie, yet reassuring, sensation that fate was steering me and my slides into the care of this Dr. Rhodes. Twice now we had had potentially problematic situations with these slides: when they were jumbled around in the box and when my daughter wanted to take the ski trip slides to school. If I had waited to get an appointment with Dr. McCool or if I had been inattentive to the disorganized slides in the aftermath of the move, I might have had an embarrassing situation. Thus I began to look forward to the prospect of handing the slides over to Dr. Rhodes. It seemed as if fate was telling me that Dr. Rhodes had been chosen by higher forces to see me naked.

At Dr. Rhodes' office, I gave the box to the receptionist and was ushered into an examining room where the slide projector and screen were ready and waiting.

"Should I get undressed?," I asked.

"No. The doctor will probably want to talk to you for a bit first, since this is your first visit."

Now I knew that fate had delivered me to the right place. In the past, my dermatological concerns always seemed to lead me to meet and converse with people while I was clothed only in goose bumps. This time I would have a chance to relax, get acquainted, and become acclimated before heading into the discomfort of the examination. My relaxed state was shaken, however, when Dr. Rhodes entered the room. She was so young, shapely, and attractive in appearance that I was momentarily struck speechless when she greeted me with a warm smile and a welcoming handshake. If I said she was gorgeous that would be an understatement. Her striking physical beauty was enhanced by an alluring charisma that movie starlets aspire to exude. She looked far too youthful and well-dressed to be a doctor, let alone a busy specialist. She had a dazzling smile. Not one hair was out of place. And she looked as if she just stepped out of the pages of a fashion magazine. In feeling overwhelmed by her good looks, I wasn't falling prey to some old-fashioned negative stereotype about doctors all being men. This woman could pass for twenty-one easily. Did she attend medical school as a teenager? How could she possibly have done a lengthy specialized residency without appearing to be at least thirty-something? Any feeling of attraction that I might have felt toward her was pushed to the back of my mind. In fact, I was deathly afraid of her. I wanted to shrink back into the corner in horror at the thought that this beautiful woman was going to examine my body which was, in the words of my former student's mother, "pale and scrawny." What if I turned beet red when she began to examine me? What if she touched me and some part of my body moved involuntarily? What if I babbled like an idiot when she tried to talk to me? I had hoped for a male doctor, but this was clearly the worst-case scenario. I could never explain this to my wife.

I was stricken with terror. Many men may look at models in *Glamour*, *Vogue*, and more revealing publications because they enjoy seeing shapely female bodies. But that doesn't mean most men would actually want a glamorous-looking model to view their middle-aged, out-of-shape, pale, scrawny, and "you-really-ought-to-wear-a-shirt-at-the-beach" bodies. A scene that had conveyed reassurance only moments before now clobbered me with an unprecedented level of anxiety and anticipatory embarrassment.

Dr. Rhodes began to interview me about my medical history. She stopped suddenly and looked closely at my face and neck. "Are you feeling hot or otherwise ill? Your cheeks and neck are quite flushed right now."

"No. I always get a little nervous at a doctor's office."

"Well, we'll try to make this as quick and painless as possible. Why don't you get undressed. The nurse will be right in to put your slides in the projector and I'll be back momentarily."

I disrobed quickly and wrapped myself tightly in the hospital gown which was lying on the examining table. Moments later, there was a quick knock on the door followed by the immediate entry of a tall, muscular young man carrying the slide try. My look of bewilderment was too transparent.

He smiled in amusement. "I'm the nurse. I always run the slide projector for male patients."

I was embarrassed that my facial expression had given away my gender-stereotyping thoughts about nurses always being female, but I felt better that this office had some gender sensitivity when patients were about to disrobe.

"Does Dr. Rhodes have a male partner who handles the examinations of male patients?" I asked, in a voice that tried but failed to sound matter-of-fact.

"Nope. Sorry. Don't worry. She's a great doctor. Very professional. She has lots of male patients."

Silently I thought to myself, "I'll bet there's a whole bunch of male patients with exhibitionist tendencies flocking to her office."

The doctor reentered the room and strapped on the magnifying glass headpiece that all dermatologists seemed to wear. "Okay, you can remove the gown and stand next to the screen. John, hit the lights and let's get started."

I stood up by the screen and closed my eyes. There was no way that I could watch her as she examined me. I decided to pretend that she was old Dr. Benson. He was such an unpleasant memory that I hoped to shift my mood from a feeling of anxiety to a state of detached annoyance. I stood perfectly still and heard the telltale click as the slide projector came on and the first slide moved into place. Within a second, I heard the nurse snicker and then remark sarcastically, "So you think you're blessed with monumental proportions do you?" He placed exaggerated emphasis on the word "monumental" as if spitting out each individual syllable. Simultaneously, I heard Dr. Rhodes exclaim, "What the….? Is this some kind of joke?" I opened my eyes and saw them both staring at the screen so I turned my head quickly and felt my breath taken away by what I saw. There on the screen was a picture of the Eiffel Tower.

Dr. Rhodes spoke quickly. "We don't appreciate these kinds of jokes. It wastes our time and needlessly takes us away from patients who actually need medical services. You'll be billed for this session and I will talking to your doctor about the extent of your obvious problems, mental as well as physical." Then she slammed my file shut with a look of disgust and stomped out of the room muttering something about "psych eval." Meanwhile, the nurse shut off the projector, still suppressing a smirk, while saying, "So this is supposed to be a medical photo of some part of your body?" I stood frozen in place, arms outstretched like a naked scarecrow, staring at the blank screen yet still seeing in my mind's eye the picture of the Eiffel Tower from my high school tour of Europe. Just then I remembered that my daughter had taken a slide tray to school and for a moment my mind imagined it heard faintly in the distance my daughter's teacher yelling something about "pornography."

*   *   *

As it turned out, when my wife had double checked the slides, she placed the Europe slides in the box marked "MED" because she thought it stood for "Mediterranean." She put the medical photos in the box marked "SKI" because she thought it stood for "skin." And she put the ski trip photos in the box marked "TRIP." This, of course, explains why I took the Europe photos to the dermatologist. It also meant that my daughter took my medical photos to show at school. Fortunately, after viewing a few close-up photos that the students erroneously perceived to be a vast snow-covered landscape interrupted by the brown dots of protruding rocks (thank heavens I'm so pale!), one of my daughter's classmates remarked, "Doesn't that look like hair growing out of that rock?" The teacher took a closer look, removed a few slides from the tray to hold up to the light, and then quickly turned off the projector and gave everyone a spelling test. She claimed that she shut off the projector when she saw that some of the slides had my face and chest clearly revealed, but I couldn't help squirming during parent-teacher conferences at the thought that she had seen more than that. I wrote a long, apologetic letter of explanation to Dr. Rhodes, which she graciously accepted, but she still recommended a psychiatrist for me anyway. I also switched over to Dr. McCool at my wife's insistence, although I was going to make that switch on my own.

Unfortunately, the slide tray my daughter took to class became the talk of the school among teachers and, eventually, a few parents. I wish the teacher would have kept the incident to herself, but I guess I can understand that people like to talk about bizarre incidents, and this one was certainly bizarre. I arranged a meeting with the principal to express my concern about how this mix-up might cause problems for my kids, especially if other students heard about it and began to tease them. After I explained the entire story to him, he apologized for any discomfort that may have been caused by the teachers' discussions about the incident. In a most empathetic manner, he said "You have gone through a horribly embarrassing episode and I really feel for you.

But don't worry. It will all blow over and be forgotten. As I always tell our students, no matter how bad something seems, you must keep everything in perspective. Remember, although this was a horrible experience, at least you have your health."

True. It's mine, but sometimes I think I'd love to trade with someone else.

Chapter Two

Streaking at Harvard

"You only go to college once, you know."

Those were life-altering words. I had always planned to enroll at Michigan State University after high school. I liked the campus, my parents were alums and it would put some distance between me and my brother at the University of Michigan. For two years, however, certain people encouraged me to seek a broader horizon. "You have good grades, varsity letters, church choir, blah blah blah, so you should apply to a competitive East Coast school." Having dedicated my life to accommodating suggestions and avoiding conflict, I decided to apply (just so people would leave me alone). And, as long as I was going to do this, I might as well apply to the very best. Not because I thought I deserved to be among the very best. It just wouldn't do to get turned down by Tufts or Williams, places that hardly anyone in Michigan had ever heard of. Did these schools even have football and basketball teams? Instead, when I inevitably got turned down by Harvard and Yale, there would be no sense of embarrassment. I would have taken my shot for the farthest horizon, so no one could complain about me limiting myself.

Just when I thought it was all sorted out, my high school history teacher asked me where I was going to go to college. When I said, "Michigan State," she said, "I thought you were applying to Harvard."

"I'm applying, but even if I get in, it's really just too expensive to go."
Actually, I was thinking to myself that I would never get in. What little
I knew about the place conveyed an impression of the rich, the famous,
and future presidents of the United States. I felt no connection to the
mythical and intimidating place that I saw in my mind's eye. I actually
hoped I would get turned down quickly so that I could move ahead
with my plans to attend Michigan State without any more helpful
suggestions from the many people who believed that I needed advice.

She frowned. "You only go to college once, you know."

For some reason, those words froze me in my tracks. Maybe I was
selling myself short? Maybe I should hope to get in? What if I did get
in? Maybe I should beg and borrow the money that it would take to go?
From that moment onward, whenever I thought about college, my
history teacher's words rang in my ears. When it eventually came down
to making a decision, I couldn't escape those words as a powerful force
shaping my future.

*   *   *

Unbeknownst to me, my prospects for acceptance at Harvard had
been shaped by events during my junior year in high school. I had
received encouragement to look at the possibility of applying to East
Coast schools, but I had been too busy (and ambivalent) to follow
through in gathering information and applications. One Saturday
afternoon, I had my first encounter (of sorts) with Harvard and the
experience neither whetted my interest in the famous institution nor
encouraged any expectation that I might belong there.

On Friday, my high school basketball team lost a tough game to our
arch-rivals from across town in the championship of the local holiday
tournament during Christmas vacation. As usual, I spent most of the
game on the bench, but I saw a few minutes of action in the first half to
let the good players have a little bit of rest. As fate would have it, the

starters were in foul trouble as the final minutes approached in an unusually tight game. As players began to foul out, the coach sent in substitutes who, invariably, committed some horrible error such as taking a bad shot or letting an opponent score an easy basket. With two minutes to go, we were down by five points and the situation looked bad.

The coach paced the sidelines in exasperation, scanning the faces on the bench without masking his visible displeasure at the disappointing choices of available players. I tried not to make eye contact with him. I wanted to play, but my ego didn't need to be deflated by seeing his lack of confidence in me. When yet another starter fouled out, the coach was silent for a moment. Then he muttered to himself, "Oh, what the hell," before yelling "Smith!"

I jumped up and headed for the scorer's table to check into the game. When I entered the game, an opposing player missed his first free throw and then hit the second to give our opponents a six point lead. The ball was thrown to me and I dribbled at moderate speed straight up the court. I foolishly stopped dribbling a few feet above the foul circle. I started to throw it to a teammate standing at the free throw line, but he waved his arms and shook his head as if to say, "Hey, you're the one who's stuck. Don't try to drag me into it." As he turned to move back toward the basket, I saw that all of my other teammates were covered. So I launched a reckless shot from 25 feet away. I could hear the coach start to yell, "What the hell do you think that you're…," but he was drowned out by the cheers when, unbelievably, the shot hit the backboard and banked in.

When a teammate rebounded the opponents' next missed shot, I dribbled the ball up and passed to another teammate who immediately scored. When we stopped the opposition again on their next possession, I took the ball and made another shot. Now the game was tied with only twenty seconds left. As our opponents tried to work a play, I stole a pass and dribbled full speed down the court for what everyone believed would be the game winning lay up. Unfortunately, there was an oily, wet spot on the floor (I swear!) which I hit full stride. I went sprawling and, after sliding for ten feet, the referee called me for traveling and awarded the ball to the other team. To make a long story short, they threw the ball in from out-of-bounds and made a shot at the buzzer to win the game. I was within seconds of being a huge local hero and instead I ended up the goat. The students from the other high school started chanting "Traveling, traveling, traveling" as I walked off the court after the game. Naturally, the local paper had a huge story on the hotly contested game. Tragically, for me anyway, the front page picture showed me falling to the floor at the key moment with the caption, "Traveling to Defeat: Exciting Ending to Championship."

I would have preferred to hide in my bedroom for several weeks or, better yet, years. Not only was I embarrassed about the game's final moments, but I also had a terrible cold. I was coughing and coughing, but the following day I had to work at my movie theater usher job at the mall. Wearing our blue movie theater sport coats, white shirts, and ties, my friend Art and I wandered silently through the mall on our way to work. As we passed the sporting goods store, Art said, "I hate to bring this up, but you know there are some really good, new basketball shoes that can help keep you from slipping."

"Are they any good?"

"I heard that they're real good. Come on. Let's go in for a second and see if they have them."

We walked through the sporting goods store on our way to the shoe department when Art stopped to admire a particular tennis racket. He pulled it off the wall from among the tennis rackets, racquetball rackets, and other kinds of rackets, and he moved to an open area by the bicycles and began swinging the racket to test its feel. I stood staring at the wall of rackets, not really looking at them, because I kept running the previous night's game through my mind over and over again. It was so depressing. The moment was broken when an unfamiliar voice said, "Excuse me, young man, aren't you Chris Smith from the high school?"

I turned slowly, half expecting to see the face of some hostile basketball fan. Instead, I found a well-dressed sixty-ish gentleman extending his hand for a formal handshake. I numbly shook his hand with a puzzled look on my face.

"My name is George Winthrop. I am a local attorney and the chairman of our regional Harvard club. I've heard very good things about you. People have told me that you're a fine student and that you're going to apply to Harvard."

"Well, I...*hack, hack*," my response was interrupted as I tried to suppress a cough. I had heard his name many times. He was the former mayor of the town and was the head of nearly every country club and civic board. I was surprised and more than a little intimidated, so I didn't know what to say.

Before I could continue, he said, "I'm glad that I bumped into you. Let me ask you a little bit about yourself." As he pulled out a small notepad and a gold-plated pen, I glanced at the wall clock and began to worry that Mr. Winthrop would make me and Art late for work. With pen in hand, Mr. Winthrop scribbled notes as he started to speak. "All right, Mr. Smith, what are your interests?"

As he asked the question, my eyes caught sight of Art standing a few feet behind him making funny faces at me and pretending that he was going to hit Mr. Winthrop with the tennis racket.

"Art!," I said loudly, while simultaneously trying not to show my anger as the word escaped from my lips. Then I pulled myself together to try to answer his broad question. "It's kind of abstract but...."

"GEORGE! GEORGE WINTHROP!"

Mr. Winthrop and I simultaneously turned to see a well-dressed man standing at the door to the store waving his hand in our direction. The man began walking briskly in our direction. Mr. Winthrop looked back at his notepad and mumbled to himself, "He's a bit early." Then he looked at me and asked, "What do you really like to sink your teeth into? Squash?"

I hesitated momentarily, not sure what to say. Did Harvard examine applicants so thoroughly that they worried about what vegetables people preferred? At Michigan State, you just sent your application fee and a copy of your grades to the admissions office. I had heard that Harvard used an elaborate, complicated admissions process but this seemed far-fetched. Then it occurred to me that Mr. Winthrop may be asking questions just to test my reactions. If he wanted to catch someone off-guard during an interview, I guess it made sense to ask about a vegetable. So I said, "Sure, I like it okay… *hack, hack, hack.*" My attempt to answer was swallowed up by another coughing fit.

He hurriedly scribbled more notes and, without lifting his eyes from the notepad, said, "Prepping?"

I hadn't really thought about studying for the SAT exam yet. After all, I wasn't scheduled to take it until the fall of my senior year. However, "No" wasn't going to sound like a good answer, so I thought I better exaggerate how much preparation I had been doing. I started to cough again as I nodded my head and said, "Over..*hack, hack*.. and over and over and over."

"And over, you say," he said with a smile. "Excellent choice, son."

I nodded my head and, "*hack, hack, hack,*" tried to choke back another coughing fit.

He kept scribbling and said, "Now, is there something about traveling?"

My stomach sank. Why did he have to bring that up? On the other hand, it was on the front page of the morning's paper, so how could he not know about it. He didn't say it in a way that seemed mean. In fact, it seemed more like friendly curiosity. I began to respond with, "There's this spot of grease…." when Mr. Winthrop's acquaintance reached our location by the wall of rackets.

Mr. Winthrop greeted him with a hearty, "Well, are you finally ready to go?" and then quickly turned to me and said, "Nice to make your acquaintance, Mr. Smith. I must go now. Best of luck to you. I hope we will be able to talk once again." With that, he headed out of the store with the other man. Art and I went to work at the movie theater and life continued as usual, except for my lingering feelings of depression from thinking about the basketball game.

I never saw Mr. Winthrop again. Sadly, he passed away a few months later in a skiing accident in Colorado. When I actually applied to Harvard in the fall, a different member of the local Harvard alumni club interviewed me as part of the application process. I never thought much about my brief encounter with Mr. Winthrop until my sophomore year at Harvard when I began making an annual pilgrimage to the Registrar's Office to check my personal file. I discovered that I needed to ensure that my file did not improperly receive grade reports and financial aid forms that were supposed to belong to the two other students in my class named Christopher Smith. When I first looked through my file, I was shocked to find that it contained a letter written by Mr. Winthrop. The letter read:

January 5, 1975
Mr. Samuel Endicott
Harvard-Radcliffe Admissions Office
Byerly Hall
Garden Street
Harvard University
Cambridge, MA 02138

Dear Sam:

I am pleased to report that I have finally found a promising prospect here. Several people had told me that he was an outstanding student and a fine athlete, and I was happy to discover that the positive reports seem to be accurate. His name is Christopher Smith and he is a junior at Kalamazoo Central High School. Once he applies, you will be able to see his grades and list of extracurricular activities. At present, I just wanted to drop you a note to let you know that he seems to have all of the qualities of a real Harvard man; the qualities that seem so sorely lacking in most Midwestern youths. I encountered him while he was examining squash rackets at the local sporting goods store. You cannot possibly know how refreshing it is to meet someone around here who is interested in the civilized competitive sport that builds the character of fine young men on the East Coast. I have no doubt that it is my weekly squash match that keeps me mentally as well as physically fit. I am looking forward to challenging him to a match. I am also happy to report that he was quite well-dressed, wearing a proper navy blue blazer on a Saturday afternoon. One never sees that around here. In fact, I doubt that there are many youngsters around here who will ever deserve to be called "gentleman." Very few of them even seem to own a blazer. But this young man seems quite different from all the rest. It became even more obvious when I asked him about his plans for prep school and he indicated that he would be enrolling at Andover for his senior year. He was so excited about it that he kept saying "Andover, Andover, Andover." As you know, the graduates of Phillips Andover Academy are, year after year, among the finest members of the entering class at Harvard College.

Moreover, when I asked him about his interests, the first thing he said was art. In fact, I think he made reference to abstract art. Everyone else around here is obsessed with sports and television. He obviously is a budding intellectual with refined tastes. In addition, he spoke of traveling in Greece. Our conversation was interrupted so I don't know if he was saying that he has already traveled in Greece or that he hopes to travel in Greece. In either case, he obviously has a taste for classical education and there is no better place for that than Harvard. Please take note of his name and send him the relevant information. I am quite hopeful that I have finally found someone out here who truly belongs at Harvard. I hate to press you for a favor, but I have worked for so long trying to locate any deserving applicants out here that I really must ask you to promise not to let this one get away. Thank you very much.

Best wishes and "fight fiercely Harvard."

George L. Winthrop, Jr. Class of '35

Attached to the letter in my file was a handwritten note on stationary from Harvard's Admissions Office which said: "Fellow Admissions Committee Members, George Winthrop '35, a loyal alumnus and dedicated schools committee member from Michigan died tragically in a skiing accident. Although he was in the class ahead of me when we were in college here, George was a close friend of mine when we were both undergraduates in Lowell House. As his last request for his alma mater, we should take seriously his wish that Mr. Smith receive special consideration for admission. It is the least that we can do as a tribute in remembrance of George. He was a dear friend of mine and a loyal son of Harvard. Thank you for your understanding. Sam."

And thus I was admitted to Harvard. As result of a jarring misunderstanding, including a slip-and-fall, a job as a sport-coat-wearing movie usher, a cough, and chance encounter by the tennis rackets, somehow I was turned into (on paper anyway) an art-appreciating, world-traveling, squash-playing preppie. Some people get into Harvard through intellectual brilliance. Others make it through wealth and family connections. I did it the old-fashioned way: sheer dumb luck. Thank you, Mr. Winthrop, wherever you are.

*　　　　　*　　　　　*

As I prepared to leave for that mythical, mystical place called Harvard, various relatives called with advice. One of my aunts said to me, "I want you to date Caroline Kennedy. I'd like to get invited to dinner at their family compound in Hyannisport." For those of us entering Harvard in the fall of 1976, this was no idle joke, because the newspapers had reported that Caroline Kennedy, daughter of the late president, was to be one of our entering classmates in Harvard's brand new Class of 1980. I'll admit to daydreaming about the possibility of meeting her. Of course, when I moved into my dorm room in Harvard Yard, it became immediately apparent that several hundred of my male classmates had received similar instructions and suggestions from their relatives. Many of them had formulated actual plans for meeting Ms. Kennedy and asking her on a date. My roommate's father had told him, "Just go up to her and tell that her that your father voted for her father in 1960." While he was optimistically envisioning that this announcement would elicit a particular response from her, such as "Really? Then let's get married," it didn't seem like a particularly effective pick-up line to me. The bolder and more obnoxious members of the freshman class discovered her dorm room number at Radcliffe Quad and simply marched up there to knock on her door and introduce themselves. I never heard that this strategy was successful. In fact, I never heard about her actually answering the door when strangers were knocking.

As I listened to the foolish obsessiveness of my classmates (and I can only imagine how this scene was repeated in later years when, amid wide publicity, actresses Jodie Foster and Brooke Shields enrolled at Yale and Princeton respectively), I gave up any realistic hopes of meeting Ms. Kennedy. As it turned out, I surrendered too soon because I actually got my shot at meeting her.

During freshman orientation week at Harvard, there is one morning reserved for welcoming speeches by the president of Harvard, the president of Radcliffe, and various deans. Unfortunately for the University, there is no location on campus, except for the outdoor football stadium on the other side of the Charles River, which is large enough to hold all 1,600 members of a Harvard entering class. Thus, for the purpose of this orientation event, the University rents the Harvard Square Theater, a large and tired-looking movie theater across the street from Harvard Yard (the theater has since been renovated into several small theaters).

I wandered over to the theater with several guys who lived in my dorm. The place was nearly full when we arrived so we headed up to the balcony. In the fourth row, one person sat right by the aisle, but there were several empty seats available, so we squeezed past our inconveniently placed classmate and sat down. After we sat down, there was one empty seat left between me and the guy by the aisle. Suddenly, Caroline Kennedy appeared in the balcony right in front of the already-full first row. She turned her head back and forth, scanning the balcony for an empty seat. Then her eyes settled on the empty seat next to me. She made slow progress in walking toward the seat because so many people were standing in the aisle, either talking to their friends or else looking for seats. Fortunately, most people apparently came to the event with roommate groups because the single seat next to me remained empty as Caroline headed in my direction.

I tried not to stare at her, but she was so recognizable and indeed famous, with her face's elements of resemblance to both of her parents, that I could not take my eyes off of her. It did not appear that others recognized her (or at least they didn't let on that they did) and because she was casually attired in faded jeans, she could easily mix right in with the rest of us. As she came closer, with her eyes clearly fixed on the empty seat next to me as her destination, I quickly began to think about what I would say.

"Here, let me help you. It's a little crowded in here getting past that aisle." No. She may be from Camelot, but chivalry was clearly quite dead by 1976, so it would be too obvious that I was initiating contact.

"Hi, my name's Chris. I'm from Michigan. Who are you?" No. Maybe she would think I was an idiot if I didn't recognize her.

"Ms. Kennedy, I hope all of these guys around here aren't bothering you too much. It must be terrible that some people won't let you just be a regular student." Nope. Too formal. Too obsequious.

Then I got another idea. I would wait until the speeches started and then I would lightly tap her on the arm (yes, physical contact with a celebrity!) and whisper, "Can you believe that they made us get up so early this morning just to hear this?" She could chuckle or commiserate or whatever. Then we would introduce ourselves. Then we could keep chatting in hushed whispers throughout the speeches, making little jokes about the inane comments being presented by some windbag administrator. By the end of the speeches, we'd have a friendly acquaintanceship developing and I'd ask her if she wanted to have a cup of coffee. I didn't actually drink coffee, but for Caroline Kennedy I would willingly become addicted to caffeine if necessary. Then we'd agree to see each other later at one of the other orientation events. I'd end up walking her back to the Radcliffe Quad. It was about ten blocks away so we'd really be getting acquainted by then. I was sure she would want to get to know a regular guy from the Midwest (a loyal Democrat, no less) after spending her school years with rich girls at an exclusive prep school. In fact, I would be a breath of fresh air compared to some of the rich kids I'd seen walking around with their preppie affectations. Before long, we'd be meeting each other for lunch and dinner. I would be quite happy to hike up to the Radcliffe Quad to have dinner with her if she didn't want to eat at the Union dining hall in Harvard Yard. Before long, she'd want to invite me along to some family gathering, perhaps at Hyannisport, where the rest of her relatives would also find my "regular guy" qualities refreshing and appealing.

In my mind's eye, I was just getting ready to throw a pass to one of Caroline's cousins during one of those famous Kennedy family touch football games on the lawn at Hyannisport. Then, just as Caroline reached my row, was but six feet away and preparing to sit down, some jerk with thick glasses and a pocket full of mechanical pencils and slide rules pushed her out of the way and plopped down in the seat.

Oh, the agony! In the short period of twenty seconds while Caroline Kennedy walked toward me, my whole life had finally begun to fall into place. Now, in one evil second, this interloper had taken the pointed end of his mathematical compass and popped my lovely balloon. I actually jumped up and yelled, "No, wait!" But the auditorium was so noisy that Caroline didn't hear me as she moved quickly away and out of the balcony still looking for a seat.

One of the guys from my dorm said, "What are you doing? I thought you didn't know anybody at Harvard."

"I don't. But I was on the verge of meeting and marrying Caroline Kennedy and this guy" (I pointed with my thumb at my other neighbor) "just messed up my entire life."

My new friends laughed. "Where was Caroline Kennedy?"

"She was walking right over here to sit next to me."

"Sure she was. Yeah, right."

"I swear. She really was."

They just laughed harder. "Man, it's so dark in here, you wouldn't recognize Caroline Kennedy if she sat on top of you."

"Let them laugh," I thought. "There's something fateful about this. I'll show them. They'll sing another tune when I do meet her and I bring her around to the dorm to casually introduce her to them." I turned to glare at the guy who ruined my life at that moment. In retrospect, he looked just like Bill Gates, the founder of Microsoft and the richest man in the world. But it couldn't have been Bill Gates, could it? I mean, he was a student at Harvard then, but he would not have been a freshman. In recent years, I have stayed awake many nights wondering if fate had another plan for me, but I missed it. Maybe Caroline Kennedy was headed my way to get my attention and get me focused on the neighboring seat. But then someone even better than Caroline was delivered, almost literally into my lap. What if I had struck up a conversation with Bill Gates? What if we had become friends? What if he had invited me to join him in founding Microsoft? What if I now would have billions of dollars if I hadn't been so obsessed with Caroline Kennedy? I try not to blame Caroline for all of this, but sometimes it's tough when I think about all of the money that Bill and I could have made together.

*   *   *

As classes began that first semester, I still believed that fate intended for me to meet Caroline Kennedy. Sure enough, there she was in my biology class. Actually, it was a general studies science course, Natural Sciences 4. It had something to do with sociobiology. I stared at her during every lecture, all the while trying to pretend that I was not staring. She never noticed. The class wasn't exactly an intimate educational setting. There were 350 students in a large auditorium. At least I didn't kid myself into thinking that our presence in the class meant that we had shared interests. I was only enrolled because it was the lone general science course that did not require a lab. She may have been there for the same reason since I think she was an art history major or something like that. Unfortunately for my academic progress, my fascination with Caroline detracted from my ability to listen to lectures. In fact, at this moment more than twenty years later I have as much understanding of what that course was about, which is to say virtually nothing, as I had as a college freshman taking notes and studying (supposedly) for exams. I remember the instructor showing the same slide over and over again of two frogs mating on a tree in Jamaica. But that's about all I knew then or remember now.

I was so distracted, anonymous, and unsuccessful in that class that the professor's graduate assistant wrote my name in large letters on the blackboard one day and announced that I should talk to him after class. Apparently, I was so preoccupied watching Caroline across the room that I never heard the announcement. Indeed, I never even looked forward at the blackboard. A few weeks later, an acquaintance from the class asked me why they had written my name on the blackboard.

"What?"

"Don't you remember? They wrote your name on the board and said that you were supposed to talk to the head teaching assistant. I know you were there that day because I saw you across the room."

"I must have missed it. How long ago was it?"

"I dunno. Maybe two weeks. Not more than a month."

A month? I felt panicked. What kind of trouble was I in? Before I had a chance to attend the next class meeting, my academic advisor stopped me on the sidewalk in Harvard Yard.

"Are you having problems, Chris? I got a notice that you skipped an exam in your biology course."

My heart started racing. "I never missed an exam. I was there."

"Well, there is no record that you took the exam. You better get this straightened out."

I rushed to my room and dug through the papers on my desk. Ah ha! I found my exam. At the next meeting of the biology class, I went straight up front to the graduate assistant.

"Hi. I'm Christopher Smith. I heard that you were looking for me a while ago."

"Looking for you?"

"Yeah, I heard you put my name on the board. I must have gone to the bathroom or something right then," I said, lamely trying to think of an excuse.

"Oh, yes. Smith. Well, the problem is that we couldn't find any grade for you on the midterm exam. Did you take the exam?"

"Sure. I never miss class or anything like that."

"I apologize if we forgot to record the grade. With 350 students, it's difficult to keep track of everything. Can you show me your exam?"

I eagerly thrust the exam in front of him.

He glanced at the front. "What score did you get? I don't see the grade."

I turned to the second page and pointed to the red numbers scrawled at the bottom. "See. I did take the exam." I said excitedly. "See, right here—I got twelve and a half points."

"Twelve and a half out of fifty?," he exclaimed with a combination of incredulity and embarrassment. I wasn't embarrassed by the score, although I should have been, since I was more worried about getting into trouble if people thought that I skipped an exam during my first semester.

"I heard that the exam was so tough that when you curved the grades a twelve and half turned out to be worth a D plus. Is that right?," I asked eagerly.

He managed a weak smile and nodded affirmatively as he recorded the grade in his book. "Thanks for bringing the exam. Sorry about the mix-up," he said, still obviously embarrassed for me. In fact, he was so obviously uncomfortable about making me talk about my terrible score that his face flushed with embarrassment as he tried to hurriedly end our conversation. He was so strikingly embarrassed for me because of my poor performance that I actually found the scene amusing for a moment.

However, my sense of amusement lasted for exactly one fleeting second because when I turned to walk away, who should be standing next in line to see him, a mere two feet away and clearly within earshot of our conversation the entire time, but Caroline Kennedy. I froze momentarily and stared at her. I wish I could say that I stared at her face-to-face, but then our eyes might have met and they never actually did. Since she was looking right past me or through me or in a manner that was otherwise oblivious to me, there was no reciprocity when I looked into her eyes (or tried to anyway). Now my cheeks and neck were flushed bright red, especially since she obviously heard the entire conversation about my horrifyingly bad exam grade. I couldn't help but be concerned that the "regular guy" charm that I eventually intended to use to woo her might now be drowned out by her impression, confirmed by solid evidence, that I was a stupid idiot. With all of the effectiveness of Barney Fife attempting to remedy a bad situation, as I walked past her, I cleared my throat and said loudly, as if to myself alone, "Boy, if I hadn't been in the hospital with pneumonia for those two weeks, I probably would have done better on that exam." She was already speaking with the graduate assistant so I'll never know if she heard me (although I'm pretty sure she would not have believed me even if she had heard me).

When I went home for Thanksgiving break, my relatives were clamoring to know if I had met any of the Kennedys or other famous people. "Well," I replied, feigning an air of casual confidence. "I am in a class with Caroline Kennedy."

"Do you ever talk to her?," came the excited response.

"It's a big class so I don't really know her well. But I do frequently exchange a word or two with her on certain occasions. That's how my life is at Harvard. I'm right there mixing in with the rich and famous."

"Wow, that must really be something."

It sure was, and I wasn't even lying to them. Virtually every day, I spoke to Caroline or her cousin Michael Kennedy or various other sons and daughters of foreign royalty, millionaires, and famous people. It wasn't that I had become socially smooth and connected in the months between the opening of the semester and Thanksgiving. It was just that I had been given the important responsibility of asking, "Would you like gravy on that?" as I wore a little red serving jacket and watched all of my Harvard classmates file down the *other* side of the serving line at the dining hall. I saw the rich and famous up close every single day, but it didn't take me too long to figure out that the gravy-stained serving jacket, which was required attire for us dining hall employees, was not much of an asset for getting myself invited to play touch football at Hyannisport.

*   *   *

I was not very popular in high school. Sure, I had a few friends from the basketball team and the neighborhood, but I was too shy to ask girls out on dates. I attempted to mask my shyness by being aloof; a strategy which naturally led everyone else to believe that I was arrogant and condescending. In addition, because I didn't drink beer or smoke dope, I was almost never invited to any high school parties. My mother practically twisted my arm to make me ask someone to the prom. Thus, when I went to Harvard, my mother said, emphatically, "You're traveling so far and paying so much money to go to Harvard that you really have to be more outgoing. You'll be all alone out East and you'll be missing out on the benefits of college if you don't put forth the effort to make friends." I knew she was right so I vowed to put forth an effort to become "one of the gang" at Harvard. Even though obstacles kept impeding my efforts to join the Kennedy gang, I had ample opportunity to become friends with my roommates and the other students in my dorm.

One cold October night, we heard yelling from out in Harvard Yard. We rushed to the window and saw a large crowd of people standing at the far end of the Yard near the gates leading to the Science Center. Immediately we noticed that the crowd was cheering wildly for a group of a dozen young men who were running a lap around the interior quadrangle of Harvard Yard while naked. Mind you, Harvard is not located in some quaint, quiet college town. In Harvard's location, if you run naked around Harvard Yard, which is an area the size of a city block, you will encounter many people. Even if you remain entirely on campus, you will encounter dozens and dozens of people walking across the campus on their way to the subway stop, restaurants, stores, and other establishments in neighboring Harvard Square, which is one of the busiest commercial spots in metro Boston. My roommates and I watched in mirthful amazement as these young men, all of whom we recognized as fellow freshman residents of Harvard Yard who ate with us at the Union dining hall, ran quite quickly and quite nakedly through the chilly night air.

The event was not entirely surprising because the 1970s was the era of "The Streak." It became commonplace for naked people, called "streakers," to run through public areas or out on the playing fields at televised sporting events. I never understood the true purpose of streaking, but it attracted attention and it made the streaker seem bold and carefree. In fact, when I went to see the Paul Newman-Robert Redford film, "The Sting," while in high school, some naked lunatic ran down the aisle and jumped up and down in front of the screen while yelling, "How's everybody doing?" The audience responded by shouting, "Get out of the way. We can't see the movie," and the streaker ran out an exit door just ahead of two ushers (thank heavens I was not working that night) who were assigned to chase him away.

As the streakers passed in front of our window and headed back around the Yard, one of my energetic roommates said, "Hey, that's cool. Why don't we streak?"

While one other roommate enthusiastically agreed, I found myself suddenly joined by two miniature versions of my mother. Each was standing on one of my shoulders and one was wearing angels' wings and, as it turned out, so was the other one. I found myself listening to a debate, not between good and evil or right and wrong, but between parental priorities.

One angel momma said, "Go ahead. You need to make friends. Be part of the gang. If this is what these smart kids do at Harvard, then you can go ahead and have some fun at least just this once."

The other angel momma responded, "Maybe I oversold the point about belonging to the group. Remember, when you were a kid, I always used to say, 'Would you jump off a cliff if all of the other kids were jumping off?'"

"Don't exaggerate. We're not talking about jumping off a cliff here," retorted the encouraging angel.

"No. We're talking about getting arrested for indecent exposure," replied the other angel sternly.

"Look. Let's be honest. You were a social loser in high school. Nobody here knows that. Here's your chance to show people that you're really a fun person inside," came the quick, angelic response.

"Did you really go through this entire application process to compete for a spot at Harvard and then take out thousands of dollars in student loans, not to mention burning yourself on hot gravy in the dining hall, just so you could run naked around Harvard Yard?" That comment made me pause.

But then the opposing angel momma interjected, "I'll bet you anything that Teddy Roosevelt and John F. Kennedy ran naked around Harvard Yard. You're probably just joining a grand Harvard tradition." As I later learned, there was a Harvard tradition, at least as an initiation in one social club, of running naked through Harvard Square to buy an apple at the corner fruit market and then running naked to Lamont Library in Harvard Yard to check out a book. I didn't know about this tradition at the time but I was a bit tempted by the thought of being able to brag about having run naked through Harvard Yard on the same grounds trod by Teddy Roosevelt, Franklin Roosevelt, John F. Kennedy, and many other famous folks.

The other angel momma retorted, "Shouldn't you be studying right now?" and that turned the tide. I was out the door and running down the stairs with my roommates. If college served any purpose, it was to rebel against paternalistic parental guidance. Such rebellions are not necessarily a good thing, (don't I know that now, since I'm a parent) but there's a certain inevitability about it.

We ran from our residence at Grays Hall over to the darker, less well-lit side of University Hall, the administration building that has the statue of John Harvard on the other side. We each took off our clothes and rolled them into separate bundles before hiding them in the bushes next to the building. Then we came back around the building and did our lap around the Yard, whooping and hollering the entire way. By this time, the other streakers' cheering crowd had disappeared so our audience consisted only of our small band of friends yelling out the third-floor window of Grays Hall as well as a few other isolated individuals who peered out from various dorm windows. We also had the involuntary audience of various citizens of Cambridge, Massachusetts who happened to be walking past as we came sprinting by, flapping in the breeze. The most notable aspects of the actual streaking experience were: 1) how much faster you can run while naked than you can run with clothes on (I think Olympic sprinters are really missing out on the extra advantage needed to set new world records); 2) how much colder it is at night in October than you realize when you usually spend those nights indoors; and 3) how much a young man's body changes dramatically (shrinkage here and gigantic goose bumps there) as a frigid breeze sweeps across sectors that have never before seen the light of day, let alone the chill of an autumn night.

After running our lap, we went back to the bushes by University Hall and, *Oh No!*, discovered that our clothes were missing. In an instant, youthful pride at boldly breaking with conventional behavior gave way to major embarrassment and worry (not to mention further shrinkage and goose bumps) as we tried to figure out what to do. We crouched in the shadow of the building's stairway, futilely attempting to cover our significant nakedness with our relatively insignificant hands.

"Oh, man! Where are our clothes?"

"I don't know. What are we going to do?"

"Somebody took them!"

"Obviously, Mr. Genius."

"Let's run back over to Grays and rush up the stairs to our room."

"I don't know. It's so well lit over there and there will be all of those women standing in the stairway and hallways."

One of my roommates spied several newspapers in a nearby trash barrel. "Here," he said, distributing them equally among us, "cover yourselves with these while we run back to Grays." We each used one hand to hold a newspaper in place strategically in the front and the other hand to hold a newspaper strategically in the back as we sprinted toward the dorm. When we arrived at Grays Hall, one of my roommates necessarily exposed his behind when he removed his hand in order to grasp the door handle.

"Nuts! It's locked!," he yelled.

Just then, we heard hysterical laughter from up above. We looked upward simultaneously just as a five-gallon trash can filled with cold water was dumped on us from a third floor window. If only we had thought in advance about inviting the people from the *Guinness Book of World Records*, we might have gained acclaim for having the world's largest goose bumps.

As we stood sputtering and cursing, gripping our now soggy and deteriorating newspaper sections more tightly against our soon-to-be-frostbitten bodies, several people came walking around the corner of the building and began to pass by the steps where we stood shivering. As they came into the light, I saw with horror that it looked like (could it really be??) Caroline Kennedy with two preppie-looking guys. I averted my eyes and attempted to obscure my face by looking downward. I still wasn't sure if it was really her.

They stopped and stared from six feet away. Who wouldn't stop and stare in such circumstances? As one of my naked roommates slammed his shoulder repeatedly against the door while yelling, "Open up. We're freezing," I couldn't help but look at the woman (Caroline?) out of the corner of my eye. One of her companions yelled up to our so-called friends, who were still laughing and leaning out the third floor window, "What did you guys do?" At that moment, I thanked my lucky stars that Caroline had never noticed me despite our close encounters. With my hair soaking wet and only small sections of my body covered by soggy newspapers, I knew that even if it was her and she might have recognized me from class, I looked completely different on this cold night. Indeed, as her friends joined in the laughter, the woman just shook her head and turned away from us with a mild look of disgust.

Just as one of the few compassionate residents of Grays Hall finally opened the door to let us in, the woman's most vocal companion yelled up to our third-floor dorm compatriots, who were still speechless with laughter, "It looks like you served these guys a big helping of ice-cold streaker gazpacho with a little bit of soggy newspaper on top." I turned and glared at him as I began to enter the doorway. "It can't be Caroline. She wouldn't hang around with an obnoxious idiot like that," I thought to myself. Then, just as the door began to close behind me, I heard the woman say in a loud voice (that I fearfully imagined to be Caroline's), "Maybe you should have asked him if he wanted gravy with that." I guess somebody recognized me after all. Perhaps I had become a little too well known as the gravy guy at the Union dining hall. Probably not a big asset for my plans to meet and marry someone rich and famous.

I don't know if it was Caroline Kennedy who saw my regrettable streaker moment. I don't want to believe that it was. But if it was, I guess that was just her way of letting me know why she would rather not hang out with a foolish idiot like me. I can't say that I blame her, whoever she was.

*   *   *

Somehow I survived and passed my classes along the way to senior year. I had accumulated extra credit in order to give myself the freedom to take whatever courses I wanted as a senior. No more required courses. I would only study subjects that would be really useful to my future. Because I thought I might go to graduate school in social sciences, I decided that I should take statistics. I went to visit Statistics 100. When I say visit, I mean visit. At Harvard, you don't enroll in classes until you have visited them for two weeks. Thus students begin with a list of ten or so classes to visit and gradually eliminate choices as they settle on which four classes will comprise their schedule for the semester. Only then do students file the paperwork to enroll in the courses. Students' choices of classes are based on the performance of the professors during the first two weeks (entertainment value ranks high) as well as the students' assessment of the burdensomeness of the course requirements. As a senior, I wasn't too concerned about course requirements. I had become very adept at writing research papers in one sitting during a single evening (I didn't say that they were good research papers). I had also figured out how to answer effectively the essay exams typically given in Harvard courses, even if I hadn't actually read all of the assigned material.

The first meeting of Statistics 100 on Monday seemed pleasant enough. I reviewed the syllabus, noted that there were a couple of exams and no writing assignments. The workload didn't appear to be too burdensome. The professor was some famous statistician, but for my purposes, he just seemed like a friendly, gray-haired old guy. Good enough for me. I settled into a seat in the back row of an auditorium filled with 150 students and read my *Newsweek* while the old guy droned on happily about something or other. During the second class meeting on Wednesday, I glanced up from my *Time* magazine occasionally and noticed that the old guy was now writing equations on the board. I had no idea what this was all about, but I figured that I would sort it all out during Reading Period. Reading Period is the two-week study period each semester at Harvard between the end of classes and the beginning of final exams. Generally, it is the time when Harvard students undertake all of the assigned reading that they were supposed to have done throughout the semester. It is easier to do the entire semester's reading during Reading Period because there aren't any annoying class meetings getting in the way.

Readers unfamiliar with Fair Harvard may be noticing that my esteemed alma mater does not appear quite so taxing for young scholars as is generally assumed. In addition to "Shopping for Classes" and Reading Period, a full courseload for students at Harvard consists of only four classes rather than the five classes that more typically constitute a full schedule at virtually every other American university. Harvard believes that its courses are more difficult and therefore four Harvard courses are presumed to equal or exceed five courses at lesser institutions (including Yale). However, no matter how many hours they meet or how many requirements they have, all Harvard courses count the same on the student's transcript: they count as one course (or one-half course if they last only one semester). Thus my English course, which met for two one-hour lectures each week, had no writing assignments, and merely a midterm exam and a final exam, counted the same on my transcript as the chemistry and biology courses taken by pre-med students that required three hours of lecture each week plus six or eight hours of work in the lab. The shrewd (and lazy) student at Harvard thus has the opportunity to shop around for four courses that meet only two-hours each week in order to have minimal academic burdens. Thus, in effect, if you played your cards right, you would have a full course load by spending a mere eight hours each week in class with ample opportunity to put aside all of the actual work until Reading Period at the end of the semester. Most Harvard students are too ambitious to follow exactly this path-of-least-resistance, but don't let anyone tell you that they don't work these factors into their calculations when they develop their study plans. How else would they have all that time to run political campaigns, direct and produce dramatic productions, and undertake all of the other extracurricular activities that are, in many respects, the real education at Harvard?

Anyway, I eagerly entered the third class meeting of Statistics 100 on Friday armed with the latest copy of *Sports Illustrated*. "This class is really a godsend for letting me catch up with my important reading," I thought to myself. I settled in at my usual spot in the back row of the auditorium and became engrossed in an article about the just-underway college football season. As I read the article, my ears (by now well-trained, not unlike a dog's, to detect signs of trouble in the swirl of sounds around me during class) detected the old guy saying, "Does anyone have any questions?" I glanced at the blackboard and noticed that in the short span of the first week, the equations had become impressively complicated. I made a mental note that I needed to find people back at the dorm who had taken this course previously so that they could explain it to me during Reading Period. No one asked any questions at that moment in class. Just as my eyes and mind re-focused on my magazine, my ears went to "High Alert" status as I heard the old guy say, "Does everyone understand?"

This was different. Usually, professors asked once about questions and then moved on. In my four years at Harvard, I had never before heard any professor ask, "Does everyone understand?" because it was a given that no Harvard students would want to debase themselves by publicly admitting that they didn't understand something, especially something about which they had just been invited to ask questions. When (predictably) no one responded, the old guy did the unthinkable: he called on someone involuntarily. How could we be procrastinating, distracted, and passive Harvard students, if someone was going to call on us? This was unprecedented. I bolted upright in my seat and peered down the steep sweep of the auditorium. I watched in empathetic horror as some poor schmuck in the second row was suddenly put on the spot trying to explain an equation that he obviously didn't understand. I felt my heart rate increase as I surveyed this unfamiliar and mildly threatening scene. The professor had now shed the label "friendly old guy" in my mind because I was starting to feel uneasy and, indeed, frightened about his approach to teaching. The professor's victim actually handled things quite well (benefiting from a burst of adrenalin no doubt) by suddenly thinking of questions that he had meant to ask the professor about the equation. The professor seemed to glare at him momentarily before providing elaborate explanations (probably re-explanations, if I had been paying attention) about the equation. Then the professor asked again, "Does everyone understand?" The threat of public humiliation apparently trumped the fear of debasement from admitting ignorance because suddenly there were several hands in the air and a multitude of questions followed. I was not listening to the questions or the answers. I merely evaluated the scene to calculate whether my well-being was actually at risk.

After answering all of the questions, the professor asked again. "Now, does everyone understand?" No one spoke. No one stirred. Everyone sat frozen, silently chanting "Not me, please, not me." Then the professor whirled to his left and pointed to a woman in the front row and barked, "You. Explain this equation." The woman provided a detailed explanation which apparently satisfied, and may even have impressed the professor. Thus he continued with his lecture and drew more equations on the board. After he presented each equation, he fell into a now predictable pattern of soliciting questions, asking if everyone understands, and then calling on someone in the first four rows for an explanation. Now that I had identified his *modus operandi*, I took my ears off "High Alert," made a new mental note to find someone *before* Reading Period who had previously taken this course, and settled back in the comfort and safety of the last row, high above and far away from the threatening action near the blackboard. I resumed reading my *Sports Illustrated*. As I was drawn into the football article again, I was aware that the professor was again asking if everyone understood. Moments later, however, I was shaken from my feeling of security and thrust into danger when I saw the professor marching up the aisle of the auditorium toward the back rows where I was sitting. Instantly, I hid the magazine behind my notebook and frantically began making completely nonsensical notations and marks across the page of my notebook. I put my head down and wrote furiously with my illegible scrawl, desperately hoping that he would stop along the way to call on someone else. Unfortunately, his footsteps came closer and closer as he moved to the far reaches of the hushed auditorium. All eyes followed his progress until he came to the back row and stopped right next to my seat. I knew he was there because with my head locked in a downward gaze, even amid the furious and desperate scrawling, I could see his shoes right next to mine and pointed in my direction. I wrote and wrote and wrote, as if my life would somehow be saved if I could set a record for putting ink on one page within twenty-five seconds. My armpits were wet with perspiration, my respiratory system kicked things up two notches, and I actually started to feel a bit dizzy.

The professor's shoes stood motionless next to mine for a long time. It was as if he was trying to torture me until I actually experienced the cardiac arrest that he apparently wanted to see. Suddenly, the silence was broken as he practically shouted (apparently so that everyone in the auditorium could hear) "YOU! EXPLAIN THE EQUATION."

My pen stopped moving, not because I froze in place but because my sense of self, my confidence, my security, and my willpower had instantly wilted away. I felt myself surrender, physically and mentally. My mind didn't even attempt to think of some self-protective distracting comment. It was clear that asking questions at this point, after the opportunity had been previously offered and declined, would only enrage my antagonist. I had no choice but to meekly prostrate myself before him (and all of my classmates) and admit that I had no idea what the equation was about. A chill rolled through my body, as if the man's shadow had suddenly blocked my access to the room's warmth and light. Like a man in the moment before his execution, I slowly lifted my head and saw...YES! THERE IS A GOD!...he was pointing at the poor slob sitting next to me.

Actually, the guy next to me (some nondescript fellow whom I had never even noticed) gave a very impressive answer. To which the professor announced, "That was outstanding!" The professor turned on his heel and began to walk back down the steep aisle steps toward the blackboard. Before he had taken two steps, I was running out the back door of the auditorium.

I felt as if I had been in a train wreck, yet survived. I was so grateful for having escaped with my life that I vowed to make a new start by giving money to the poor, volunteering to tutor poor kids, and delivering meals to elderly shut-ins. As it turned out, I never did any of these things, but I sure took a lot more care in selecting classes that were non-threatening and comprehensible. As I headed across Harvard Yard from the Science Center, I realized that I needed to find another course since, having settled prematurely on Statistics 100, I had not been visiting alternate selections. I ran into a friend of mine walking in the opposite direction; another senior, wise in the ways of course selection.

"Paula, I need a course."

"What are you looking for?"

"I need Monday, Wednesday, and Friday at 10 a.m., preferably in the social sciences, with no required paper and not more than two exams."

Like a modern computer processing information, she paused only momentarily before saying, "Psych 1550. Meets at William James Hall."

"What's it called?"

"Stress and Disease. Looks pretty easy."

"Thanks. I'm there," I said gratefully as we parted company. It all seemed pretty appropriate after what I had just gone through. I had learned much about stress in just a few short moments and now it was time to advance my disease, senioritis, by finding a comfortable place to keep up with my reading. Thank heavens there were always experienced shopaholics around to rescue those of us who were inattentive during the course selection process.

*   *   *

One night I was in my dorm room hunched over my typewriter. During my final three years at Harvard, I lived in Leverett House, a set of buildings that included two eleven-story glass towers. The entire external wall of my small cubicle of a dorm room was a glass wall with a view of the Boston skyline. The rooms provided a great view, but had drawbacks when trying to get dressed behind wrinkled old curtains that did not entirely cover the room from outsiders' eyes. (One Leverett resident discovered another drawback when he was growing marijuana plants in his window and the police could not help but notice). Periodically, I would glance at the skyline and wish that I didn't have this stupid paper due the following day. As I typed my thoughts on the page, my desk lamp flickered briefly. "Stupid, cheap lamp," I thought to myself as I continued typing. Then the lamp flickered again. Now I was really annoyed. I didn't want to write this paper anyway, and now I had to deal with the lamp as a distraction. When the lamp flickered for a third time, I reflexively and angrily slapped it, the way people hit the side of a television to try to persuade it to provide better reception.

WHOOSH. Darkness fell across metro Boston in a flash. When my hand struck the lamp, all of the electrical power in the Boston area disappeared. No streetlights. No skyline. No nothing. Just an eerie silence, except for the headlights of passing automobiles. I froze with my arm in mid-air. "*What have I done?*" I was stricken with fear. "What if someone finds out that I did this?" If there is such a thing as one's blood running cold, then I now knew what that meant. (By the way, I only mention this incident because the time limit set by the Massachusetts statute of limitations has now passed for prosecution of any crime related to causing the great Boston power failure). The fear passed quickly, but not the guilt. "Could anyone find out that I caused this?," I thought. Maybe they could trace the circuits or something back to my lamp, but that didn't seem likely. They would be too busy trying to restore power and clean up all the problems that developed when

Boston was plunged into darkness. My sense of guilt and responsibility grew with each passing moment, so it seemed that the least I could do was get out into the streets and help some of the people who were being victimized as a result of my impulsive assault on the desk lamp.

The dorm hallway was pitch black and I felt my way along the hall and the staircase while trying not to listen to (and be too guilty about) the screams I heard from fellow students trapped in the claustrophobic confines of dark and frozen elevators. Near the front door, which was illuminated by moonlight, I saw a crowd of students trying to yell through the elevator door and up the shaft, "Just relax. The power will probably be on in a few minutes. Stay calm." I thought I better move on. I think the police always look for perpetrators to return to the scene of the crime so it seemed better to help people elsewhere.

At the corner, I was relieved to see that no one was injured in the car crash caused by the failure of the traffic lights. That would have weighed heavily on my conscience, but what could I do? I didn't know that smacking a desk lamp could cause a power failure.

As I rounded the corner in the darkness, I ran into (literally) a man who was carrying something.

"Ooof." I heard the air expel from his lungs by the force of our collision. I also heard him drop something as we collided.

"Oh, I'm so sorry. I didn't see you." I reached out to help him regain his balance, but he had dropped to his knees and was feeling around the sidewalk in desperate, frantic motions.

"Did you lose something?," I asked.

"Yes. Yes, I did. Something very important."

"Let me help you look."

"No, really. I can handle it."

"I'll help. It's my fault."

"No, really. Just stay where you are."

Because I felt very responsible for the collision and for the darkness that caused the collision, I stepped over him to find a spot to help with the search. Unfortunately, in the darkness I miscalculated where he was crawling. Thus I stepped on his leg and then fell heavily on top of him.

"Ouch. You idiot!," he yelled. "Watch what you're doing! I think you broke my ankle or something!" He was doubled over holding his leg and cursing me vigorously under his breath.

As I rolled off of him, I heard the sound of breaking glass. Suddenly, he froze and whispered loudly, "Oh my god, no." This didn't sound good, so I leaped to my feet and felt (and heard) more glass crunch beneath my shoes. "Freeze!," he screamed. "You're smashing the test tubes containing the research for my Ph.D. dissertation. That's five years worth of work that you're destroying. You're ruining my life!"

At the sound of his screaming, several people with flashlights ran to where we were. "Are you two all right?," they asked anxiously. "Should we call an ambulance?"

"No, I'm not all right. This idiot has destroyed the research for my doctorate. I'll probably have to spend three extra years here living as a starving student just to undo what this moron managed to destroy in five seconds."

Suddenly, all of the flashlights were on me. I felt like one of those prison escapees suddenly cornered in the searchlights. "I didn't mean to…it was an accident…I was just trying to help."

As the excuses tumbled forth from my lips, I suddenly heard my poor victim exclaim, "Say, I know you!" I peered more closely at him in the darkness and then, as a flashlight beam fell across him, I recognized him as the graduate assistant from the biology class I took with Caroline Kennedy during my freshman year. Before I could say hello, he said, "Aren't you the guy who got a twelve and a half on the easy exam in freshman general biology?"

It wasn't exactly the way I wanted people at Harvard to remember me, let alone the way to be introduced in front of a group of strangers on a sidewalk. However, I had little choice but to say, "Yes, I am."

His next words, formulated as an obvious attack, struck deep into my being. "*What in the world are you doing at Harvard?*"

In an instant, my mind reviewed the misadventures of the previous four years, including George Winthrop, Caroline Kennedy, gravy, streaking, Statistics 100 (the actual list went on and on) as I struggled to find a response. Suddenly, I heard the words of my high school history teacher, and I responded by blurting them out, tentatively, almost as if answering with the uncertain hope that the listeners might agree that this was the correct answer: "Because you only go to college once?"

With a look of disgust, he muttered, "Well, some of us wish that you had never come to Harvard at all."

As I looked around and my senses absorbed the sounds of traffic accidents at every intersection and screams emanating from every elevator, I almost thought I heard two million people in the metro Boston area simultaneously mumble, "Amen."

Chapter Three

The Roots of My Family Tree

You must know your history in order to understand yourself.

Maybe that's the essence of my problem. I can't understand myself because I have so little connectedness to my ancestors. Genealogy helps Americans distinguish themselves from their fellow countrymen (and women). We are all perfectly equal as Americans. Yet, while chanting the mantra of "equality, equality" as required by our national ideology, we seem to look for ways to elevate ourselves above those around us. Our ancestral pasts (or at least the pasts that we claim for ourselves) provide us with claims to nobility, dignity, courage, perseverance, and ingenuity. Through our ancestors, or perhaps more accurately, through the myths about our ancestors, we achieve all of these elements without actually having to display any of those qualities for ourselves. We feel proud about the admirable qualities evident in the portraits of our ancestors that we paint for others to behold.

At Harvard, "roots-talk" provided the opportunity to distinguish one's self from the surrounding horde of overachievers.

The person who said, "My ancestors sailed to America on the Mayflower" might hear in return that "My great-great grandfather escaped from slavery on the Underground Railroad and established a school for freed slaves in New York." These competing claims provided distinctive sources of pride.

For others, ancestral claims pointed to particular geographic locations and historical moments to connect contemporary souls to a monumental thread of history. Thus students saw themselves deeply connected to their ancestors' trials and tribulations that spurred journeys to the United States from the impetus of the Irish potato famine, slavery, or the Holocaust.

So what connection did I have to an interesting or noble past? I had to ponder that question. How can you join in the "roots-talk" and feel ancestral pride when you're a regular middle-class guy from the Midwest with the most mundane of WASP names, Smith? I felt left out of the conversations going on around me. As I began to hear everyone else's claims to distinctiveness, it seemed as if I was the one anonymous American at Harvard. Everyone else was standing on the high branch of a unique family tree. Meanwhile, I was wandering through the genealogy forest looking at each tree and hoping that I would find my initials carved on a giant redwood rather than on some nondescript shrub, or worse yet, on the moss growing on the north side of a stump.

One night at dinner, the conversations revealed that everyone at the table (except for me) was an immigrant or the child of an immigrant. These students had their own personal memories and direct links to Trinidad, Jamaica, Haiti, Mexico, and China. It was odd to realize that they all came to the United States in order to become Americans like me, but they weren't really Americans like me. They were Americans like I wanted to be. They had individuality. They were connected to interesting geographic roots. They had witnessed or participated in the struggle to seek security and upward mobility in a competitive society. Because their families had escaped impoverished circumstances in recent memory, they exuded the pride of familial accomplishment and that air of superiority (or so it seemed to me in my jealous state) of people who had earned every bit of their success in the face adversity.

One of my friends realized that I was sitting silently throughout the sharing of lineage and Horatio Alger stories. He said to me, kiddingly,

"So how does it feel to be a stereotypical white male who can't relate to the heritage and struggles of Third World peoples?" As my other friends chuckled about my misfortune in being disconnected from any noble past, I suddenly saw my tree in the forest and I quickly climbed aboard.

"Actually, my family is from the Third World and rose from poverty just like you guys."

"The Third World? Get real. You're from Michigan."

"Ahhhh. But my father's family is from West Virginia!" It was just like laying four aces on the table in poker and I rose halfway out of my seat as if to collect my chips for winning. But for some reason my friends' expressions indicated that my gambit had not won them over. They sat staring at me with bemused expressions. They weren't opening the door to their fraternity for me just yet.

"West Virginia is part of the United States. It is not in the Third World."

"Ah hah. You're not recognizing the internal colonialism that has held my people in figurative chains for centuries. Well, for decades anyway."

The expressions began to change to annoyance. "Don't talk about colonialism. You don't know what it is unless you go to a real Third World country."

"But we've got it all: rampant poverty, exploited natural resources, corporate control, and corrupt politicians. We're there in the struggle for liberation." I could tell from my voice that I was starting to plead for acceptance.

The jury was unmoved. Well, one of them was moved to sarcasm. "Wrecked cars parked in everybody's yards, rampant intermarriage within families, and demented mountain men who capture hikers to make them 'Squeal like a piggie' does not the Third World make."

At the derogatory reference to a certain unforgettable scene in the film *Deliverance*, I sat up straight in a full defensive position. "I'll have you know that *Deliverance* took place in Georgia, not West Virginia. Hey, think about how it really is. The poverty. The coalminers. My ancestors, pulling themselves up by their bootstraps. Don't tell me that we haven't got it all. Have you ever been to West Virginia anyway?!?"

"Have you?"

Oops. They had me there. As they all collected their trays and began to depart, I called after them. "Hey, we've got a national anthem. Well, a song anyway." I started singing. "Almost heaven, West Virginia, Blue Ridge Mountains…." Of course, I didn't realize how loudly I was singing until I noticed that the dining hall had grown completely silent and eight hundred people were staring at me. "Shenandoah…." My voice trailed off meekly and I quickly sat down. As I watched my friends disappear across the room, I was left alone, figuratively anyway since there were eight hundred other diners in the room. I felt a yearning for that which seemed missing in my life yet was so central to the lives of so many of my Harvard friends. At that moment, I vowed that I would travel to my ancestral past and discover my roots.

*   *   *

After graduation, I set off with my friend and classmate Abe to drive across America (well, from Boston to Denver anyway). Along the way, we would stop in West Virginia to see if I could find some long-lost relatives. Actually, it's a little awkward describing them as "long-lost" since they presumably knew right where there were and had been there for their entire lives. It was my father who had moved away as a child. Thus I was the offspring of the "lost sheep" and this was my moment to reestablish my connection to my ancestral flock.

My father made a call to a distant cousin of my grandmother who had appeared at my grandmother's funeral. He didn't know her well but she had been very friendly and she made an admirable effort to come north for the funeral a few years earlier. After spending a night with her family, the next day we would drive into the hills to look for a great-aunt (on the other side of the family from the distant cousin) whom my uncle had discovered was still alive and living alone on a farm in country.

On the drive across West Virginia, Abe began to express some concern about the unknown world into which we were entering. "How well do you know this distant relative?"

"She's my late grandmother's cousin and I don't really know her at all."

"Have you met her?"

"I vaguely remember her from the funeral a few years ago."

"What's she like?"

"All I remember is that she kept saying that I looked just like Robert Redford."

He frowned at me. "So, other than her poor eyesight, what else do you remember?"

"I don't remember anything. But don't worry, My father thinks she's very nice."

We drove in silence for a few more minutes before Abe said, "What if they don't like Jewish people?"

"How will they know that you're Jewish, for heavens sake?" I was surprised by the question.

"Hey, lots of times people can tell things. My name is Abraham, you know. Very Old Testament. It's not that hard to make a guess."

"They probably don't know anything about Jewish people."

"Look, you don't really have much understanding of the rampant anti-Semitism in some parts of the country. There are a lot of fundamentalist Christians who refer to Jews as 'Christ-killers' for betraying their Jesus."

Because I was trying to be reassuring, I did not want to admit that I, unfortunately, knew this to be true because I had heard such comments from some kids in junior high school when I was growing up. "Let's not worry about anything prematurely. If it's a bad situation, we can always leave."

After a few more minutes of silence, Abe said, "What if they serve ham for dinner?"

Actually, this very thought had occurred to me, but I was hoping that he would not be thinking about it. "Well, I don't know. What are you going to do?"

"I guess maybe I might have to eat it. To be polite or something."

I turned toward him with a look of surprise. "Are you serious? Have you ever eaten ham before?"

"No. I'm just not sure what I would say."

Again, I tried to be reassuring. "Let's not worry prematurely." Despite my words, his comments now had me worrying quite a bit about interacting with these total strangers.

When we arrived at the small house, the cousin greeted us warmly. She came out of the house and walked all the way down to the end of the driveway to meet us. I introduced her to Abe and she promptly introduced me and Abe to her husband. It was quite noticeable to me that she introduced Abe as "Abner." He interjected politely by saying, "Actually my name is Abe," but the husband ignored his comment, thrust out a beefy hand, and said, "C'mon in, Abner."

We chatted with them for a while and they kept calling Abe "Abner" no matter how many times we tried to correct them. When the cousin said that dinner was almost ready, I went into the bathroom to wash my hands. While I was drying my hands on a towel, I heard from the kitchen the very words that we had dreaded.

"Do both you boys like ham?"

I stood very still and listened intently for Abe's response. After a long pause, I heard Abe say, "He does." It's hard to remember exactly what it was we feared might happen next. I'm not sure we even knew at that time what it was that we feared. Certainly we didn't really think they'd leap to their feet yelling, "Ah ha, we thought you might be Jews!" Perhaps we feared that our hosts' dispositions would suddenly turn icy. Perhaps we feared that they'd make mysterious phone calls to organize a mob to run us out of town. It was somewhat silly in retrospect. Moreover, it was unfair for us to ascribe hostile motives to people, relatives of mine no less, who had invited us into their home. A close self-analysis at that moment might have revealed how our own stereotypes, fears, and prejudices were at work.

The cousin responded quite quickly. "You know what?," she said, "My daughter doesn't eat ham either." When I heard that, I breathed a sigh of relief. Now Abe could decline the ham and no one would think anything of it. Unfortunately, he still had to eat something, and that something turned out to be home-made, home-preserved strawberry jam. Time and again, the husband would point over at Abe and say, "Give Abner some more of that there jam." Abe would thank them politely and spread more jam over another slice of home-made bread. All the while, he kept whispering to me, "My father would kill me if he saw me eating this stuff. People who do this home canning are always growing botulism and other microscopic poisons in their food." Abe's father was a medical school professor, so he was especially well-schooled in the issues of food safety. I decided to stick with the ham. I didn't see any sign of swine in the backyard so I presumed they had purchased this item at the store.

The next morning we set off to find my great-aunt from the other side of the family. We figured we'd drive to the great-aunt's town, a small dot amid winding country roads on the map. When we reached the town or rather the intersection that had a gas station and a small post office, we thought it best to ask for directions at the post office.

"Excuse me, do you know where Mary Smith lives?," I asked the man behind the counter.

"Miss Mary? Why, of course. Everyone knows Miss Mary."

"Well, I'm her great nephew and I wanted to try to find her house."

"Hmmm." The postman eyed us carefully. He didn't seem to be suspicious of us; he just seemed to be sizing us up. "What kind of car are you boys driving?"

It seemed like an odd question, but we answered "A Chevy Vega." For those who cannot remember this extinct vehicle, it was notable for two attributes: it was very small and it was very cheap (in construction and price). It was a dependable car, but, in our situation, it was quite sluggish and slow. In fact, the little blue car was so overloaded with all of the stuff that had filled two students' dorm rooms that the body was barely traveling four inches above the roadway and the engine hardly had any pick up at all.

The postman thought about something for a minute, and then said, "I think you can make it." We didn't really think much about his comment because we were immediately listening intently to his directions. "Go down here a little ways," he said, pointing vaguely in the direction of the front door to the post office. "Then you'll see a sign for State Route 147. Turn left there and follow that road. Eventually you'll hit Route 622 and then you need to turn right on Mountainview Highway."

I wasn't sure that I understood the directions but, hoping that Abe had grasped the instructions better than me, I joined Abe in thanking the postman profusely. Abe got behind the wheel and started to drive. As we turned out of the post office parking lot, he said to me, "I hope you caught those directions because I couldn't tell what the man was talking about. He didn't even give us an address or description for her house, did he?"

Knowing that Abe tended to worry about things even more than I did, I felt forced to display an air of confidence. "No problem. I've got a clear picture in my head." A clear picture of what, I couldn't say.

At the bottom of a small hill, our road seemed to end. We stopped in the middle of the street and looked for any kind of sign. Then I noticed that off to the left was a short post with a small, softball-sized circular sign that read "S.R. 147." It was so small that it was difficult to spot amid the trees and bushes. We both remembered that we were supposed to turn left on State Route 147. That turned out to be the only part of the directions that either of us understood. But we didn't see any road next to the sign. We were quite puzzled until I noticed a faint set of tire tracks going through the waist-high weeds in the field next to the sign.

I pointed out the tire tracks and said, "It looks like the road is the field or vice versa."

Abe looked at me as if I had lost my mind. "We're not driving into that field. The weeds are so deep that you can't even see where it goes."

"C'mon, man. We've come this far and we've gotten this close. Let's not quit now. Let's just go a little ways and see."

Muttering under his breath, Abe turned left, accelerated, and drove blindly into the field, trying to follow the faint tire tracks. Very quickly the tire tracks swerved right and we found ourselves moving up a steep hill. As the weeds thinned out, Abe suddenly stopped the car. We each looked out of our respective side windows and simultaneously gasped. Clearly, a heavy four-wheel-drive vehicle had taken this path after a significant rain storm. The field was now mostly dry, but tire ruts that were nearly two-feet deep defined the path up the hill. We had been driving precariously in the middle of the tire ruts without even realizing it. If we steered off course just a few inches in either direction, our overloaded, low-riding car would fall sideways into one of the deep tire ruts and then we might not ever get the car out of there. Now we knew why the postman asked us about what kind of car we had. He must have owned stock in Chevrolet, because I think he greatly overestimated the compact Vega's off-road capabilities, especially when it was in such an overloaded condition.

Abe looked at me, partly angry and partly desperate. "Now what are we supposed to do?"

"I think we need to keep moving forward, very carefully. We can't stop here on the side of the hill. What if some truck comes rolling over the hill going in the other direction? They'll smash right into us. We can't back up. There's no way you can back down a hill and into some tall weeds without having the car fall into these deep tire tracks." I was worried but I was trying to think clearly and logically.

Abe inched forward slowly as we both glued our eyes to the deep tire tracks and literally held our breath that nothing bad was about to happen. As we neared the top of the hill, Abe informed me that we would be stopping at the first house we found and that I would go to the door to ask for some clear directions. As he talked, he also decided that we would abandon the car at the first clearing amid the weeds and woods. He did not want to risk getting stuck on the side of a mountain with no way to get his parents' car out.

As we reached the top of the hill, the ruts disappeared and we found ourselves on what seemed to be a real dirt road. There was no gravel on it, but it was well traveled so it seemed like a luxurious super highway compared to the minefield we had just traversed. Up ahead on the left, we could see a small house. "When we get to the house, you're going up there to find out how we get out of here," Abe declared firmly. "If we're going to really keep going on your little adventure, then I'm leaving the car somewhere around here. If they tell you it's too far to walk, then let's get out of here, and hopefully by some way different than the way we came in." I nodded in order to appear cooperative, but in my mind I was determined to find my great-aunt now that I had come this far.

Approaching the house, we could see chickens running around the yard and a short, elderly woman tossing feed to them. We pulled off the road across from the house and I jumped out of the car and headed toward the woman. I wanted to talk to her out of Abe's earshot, just in case she said we still had far to go. It would be easier to persuade him to keep going (i.e., lie to him) if he hadn't heard anything for himself. The woman greeted me with a broad smile. There was something odd yet refreshing about her demeanor. A couple of strangers just arrived at her house and she didn't look the least bit wary or suspicious. She became even warmer when I told her I was looking for my great-aunt

Mary Smith. I also told her that we wanted to leave the car and walk from her house.

"Oh, Miss Mary!," she said clapping her hands together happily. "She lives just on the other side of the mountain. Y'all just go on down this road and then you'll see this house. Just go and ask that lady and she'll tell you how to get to Miss Mary's. You just leave the car right there. That's fine. It won't take you very long at all."

I thanked her repeatedly and happily ran back to the car, where my partner didn't look quite so happy. He got out of the car and stretched his arms in the hot sun while shaking his head. "That guy thought a Vega could climb like a mountain goat and he was wrong. Now I'm supposed to believe it when this lady says its just down the road."

"Actually she said it's on the other side of the mountain."

"Which mountain?," he exclaimed, pointing to the numerous wooded hills surrounding us.

"The lady at the next house will tell us," I called over my shoulder as I started walking briskly down the dirt road. "C'mon."

He hadn't moved yet. He called after me, "What house? I don't see any house."

As I expected, he only let me get about thirty yards ahead of him and then he jogged after me. "This better not turn into some nightmarish experience," he muttered as we kicked up clouds of dust along the undeveloped road. Although I couldn't see any houses up ahead, I prayed that we wouldn't be required to walk too far because I detected that Abe had far less commitment to this adventure than I did. But then again, he wasn't the one trying to discover his roots.

Very quickly we came upon a house that had been hidden from view by a rise in the road. Well, it wasn't actually a house. It was a deteriorating mobile home with a barn behind it. The front yard was strewn with various metal objects, presumably the rusting inner components of several deceased automobiles. We could see cattle grazing on a hillside pasture behind the mobile home. I knocked on the door and heard a flurry of activity inside. The door opened and a small woman and three children peered suspiciously at me through the crack. I asked about Aunt Mary and, without displaying the warmth that was characteristic of everyone else who heard my great-aunt's name, she matter-of-factly informed me that Aunt Mary's pasture backed up against her pasture just on the other side of the mountain. She told us that we could just walk across her pasture to get there.

We were elated. This was much easier than we had expected. We started to walk toward the gated entrance to the pasture behind the mobile home. Abe's demeanor changed suddenly. "You don't think we'll see any snakes back here do you?"

"Snakes?"

"Yeah, I would really like to avoid large ones or poisonous ones, and especially not the merger of the two."

I didn't want any new, speculative concerns to diminish my renewed sense of optimism. "No. Those kinds of snakes really live in warmer climates down South."

He looked at me skeptically but did not argue.

As we reached the gate, we noticed that the pasture was actually very steep and it was going to be quite a walk to reach the top of the large hill that everyone referred to as a "mountain" (since Abe was from Colorado, a state with real snow-capped peaks, we were incapable of regarding these hills, albeit substantial, as "mountains"). We entered the pasture, carefully shut the gate behind us, and slowly trudged upward, trying to avoid sections of mud and muck that had been stirred up by the cattle's hooves. As we climbed higher, we both noticed that in the shade of a very large tree there were many more cattle in the pasture with us than we had originally realized. There were only a half dozen cows wandering around visible from the road in the sunlight, but there were several dozen more that we were now approaching bunched together under the tree. Naturally, these dozens of heads turned in our direction to stare at us, including one animal that had visible horns and looked much larger than the others. Maybe snakes weren't the critters that we needed to worry about.

Abe and I both caught sight of him simultaneously and we both presumed that it was a "him." "Do bulls do anything to people?," Abe whispered to me. "I mean outside of bullfighting rings or whatever."

As he asked the question, my mind flashed back to a long ago Boy Scout camping trip to New Mexico where a cattle-creature (I don't know if it was a cow or a bull because I was fleeing too quickly) charged me without warning (do they ever growl or anything first, like a dog does before attacking?) and chased me down the side of a steep hill. Fortunately, the beast got distracted by a tasty patch of clover or something, although I didn't know that until I had sprinted for a quarter-mile before looking back. With this memory leaping vividly to mind, I turned to my pal and said reassuringly, "Naw, they never do anything."

"So you're saying that the fact that this bull is starting to jog in our direction in really nothing to worry about?"

I turned my head quickly to the right and saw the extremely disconcerting sight of which my friend remarked. I grabbed his arm and pulled him along as I broke into a run. "Maybe West Virginia cattle are more aggressive. In-breeding or something perhaps."

He wasn't really listening because, like me, he was trying to run forward while looking backward at the same time. In the best of circumstances, this was not a good posture for efficient foot speed. When slipping in cattle muck while trying to move up a steep hillside, it was downright scary. We slipped and stumbled, at times reduced to falling over on all fours to pull ourselves up the grassy hill. The bull continued his slow trot, but he obviously had better traction because he was gaining on us. I began to envision the next week's headline in the *Harvard Crimson* back in Cambridge: "Recent Grads Killed by Angry Bull on West Virginia Hillside" with a subtitle, "Friends Ask: What the Hell Were They Doing There?" Meanwhile, Abe was muttering, "I can't believe you brought me out here. My parents paid $30,000 for my

Harvard education [Note: Four years at Harvard was much less expensive in the late 1970s than it is today] and now I'm going to get gored by some psychotic, Appalachian bull." Funny how Harvard pretended to prepare us for running the world but never gave us any tools for saving our own skins (they need a required course entitled Vertical Windsprints 202. I'm sure it would come in handy in other situations, too). I wasn't too keen on having my last memory be this bull's horns, but I felt oddly reassured, in a small way, by the thought that my student loan contract had a loan forgiveness provision if I should die before paying off the loan. Hopefully, I hadn't overlooked any stupidity clauses in the contract that canceled the forgiveness if one's demise occurred under exceptionally foolish circumstances.

Because of the direction from the which the bull pursued us, our flight directed us off course. Instead of heading straight up over the hill on the grassy (and muddy) pasture, we were now climbing at an angle and moving toward a wooded area on the side of the hill. As we stumbled and ran, with the bull casually jogging along while steadily gaining ground, Abe was a step or two ahead of me when I saw it. A single strand of wire emitting a slight buzzing sound that was strung knee-high to short posts along the edge of the pasture. Instantly, my mind had a flashback to a moment in my childhood when my grandfather lifted me over just such a wire when we walked across a pasture to look at some horses during a visit to his rural home in Ohio. I reached out and grabbed Abe just before he reached the barely visible wire.

"What the hell are you doing?" He turned suddenly, his bewildered eyes shifting rapidly back and forth between me and bull.

"Don't run into that wire."

"What wire?" he asked in breathless confusion, now staring only at the approaching bull.

"I think it's an electric fence."

"A what?"

"An electric fence."

"What have you gotten me into? How am I supposed to know anything about electric fences?" His anger started to rise.

"C'mon, c'mon," I said, hurrying him along. "Just step carefully over the wire and then the bull can't get after us." We both stepped over the wire with the utmost care and continued to walk briskly toward the woods, not quite trusting that a single strand of metal could stop the large beast who followed us with such obviously malevolent intentions. As we reached the shade of the wood's edge, we looked back to see bull stop short of the wire and stare at us intently. A few moments later, the bull began to wander back from whence he came. A relaxing feeling of relief washed over us as we continued to stare at the bull until he was once again a small, distant figure among his hooved colleagues in the far stand of trees.

It was clear that Abe had written off our excursion as a disastrous failure. "We need to figure out how to get back to the car. Something else bad can easily happen. I don't see any houses. We don't know exactly where we're going. This is foolish. We don't know these people around here. We need to get out of here."

"Look, we're really close now. Let's not stop." I tried to sound encouraging but there was an edge of pleading in my voice.

Abe looked down at the ground, kicking the mud and shaking his head. "This is foolish. We don't know what else is going to happen." Then he froze momentarily before reaching down to the ground. He pulled from the mud two spent shotgun shells. Holding them in his right hand, he shook them at me. "See what this is? This is our message to get out of here."

I knew he was probably picturing the movie *Deliverance* in his head, when the city-dwellers' canoe trip is horrifically derailed by their encounter with violent mountain people. I knew this because I was thinking the same thing. I tried to think of something reassuring to say. "I'm sure everybody hunts around here. Don't worry about it. It's no big deal. It's the middle of the day and that lady gave us permission to walk across her pasture."

"Okay, smart guy. Since we just climbed over an electric fence and are now on the edge of some woods, how do we know that we're still in her pasture? We could be on somebody else's land right now. Who knows how they react to trespassing?" With his last statement, he held the shotgun shells up in front of my face and waved them back and forth.

He had a point. I didn't really know the consequences of going off course. However, we couldn't very well rejoin our friend the bull by heading back over the top of pasture as we had been directed. On the other hand, the roots of my family tree were almost in my grasp. I hadn't come this far in order to stop just short of my goal. While trying to think of a response, I started walking in the direction of the downward slope at the side of the hill.

"Where are you going?," Abe called after me, still standing in the same spot.

After I had taken a few steps, I saw a path leading down the hill and into the woods. It looked as if someone had driven a vehicle on it at some point. Before Abe could reiterate his query with greater emphasis and annoyance, I yelled, "Hey, I found a road. C'mon."

"This is crazy. We don't know where we are. Let's not do this." Now his voice was pleading a bit as I continued to walk. Then he seemed to get angry. "We're not doing this. This is foolish!"

In an effort to appease him, I turned back and yelled, "Let's just go to the bottom of the hill. If we don't see a house then we'll turn around." I felt bad about lying, since I had no intention of turning back without finding Aunt Mary. He shook his head in disgust and then jogged after me. As he caught up with me, I could hear a dog barking faintly in the distance. Although it was faint, it was the deep-throated sound of a very large dog. I hoped that Abe wouldn't notice, but his senses were tuned up to high alert.

He stopped. "Do you hear that?"

"Hear what?"

"That dog up ahead."

I kept walking while pretending not hear.

He stayed put. "Don't you hear that dog barking? That is not a friendly bark."

I continued walking, again trying to think of a response. Behind me, I could hear him yelling again. "This is crazy. What are you doing?"

As I got about thirty yards ahead of him into the woods, I saw that there was a fork in the trail we were following. The dog's barking, which indeed had a threateningly ferocious quality, was in the direction of the left fork. I yelled back. "The dog's over in that direction. Let's just go this way a bit. Just to see if we find her house."

Since it was apparent that I would keep walking, he had little choice but to run after me. As we reached the bottom of the wooded section of the hill, the trail intersected with a paved road. It was beautiful black asphalt on a road that had been resurfaced quite recently. I describe it as "beautiful" because its presence made me feel as if I had reentered civilization. We turned right on the paved road, moved further away from the audible canine, and immediately came upon a small wooden house. We could hear the sound of a hammer pounding from the far side of the house so we walked through the front yard to see who we would find. We came upon a spritely, elderly woman standing on a ladder and hammering shingles on the roof of a chicken coop.

"HELLO!" I yelled, trying to get her attention.

She stopped hammering and looked down at us. She waved the hammer at us, smiled a broad, closed-mouth smile, and then responded with "Howdy."

"We're looking for Miss Mary Smith," I said.

When she quickly responded, "That's me," I was overjoyed. It was as if I had made it to the top of Mt. Everest. When I explained who I was, at the sound of my father's name she scampered down the ladder and gave us each big bear hugs. It was an incredible moment. There was no hesitation, no getting acquainted, no further questions about my identity. I was immediately swept on to a secure perch of my heretofore undiscovered family tree. As she led us into the house, talking a mile a minute about her memories of my father as a small child ("That boy just wouldn't put on his socks...."), Abe whispered to me, "Wow. That's the strongest woman I've ever met. What a hug. It almost knocked the wind out of me." For a woman in her seventies, she seemed incredibly strong and fit, which had to be the case, as we discovered, when she described running her small farm with twenty-four head of cattle all by herself.

Entering the house was like stepping back in time. Her living room could have been an exhibit in an American history museum. There was a huge black stove (I don't know if it burned wood or charcoal) in the middle of the living room. Instead of art work, there were portraits of Franklin Roosevelt, John F. Kennedy, and Jimmy Carter hanging on the wall. Seeing those pictures fused me with an instant connectedness to the loyalties and aspirations of the poor, working people who comprised my family's preceding generations.

We only stayed about fifteen minutes and she talked the entire time. Mostly she talked about her many relatives, although I couldn't possibly keep track of the names and descriptions presented to me in such rapid-fire fashion. As we were getting ready to depart, she said "I want to show you one more thing." She reached into a drawer and handed us several Polaroid pictures of huge snakes. "These are some vipers I found in my yard," she said, showing evident pride at the photograph of six dead snakes laid out side by side in her front yard. More disconcerting to us were the photographs of live snakes hanging out of trees in her pasture. Abe and I looked at each other. Without exchanging a word, our eyes grew large at the shared recognition that we still had to walk back to the car somehow.

Aunt Mary walked with us through her backyard and opened the gate to her pasture. She pointed up the steep hill and said, "Just keep walking straight and you'll be right back in the pasture you came over from."

We could see cows scattered across her pasture so I couldn't avoid asking her, "Are there any bulls that we should watch out for?"

She laughed. "Don't worry about any bulls. If you meet up with one, just show him who's boss." Easy for her to say. We didn't have her physical strength.

We received our powerful farewell hugs and headed up the hill, which fortunately was a little less muddy since it was the sunny side of the mountain. We walked briskly and turned our heads from side to side, as if we had become human radar stations programmed to monitor every movement in each direction. We were both thinking about vipers and we couldn't stop talking about the photographs of the snakes as we headed up the hill. When we reached the top and pondered whether to take the long way around the perimeter of the pasture in order to avoid the bull, we both decided to head directly down the pasture hill as quickly and inconspicuously as possible. There's something about fearing that a viper (whatever kind of snake that is) will fall from a tree onto your head that helps you move quite quickly and diminishes lesser fears, such as trepidation about encountering large, unfriendly mammals.

In retrospect, except for our paranoia about the vipers, a paranoia that did not cease until we arrived at the car *and* inspected it for hidden vipers, I can hardly remember recrossing the bull's pasture or driving the car back down the mountain. My mind was filled with two thoughts. First, I had this glow of accomplishment, and a sense of being in touch with history. I almost wanted to drive straight back to Harvard to find those guys who had disparaged my West Virginia ethnicity. At the same time, I found myself returning again and again to a second compelling thought: Since Aunt Mary lived on a beautifully paved road, why didn't the postman give us directions that would permit us to drive to that road? I have a hunch that back at the post office and gas station, they're still slapping their knees and laughing (" Did you see those two city kids try to drive a Vega up that hill? What a couple of idiots? Those boys don't have any hope of getting admitted to a college.").

*   *   *

The success of the West Virginia adventure whet my appetite for further connections with my ancestors. When I traveled to Europe and later studied for one year at a British university, one of my goals was to visit the homelands of my known forebears: the Netherlands, England, and Germany. In each country, I attempted to find and feel a sense of connectedness that would let me share the "home" of my ancestors and, hopefully, get a glimpse into the foundations of my own spirit and soul.

I arrived in Amsterdam as a member of a tour group. We were to rent bicycles at the airport and cycle our way to a campsite at the old Olympic stadium. After the rented vans were loaded with our sleeping bags and suitcases, we jumped aboard our bikes and took off. Unfortunately, within one minute of leaving the airport, I noticed that my friend's bike tire seemed to be coming loose from the wheel. He and I stopped to see if we could fix the tire. Meanwhile, everyone else in our group just kept going and going and going and going until they disappeared from sight. After flying all night and feeling disoriented from jetlag, we didn't even think about the fact that we were now lost and alone in a foreign city. As it turned out, we fixed the tire and biked to our campsite. Unfortunately, we were so lost that the twenty-minute bicycle trip took us nearly seven hours to complete. We were practically hallucinating from sleep deprivation so it's a wonder that we didn't fall into a canal somewhere. I was so tired, lost, and depressed that I never felt much of a connection with my ancestral homeland. In fact, I was repeatedly annoyed by seemingly circular streets and canals that always brought us back to the same spots over and over again.

After a good night's sleep at the campsite, we spent the next day sightseeing, first with a boat tour of the canals. Then we wandered through Amsterdam's red light district. Quite a sight for a young American to see, let me tell you. I decided to take a picture of the street scene, but apparently one of the local entrepreneurs mistakenly believed that I was taking a picture of her. I had no idea that someone wearing a mini-skirt and spike heels could land a karate kick like that. My leg was bruised for six months afterward. Even worse, she seized my camera and proceeded to smash it in the cobblestone street. Based on what she was yelling in Dutch, I got the distinct impression that she wasn't saying, "Welcome home, native son." This experience led me to believe that I might feel a stronger ancestral connection to one of my other homelands.

In England, I had interesting experiences such as being spat upon by a soon-to-be Duchess and embarrassing the Queen from close range (see Chapter 4). However, I never quite felt as if I had found a long-lost home. The food was (how can I put this diplomatically) not an attractive feature. For example, steak and kidney pie: what's in that anyway? They boiled vegetables into a green, mushy mass so that you never knew if it began as peas, cabbage, or something else. Whole milk with the cream on top was delivered by the milkman every morning. That might be quaint for historical memories, but it is almost indigestible to someone brought up on skim milk. My basic beverage in life, orange juice, was a luxury item in Britain. I can count on my fingers the number of times that I saw it during the course of a year. Obviously, the culinary adjustment was difficult.

The room I rented gave me a greater appreciation for things American. There was no central heating in the building and no insulation around the drafty window. Thus even with the windows closed, the curtains blew in the breeze as if I was outdoors. The only heat was provided by a small space heater which cranked out quite a bit of intense heat, but unfortunately only for a distance of about two feet.

Worse yet, you had to pay every day for the electricity in your room. There was a coin box attached to the electrical outlet and you had to feed it with coins in order to plug in any electrical devices. Imagine feeding a parking meter in your room in order plug in a radio or clock. I also had to feed the meter to use the space heater. Thus when I tried to write at the desk, I jammed coins into the box, plugged in the space heater, and moved the heater close to my chair. On one particularly cold evening, I had to move the space heater closer and closer in order to enjoy any heat. As usual, my leg got second-degree burns while my fingers were numb and stiff from the cold. The low point came when I smelled smoke and looked down to see that the space heater had caught the chair on fire yet my fingers, which were four feet from the space heater and therefore out of its range, were so stiff and frozen that I could hardly work the doorknob to get the smoke out of the room.

The English people were wonderful hosts. I had terrific English friends and basketball teammates at the university. I also saw the most interesting sights. But I never felt as if I had touched a place that was in any way "home." Almost daily, England came close to becoming my final resting place since I continually watched for cars in the wrong direction while crossing the street. Despite many fond memories, nothing about England touched me like a long-lost "home."

Germany was the site of my final ancestral homeland visit. When I set foot in Germany, I was greeted by hundreds of soldiers, searchlights, machine guns, and guard dogs. Sort of like, "Welcome home! Now you're under arrest." The problem was that I impulsively decided to visit Germany while sitting in a tiny hotel room in Stockholm, Sweden. (It really was tiny. It was formerly a closet to which they had added a sink and a mattress. In order to fit the mattress into the room, they cut a slot in the wall. Although this permitted the mattress to stretch out, there was no corresponding slot in the wall for the sleeper's feet. It was like sleeping scrunched up in a box). I took a train from Stockholm to the Swedish south coast and then the train went aboard a ferry to be transported to Germany for the final leg of its trip to Berlin. The problem, of course, was that by coming down from Sweden in 1981 I was entering the old *East* Germany.

When we disembarked from the ferry to board the train, we were accosted and interrogated by East German soldiers. I had a pretty good capacity for summoning up my knowledge of high school German in order to formulate questions and answers, but I was absolutely incapable of understanding verbal commands and questions from a native speaker. The soldiers responded to my linguistic deficiencies by pounding their hands together and yelling louder. For some reason, this did not enhance my capacity for comprehension. Eventually, a soldier stamped many papers, apparently issued me a travel visa, and permitted me to enter the train's passenger compartment.

Unfortunately, by the time I was able to disengage myself from the soldier, all of the seats on the train were taken, primarily by drunken Swedish youths who had been partying for hours since we left Stockholm. Sadly, these youths had no way to know that the East Germans would lock all of the bathrooms on the train for the entire five-hour trip to Berlin. I have never seen such expressions of pain and anguish, manifested in the bulging eyes and groans of discomfort, as I saw among those hard-drinking youths who needed to use the bathroom but could only tug helplessly on the locked door. Those Communists certainly thought of every possible means to impose control and inflict punishment.

Because there were no seats available, I stood for the entire trip in the hallway next to the bathrooms. I was joined in the hallway by a Jordanian student and an Iranian student who found that their only language in common was English. Thus I stood nearby pretending not to listen to their conversation which, from the Iranian student's perspective, seemed mostly concerned with condemning Americans. After the Iranian student went to look for a seat, the Jordanian student addressed me in Swedish (apparently they both assumed that I was

Swedish because of my northern European looks and long blond hair). However, when I told the Jordanian that I was an American and only spoke English, he fled in embarrassment, presumably because of all the critical comments made by his conversation partner.

When we arrived in East Berlin, the East Germans, who were riding in separate cars, were forced to disembark. Meanwhile, teams of soldiers came aboard and literally tore the train apart, removing every ceiling and wall panel to make sure that no East Germans were hiding in order to escape to West Berlin. Then the train rolled over the Berlin Wall from East to West, over the minefields, over the barbed wire, over the machine guns, over guard posts, and over the Wall. Somehow this first picture of Germany did not make me feel at home, let alone feel welcome. Although I met many great people in West Germany, it was difficult to get those first few hours out of my head. I found myself saying, "No wonder my ancestors left," rather than "Boy, isn't it nice to be home."

There were many things I loved about the Netherlands, England, and Germany, including people, sights, and interesting experiences. However, my visits there did not give me any sense that I had become more connected with my roots. West Virginia gave me a sense of connection to my roots because of Aunt Mary, but even there I did not really have an enduring feeling that I had paid a visit to my "home," ancestral or otherwise. I did learn something from these experiences, however. If I need to know my history in order to understand myself, then maybe I should look closer to my literal home as in right inside my house. My history is comprised primarily of four parts: eating pizza, watching sports on television, reading books, and playing basketball. I have spent more time in my life doing these things than doing anything else (other than sleeping). Perhaps these are the activities that define my ethnicity and culture. Perhaps these activities define my true roots. When I do them, I am happy. When I do them, I am me.

Dorothy had to click her heels together three times and say, "There's no place like home. There's no place like home." By contrast, all I have to do is pick up the phone to order a large pepperoni with green peppers, flip on the tube to a basketball game, and read something at halftime. Like Dorothy, I undertook incredible journeys to find my roots. But unlike Dorothy, I probably could have reached the same spot, namely the family room sofa, by just sitting back and operating the remote control and the push button phone. There's no place like home and if I lie on this sofa long enough, I'm pretty sure that I'll become rooted here. Do you think if I saw my old friends from Harvard, they'd accept my description of my culture as being comprised of elements such as vigorous ceremonies (i.e., basketball games), ethnic cuisine (i.e., pizza), traditional technologies (i.e., an old television), and repetitive rituals that preserve and spread knowledge (i.e., reading)? Maybe I'll have a shot at convincing a naive anthropologist about the depth of my roots in a unique culture, but I have a hunch that my old colleagues will still view me as rootless, acultural, and devoid of sources of cultural pride. Let them think what they want. I think I'll be quite happy rooted to the sofa, mesmerized by my cultural attachment to televised basketball, and filled with cultural pride because of my ability (gained through my tribe's traditional methods of socialization) to scarf down an entire pizza before halftime.

Chapter Four

Fifteen Minutes of Fame

Everyone will have fifteen minutes of fame.

I am a hopeful believer in Andy Warhol's famous comment. My goals and decisions have never been based on the attainment of wealth or power. Instead, I seem motivated by a desire for achievement and recognition. Frankly, I would like to be famous. Perhaps that's the reason that I have been fascinated by prominent people and I keep a mental catalogue of the moments in my life when I have come into contact with famous people (and people who subsequently became widely recognized). When my life has intersected, even for one moment, with a famous person, then I feel as if I encountered history or, if I want to characterize my role more optimistically, became a part of history. I'm not sure if I shaped history in any way through my encounters with Caroline Kennedy at Harvard. Perhaps I dissuaded her from streaking and thereby saved her family from significant embarrassment (then again, maybe not). I feel fairly confident that I helped protect her health by steering her away from gravy. The samples splashed across my red server's jacket should have been enough to convince anyone to eat their potatoes plain. In any case, by standing on the same spot on the earth with her at the same moment in time I felt as if I was only one step removed from contact with her father, the late president. What's that they say about six degrees of separation? We're all just a few contacts indirectly removed from everyone else on the earth and everyone else in history. In my mental museum of celebrity (a museum that I preserve and treasure with a curator's care), I see those moments when I was right there with a prominent figure experiencing zero degrees of separation between me and fame, me and history.

*   *   *

My earliest contacts with celebrities were from a distance. They were thrilling moments, to be sure, but I wasn't close enough to reach out and touch the magic of fame. For example, when I was ten years old, I went to my first major league baseball game and I saw Denny McLain of the Detroit Tigers strike out future Hall-of-Famer Carl Yastrzemski of the Boston Red Sox. Okay, it wasn't much, but for a kid obsessed with sports, it was a big moment. When I was thirteen and camping at Grand Teton National Park with my Boy Scout troop, we encountered President Richard Nixon and his entourage on a vacation trip. I got to snap a picture of the president from about six feet away. However, since a Secret Service agent was punching me in the stomach at the time, (yes, thrusting his fist into the solar plexus of a uniformed Boy Scout; talk about paranoia motivating your security measures) the photo is quite blurry. So some celebrity encounters do not necessarily produce happy memories. In Nixon's case maybe that just says something about the particular celebrity. A few years later, I was driving through Boston with a car full of fellow teenagers on a church youth group trip. As we stopped at a red light, I looked out the window and there on the sidewalk was a tall man with a very familiar face. I stared for a few moments and then our car began to move forward. Suddenly, I realized who he was. Walt Frazier, all-star basketball player for the New York Knicks. I opened my window and desperately yelled, "Walt! Walt!" I think I wanted him to converse with me or acknowledge my presence, but this was entirely unrealistic since the car had traveled half a block already and was moving farther away at a rapid clip. The experience did make me a hero for a week back at my junior high school in Michigan, however. No other kid in Kalamazoo had ever seen such a famous star in person.

These first moments of nearly encountering fame merely whet my appetite. They hardly qualify as touching history (well, maybe seeing it pass close by, like watching a parade). As it turned out, sports provided my first avenue for close contact with celebrities, or rather future celebrities. I played high school basketball in Michigan at the same time that Magic Johnson was leading his Lansing Everett High School teams to high rankings and, eventually, a state championship. I would like to tell you that I went toe-to-toe with Magic Johnson, stopped him from scoring, and dazzled him with my brilliant hoopster moves. However, that would be stretching truth (which I'm willing to do, but not quite that much). I did see Magic play in high school, but he was in the advanced rounds of the state high school tournament and I was sitting in the stands because my team had already lost. Although Magic was lucky that he never had to face me, two other famous names were not so lucky.

When we played Benton Harbor High School, I played against a guy named David Adkins (I think so anyway. It's funny how the active maintenance of a celebrity archive often involves retrospective reconstructing with, unfortunately, some risk of error). Anyway, I played against Benton Harbor every year and I learned subsequently that one of Benton Harbor's players during that era was David Adkins, better known today as the comedian Sinbad. I don't actually remember Sinbad, but since I had my career high scoring effort for a high school varsity game (eight points!) while playing against Benton Harbor (I actually scored three two-point baskets but through the magic of official scorer errors, history will record that I got eight), we might as well presume that at least one of those shots went up over the aforementioned Mr. Adkins. Yeah, as I remember it now, I think I rose up and dunked on Sinbad. One of those monster jams that was probably so devastating to his psyche that he quit basketball and went looking for another profession. I could be imagining all of this, of course. Especially because dunking was illegal in the mid-1970s and I can't even touch the rim. But something in my memory tells me that I managed to far exceed my usual abilities when I went up against Sinbad. Fate was probably using me to send him a message. Surely, having a short white dude dunk on him must have been something akin to a voice from the great beyond capturing his attention and steering him toward his intended path of life (and success). Come to think of it, the man ought to thank me. He had no long-term future in basketball and if not for the embarrassment of a little, slow white dude scoring major points on him (oh, all right, so it was only eight points, but believe me, that was a major scoring effort for our side in the light of the way Benton Harbor sometimes blew us out of the gym), he might never have discovered his true calling in the entertainment industry. In fact, when he writes that "thank you" note, he could stick some money in the envelope, too. I did him a really big, big, favor. Just happy to help, Mr. Sinbad. We Michiganians (or is it Michiganders?) must always help each other out.

Let me just add that, although eight points sounds pitiful as a career high, that was for *varsity high school games.* I throw in that qualification to note that I had brighter moments in my career. Such as twenty-two points, including a school-record-tying eight-for-eight from the free throw line, against Ypsilanti High School in a junior varsity game. Okay, so I was only seven-for-twenty from the field, but hey, twenty-two isn't a bad total. Later in life, when I played in England for the University of Bristol, I scored twenty-eight points in a victory over the defending national champions from the University of Exeter. I had similar totals in other games, including twenty-two in the national semi-finals against Loughborough University, so my career isn't as sad as it might appear just by focusing on my point total for the game when I think I drove Sinbad out of basketball and into fame and fortune in comedy. (Okay, I admit that the players at English universities at that time weren't good enough to play for my junior high school team, but twenty-eight points is still twenty-eight points. Isn't it? I mean that counts. Right?? Please??).

In reality, I had a relatively modest high school career. I averaged about two points per game in my varsity career. I was a varsity starter for a total of six games in two years, and making me a starter typically meant that someone else was either academically ineligible or being punished (I can just imagine the conversations that the coach had with the real starters. "You see, I'm so mad at you that I'm going to start Smith in your place. How do you like that? Are you embarrassed now? You should be! Having him in there is going to put the entire team at risk"). A funny thing happened after high school, however. Whenever I did something "notable," such as earned a degree, got a university teaching job, or won an award, the sports section of my hometown paper would publish an article about me in an effort to say to the world "See. Jocks aren't stupid." I don't consider myself particularly representative of athletes, but what can I do if they (mis)use me as an example. When they wrote articles about me during college, including the erroneous and never corrected report that I was a member of Harvard's varsity basketball team (don't ask me where that came from; I was too busy pouring gravy, reading *Newsweek*, and having traumatic encounters with Caroline Kennedy), they characterized me as "a former Kalamazoo Central basketball player." By the time they were reporting on my graduate degrees, memories of the actual details of my less-than-illustrious career had begun to fade and I had somehow become "a slick backcourt performer." In reading these reports about myself, I began to appreciate how history can add gloss to a dull object. Sort of like turning a lump of coal into a diamond over a long period of time, I suppose. When they later wrote about my university teaching positions, they called me a "former basketball star." I am anticipating that I will be a "former city all-star" when I am in my late forties. Presumably I can progress to an "all-state basketball player" during my fifties in order to set the stage for retrospective high school All-American honors as they look back at my career when I'm in my sixties. I'm not interested in any posthumous honors, so it seems clear that in order to pass through the intervening stages of "star college basketball player" and "professional hoopster," I will have to live well into my nineties in order to become remembered as an "NBA all-star" (albeit retrospectively). But hey, if I manage to live into my nineties, I probably deserve to be remembered as an NBA all-star. There won't be anyone around who will still remember my actual career, so why not? Isn't history grand? Just by aging successfully, I can become a more famous and illustrious athlete.

Looking back at what actually happened, I would simply point out that scoring is only a small part of the game. So the fact that I didn't score much does not tell the entire story of my abilities and achievements. My real claim to glory in basketball came from hustling defense plus other kinds of things that aren't visible in the box score (I was dynamite in leading pregame warm-ups). And it was through defense that I really made my mark on another celebrity. Let's just call him Future NBA Star (after all, he probably has a lawyer on retainer). He was someone who starred at a Big Ten university and then spent a decade as a very respectable player in the National Basketball Association. He played for a high school that was in…let's say it was Detroit or Lansing or Flint, and we played against his team twice each year as part of our league. At six-foot-seven, he was a full seven inches taller than me (more like eight, but my driver's license says I'm six feet tall so I guess that makes it official). Yet, when I guarded Future NBA Star he never scored. Indeed, I have no doubt that he remembers the particular game when I was such a demon on defense. How could he (or anyone else present) forget?

I came into the game early in the second quarter. I was supposed to guard one of their guards, but Future NBA Star set a pick on me and the next thing I knew, my teammate guarding Future NBA Star had switched over to cover my player. Thus I was forced to switch to the taller player. I knew that it would be tough to stop Future NBA Star because of his size advantage, but I crouched down low and glided along with him, sticking close as he tried to get open. As I guarded him, our opponents seemed stuck and unable to dribble or pass into a good position for getting a shot. Because there was no shot clock, we kept them trapped for what seemed like minutes on end, constantly harassing whomever had the ball and denying them opportunities to drive or pass near the basket. In my crouching position, I started to notice that the crowd roared whenever I came close to the sidelines while tracking Future NBA Star's every step. I crouched lower, my buttocks jutting back, my hands practically dragging on the floor as my feet kept gliding in unison with Future NBA Star's every move. He moved left, and I slid rapidly to beat him to the spot where he wanted to go. He moved right, and there I was. With each move, with each turn of my body, the crowd's roars got louder and louder. Here was an audience that could appreciate outstanding defense. Eventually, after what seemed like three solid minutes of superlative defensive effort, one of Future NBA Star's teammates threw the ball out of bounds. As I headed toward the sideline to throw the ball in, I heard the scorekeeper's buzzer sound and one of my teammates ran onto the floor and signaled that I was being replaced. I stopped in my tracks, stunned by surprise. I had just entered the game. I had stopped their best player, Future NBA Star, from scoring. In fact, the crowd was still screaming. People stood and cheered happily, some even pointing at me, as they roared their approval. Yet, the coach was gesturing frantically for me to leave the floor. I was completely perplexed as I ran toward the coach. Before I reached him, he pointed emphatically toward the far end of the bench. Turning my head, I saw the assistant coach standing at the end of the bench. He waved his arm rapidly, summoning me to follow him. When I started to run toward him, he started to jog away from me and headed toward the locker room. With the roar of the crowd still in my ears, I stopped by the end of the bench, uncertain about what I was supposed to do. He turned and motioned frantically for me to follow him. I ran after him again and caught up with him after he had entered the locker room.

"What's going on, coach?" I asked breathlessly. "We're in the middle of game."

"I know. Let's hurry," he said over his shoulder and he continued toward the supply room.

"Where are we going?"

"You split your pants."

"What?" I could barely hear him as our running footsteps echoed through the locker room.

"I said, you split your pants."

I stopped instantly and looked behind me. Sure enough, the center seam on my basketball shorts had completely disintegrated. Because we wore only jock straps under our athletic wear in those days (none of today's compression shorts even existed back then) my bare buttocks had been fully exposed, especially when I bent over in my crouching defense stance.

"Didn't you hear the crowd laughing?" he asked as he handed me another pair of shorts.

Thinking back on how the crowd's cheers increased each time I came over near the sideline, I found myself turning red with embarrassment as I replied, disingenuously, "I thought they were cheering for my great defense."

"They were cheering for your great moon," he said with a smirk.

As I changed shorts, my strongest desire was to remain in the locker room. Honestly, I would have preferred to have cleaned out my locker and transferred to a high school in a different city. I certainly didn't want to go back out in the gym. But what could I do? There was a game on and I wanted to play.

When I reentered the gym, the crowd roared, mostly with laughter, but I guess one could call it "cheers" if one wanted to be charitable. As I sat on the bench, the gym was filled with the chant, "Moon! Moon! Moon! Moon!" I had always hoped to have the fans chant my name, but this wasn't exactly what I had hoped for. Apparently, the coach decided to spare me from further embarrassing attention since he kept me on the bench for the remainder of the game. His tactic was obvious when guys beneath me on the depth chart played in the second half of a close game as I sat and watched.

After the game (which we won by the way), as we shook hands with the other team, Future NBA Star said to me, "Nice moon, man." At the time, I felt a flash of annoyance at his comment. In retrospect, however, I can see it as a compliment. Here was a future NBA player who, implicitly anyway, expressed admiration for my dedication, courage, and fortitude in the face of unsettling developments and hostile public attention. Moreover, I now realize from my subsequent university training in psychology, that he was probably subconsciously expressing grudging respect for my dogged defense which kept him from scoring. I was later told that the entire defensive sequence lasted only about ninety seconds (a time period that can seem like a lifetime when you later realize that your bare behind was waving at a vocal crowd), but I like to think of it as the crucial ninety seconds that kept our opponents from mounting a rally.

Years later when I told one of my students that I had kept Future NBA Star from scoring while guarding him in a high school game, my student asked, "How many shots did he take?"

"He didn't take any."

"Did they throw him the ball?"

I thought for a moment and said, "Well, no. They didn't."

"Well, how long did you guard him for?"

"About ninety seconds."

"You mean you're sitting here bragging about keeping some guy from scoring for a mere ninety seconds when they didn't even throw him the ball! Your basketball career must have been awfully pathetic if that's the highlight."

This, of course, illustrates precisely what's wrong with today's callow, unthinking youth. The point is that my defense was so good that I kept a future NBA player from scoring. This means that I am really connected to and in the same "club" as Michael Jordan and others who kept Future NBA Star from scoring at certain moments in later games. I have a bond with famous professional players, and Future NBA Star knew that. Remember, he said, "Nice moon, man." He might just as well have said, "You play defense as well as anyone in the NBA." It basically means the same thing. Right? Doesn't it? On second thought, don't answer that. Let's just wait until I'm ninety-five so that the hometown paper describes me as having been an "NBA all-star." Then everyone will recognize the world-class nature of my defensive effort on the night that I overcame a taunting crowd and a chilly breeze as I touched a celebrity and made my place in basketball history.

As I look back on that night, however, I am a bit a worried. Hopefully those couple of minutes with my bare buttocks exposed to the cheering crowd aren't going to use up a portion of the fifteen minutes of fame that Andy Warhol promised me.

*   *   *

During college, the field of celebrities available for contact with me expanded into the highest reaches of government. With Harvard's Democratic Club, I traveled to Washington to meet with Democratic officials. The most significant impression that I took away from our meeting with United States senators and other prominent officials was that a very big head (literally!) must be an asset in politics. For the purpose of presenting one's self effectively on television, apparently it is very beneficial to have a fat head and a fat face. I can think of a long list of politicians who, upon encountering them in person, my first, spontaneous reflexive thought was "Wow, what a big head!" President Richard Nixon, Senators Edward Kennedy of Massachusetts, Frank Church of Idaho, and Henry "Scoop" Jackson of Washington, Speaker of the House Thomas "Tip" O'Neill of Massachusetts. The list could go on and on. There is no doubt that many people have parlayed the gift of cranial girth into a bonanza of fame and power.

I also learned that dealing with the famous can be awkward when you are not prepared to apply some assuasive balm to their significant egos. I found myself in a particularly awkward position on one college trip when some genius scheduled our group to meet with two U.S. senators, Howard Metzenbaum of Ohio and Gary Hart of Colorado, in the same room at the same time. I suppose the scheduling, on its face, was not necessarily problematic. These were two Democratic allies who undoubtedly cooperated on many matters. What no one could foresee, however, was that while our group was waiting at a senate meeting room for the arrival of Senators Metzenbaum and Hart, Senator James Allen of Alabama stuck his head into the doorway and invited everyone across the hall to hear him speak to a group of visiting high school students.

As I watched my colleagues depart, I felt worried. "What happens when Metzenbaum and Hart show up?"

"Don't worry. We'll be right back," they said. Right back. Yeah, sure.

The next thing I knew, I was alone in a room with two senators. They both seemed extremely unhappy about meeting me. I have always presumed they were unhappy about meeting me alone, without the audience that they expected, but I suppose it's possible that the chilli that I had for lunch was still evident on my breath and thus the cause of their discernible dissatisfaction. I started asking questions about government, law, the weather and anything else I could think of. I desperately tried to keep the conversation going by deftly (or so I thought) firing questions to one senator and then the other so neither would have to spend a long period of time listening to the other one speak. This lasted for a few minutes before Metzenbaum left me "in the able hands of [his] distinguished colleague," as he put it, while Hart looked annoyed at being abandoned or perhaps not beating Metzenbaum to the punch by departing first. Looking back, if only I had been prescient, I could have changed American history by warning Hart to stay away from any woman he met in the future named Donna Rice and, for heaven's sake, don't go on any cruises on a boat called "The Monkey Business." Of course, I had no way of anticipating how Hart would later destroy is own presidential campaign through the appearance of careless womanizing but it sure is fun to think about how my fleeting contacts with famous figures might have changed history if only I had done something different than what I did. What I actually did was fail miserably in my effort to maintain Senator Hart's interest and attention. Within a few moments, he was gone, too. When my Harvard colleagues returned a few minutes later, they thought I was lying when I said that I had already met with both Metzenbaum and Hart. This attitude annoyed me, so I said, "You're right. I'm just kidding. Hey, I'm going over to the bathroom. You all wait here for Metzenbaum and Hart. I'll be right back." With that, I departed and as I far as I know they're still standing in the room waiting for the senators to arrive.

*   *   *

One summer I worked for a political interest group in Washington. As a summer intern, I handled all kinds of tasks, both substantive and mundane. Within my first ten minutes of entering the office on my first day of work, I was placed in charge of lobbying on the issue of making public transportation accessible to the handicapped. I was overwhelmed and intimidated, particularly because I didn't know anything about lobbying. In fact, I hadn't figured out how to get from my office to the Capitol building yet. However, I was very gratified that my superiors recognized that this twenty-year-old was obviously qualified to take a leadership role in their organization. In reality, they were quite cognizant of my qualifications. Thus I spent the rest of week (after the initial euphoria of the assignment I received in the first ten minutes had passed) running the Xerox machine. Amid the flashing green light of the photocopier and the whir of the paper sorter, I had plenty of time to fantasize about how I would change the face of public transportation and improve the lives of millions of people. Maybe this would make me famous, or so I imagined.

I received other important assignments. One day an attorney pulled me aside. "Chris, I have an urgent situation. You drive, don't you?"

"I don't have a car, if that's what you mean. I take the subway."

"No. I mean, you have a driver's license don't you."

"Sure."

"Well, here's my car keys. I'm parked right outside in the lot. You know which car it is, don't you? I need you to take these papers over to this address by the Supreme Court building."

"Sure." I was excited now. I was going to escape the Xerox machine and handle an important task outside of the office.

Unfortunately, my outlook changed when I reached the parking lot. The car was a stick shift. I didn't know how to drive a stick shift because I had only driven cars with automatic transmissions. However, there was no way that I was going to embarrass myself by going back inside to concede that I was not up to the assignment. Thus I started the car, fiddled with the clutch and the gear shift, and somehow made it out onto Pennsylvania Avenue Southeast. This was a huge mistake. I stalled out every ten feet. When I got the car started, I would lurch forward and barely miss striking other vehicles and pedestrians. I managed to pull over onto the nearest side street and park the car (illegally) by a fire hydrant. Then I jumped out of the car and began to sprint the eight blocks or so to the cluster of buildings across from the side of the Supreme Court. Sprinting is never a good idea while wearing a coat and tie. This is especially true in the ninety-degree heat and humidity of Washington, D.C. in July. Suffice to say, by the time I returned to the office nearly an hour later, I looked as if I had fallen into a swimming pool or (more accurately) a cess pool, since my aroma left something to be desired. Worst of all, I was still trying to think of an explanation for why the lawyer's car was towed away. In Washington, of course, one can always rely on the ubiquity of famous and powerful people in thinking of excuses, so I naturally blamed it on some unnamed prominent politician. Fame has its benefits, even for those of us who don't share directly in its blessings.

"There was some motorcade blocking Pennsylvania Avenue between here and the Capitol. It could have been the President or some foreign head of state or ambassador or something. I knew this delivery was urgent so I had to abandon the car on a side street, only because of how important I knew this was, and I ran all the way to the office. By the time I got back...." He had a very pained and disgusted look on his face as I spun out my story. I don't know if he believed me, but he never bothered me with any assignments again, except when he needed thousands of pages photocopied.

I finally got a significant assignment from a different attorney when the office was attempting to blitz the U.S. Senate with a coordinated lobbying effort on the eve of a vote on controversial legislation. Most members of the Senate had already announced publicly how they would vote on this legislation, so the outcome of the vote hinged on how a few undecided senators cast their ballots. Each intern was assigned one of these undecided senators. We studied their voting records. We examined how the legislation would affect each senator's home state. We played devil's advocate with each other in staging mock debates about the legislation. Our intent was to be prepared to handle any question that might be posed to us by the senator's staff or, if we were lucky, the actual senator. After days of preparation, I felt that I was ready to handle any question or argument posed by people at the senator's office. I had been assigned a senator from (I don't actually remember) North Dakota or Montana or one of the other exotic, frozen locales along the top of the country's western midsection. I hadn't been particularly familiar with the senator or the state, but my intensive study made me feel supremely confident that I was positioned and prepared to help shape the country's future on this issue. I believed that I could have persuaded anyone, absolutely anyone, to agree with our position on the legislation.

We each made brief appointments with our respective senators' legislative assistants. I was surprised at how easily I secured my appointment. As I dialed the number, one of the interns started to talk to me so I couldn't hear what the receptionist who answered was saying. "Shhhh," I whispered. I was momentarily worried that I might have dialed the wrong number, but I was reassured when, after identifying myself and asking, "May I have an appointment with the senator's legislative assistant?," the receptionist gave me the office number for my designated senator as the place to meet the legislative assistant. When we departed for the senate office buildings, we carried packets of informative, persuasive material about the legislation. We were instructed to ask the legislative assistant to "Please ask the senator to read these materials as soon as possible. It is most urgent." I hoped to be able to utilize my intensive preparation by discussing the issue with the legislative assistant or, better yet, the senator. I knew the legislative assistant might be busy, but we were told that the ease with which we gained appointments probably indicated that the assistants wanted to hear what we had to say.

As I walked down the corridor toward the office, a young man (well, he was older than me, but he was still young, probably in his twenties) stood in his shirt sleeves reading a file. He saw me coming, glanced at his watch, and asked, "Are you Smith?"

I nodded and he introduced himself as the legislative assistant. He quickly ushered me through an unmarked side door that went directly from the corridor to his office within the senator's suite of offices. He offered me a comfortable chair and then asked me to wait for a minute while he gathered several other assistants to hear what I had to say about the issue. When a group of seven or eight assistants had gathered around me, the legislative assistant glanced at the packet in my hand and said, "Well, what have you got?"

I handed him the packet of papers. Prominently positioned at the top of the packet was a letter addressed to the senator from me which laid out our arguments in quick succession. The rest of the packet contained position papers and studies that backed up our arguments. As I watched him look at the letter and frown, I found myself relishing the prospect of debating and persuading someone who was skeptical of our policy position. The look on his face made me anticipate that he would ask a probing, challenging question. He looked at me quizzically and then walked around the room briefly showing the letter to each of his colleagues. I waited in silent anticipation believing that I was thoroughly prepared for anything he might say.

He looked at me seriously and then, after a long pause, said the one thing that I never expected. "The senator is dead."

I felt my eyes open as wide as they could go. "Dead?," I murmured as if talking to myself.

"Yes. In fact, he died more than six weeks ago of a heart attack and a new senator was appointed by the governor to replace him."

I wasn't prepared for this news. In fact, this news proved beyond a shadow of a doubt to everyone in the room that I wasn't adequately prepared at all. Instantly, I resented the senator's death and its interference with my assignment. If all of these senators weren't so old, they wouldn't be dying all the time. Moreover, if they weren't from such inconsequential places, then maybe I would notice these events in the news. I also felt embarrassed that I had missed this small, but admittedly important, detail during my many recent hours of intensive preparation. I fumbled for something to say. "Do you want to talk about the policy issue?," I asked hesitantly.

"No, Mr. Smith. I'm afraid that if you don't even know which senator we work for now, we don't think you are likely to know anything useful about this legislation." With that, they all stood up and left the room. I sat silently for a few moments trying to think of what to tell my superiors back at the office. A part of me was disappointed that I didn't get to meet the late senator. Now that I had studied him so carefully, I had hoped to add him to the list of famous people I had encountered. Most of me, however, felt a rising concern that the legislation would fail by one vote because I had failed in my assignment. As it turned out, I can't even remember what the legislation was about, let alone whether it passed, so I guess I wasn't too scarred by this particular near-brush with celebrity.

*   *   *

The interest group sent me one day to serve as its representative at a meeting of dozens of interest groups working in a giant coalition to ratify the proposed Equal Rights Amendment, the effort during the 1970s to add a provision to the U.S. Constitution guaranteeing equal rights for women. I hated being sent to meetings about ongoing issues because I never knew what discussions had taken place previously and I worried that someone would call on me to make a statement on behalf of my organization. "I'm just a stupid summer intern" didn't seem like an adequate response to a request for a statement about my organization's official policy position, so I spent hours in anticipation of such meetings just planning what I might say if called upon. When I arrived at the large meeting hall at AFL-CIO headquarters, I decided to mix into the crowd in order to remain as inconspicuous as possible. I noticed that many tables had been pushed together to form a huge rectangle with a large open space in the middle. The perimeter of the rectangle was so large that there were probably more than sixty chairs going all the way around. When I noticed that several well-dressed men and women were talking in an animated fashion while sitting in the middle of one side of the rectangle, I decided that I should sit as far as possible away from these people who were obviously leaders of the coalition effort. So instead, I sat on the opposite side, in a row of chairs along an empty side of the rectangle. As more people filed into the room, they began to distribute themselves around the tables. A woman sat next to me and soon began asking me questions. She would point at someone sitting elsewhere and ask, "Do you know what organization that person is from?" I would then respond, "I really don't know." We went through this exercise five or six times before she apparently figured out that I really didn't know much.

After the chairs around the tables were nearly all occupied, I waited for the people across from me to begin the meeting. However, they continued to talk with each other. I looked at my watch with obvious impatience. I hated to waste my day just sitting and doing nothing. The woman next to me noticed me checking my watch. She leaned toward me and whispered, "Seems as if this meeting really ought to get going."

I nodded my head in agreement and whispered back, "I get sick and tired of people who are supposed to be in charge of meetings just letting things drift along. Meetings should start on time so that people aren't inconvenienced."

"I agree," she said. Immediately she stood up and shouted in a loud voice, "Welcome everyone. Please take your seats. My name is Eleanor Smeal. I'm the President of the National Organization for Women and I am chairing this meeting."

I nearly fell out of my chair. For the first time, I actually looked at my neighbor. It really was Eleanor Smeal and I knew I would have recognized her if I had paid attention. Unfortunately, I had blown my opportunity to really get connected to this famous person. She had initiated a conversation and I had ignored her. Now I was stuck staring at her, wrenching my neck in an awkward position, with the pretense of rapt attention because every eye in the room was focused on our head table. Every moment of fidgeting on my part would be seen by everyone in the room. Thus my punishment for being oblivious to a famous person who sat just inches away from me was a sentence of sitting perfectly still and pretending that I was deeply involved in the meeting. I made a vow to be more attentive to my surroundings, especially people sitting next to me. Who knows, perhaps I may have sat next to Mick Jagger or somebody else along the way and simply never knew it.

*   *   *

During my year at the University of Bristol in England, I gained exposure to a new and unanticipated realm of celebrity contacts: British royalty. This was an opportunity to open an entirely new exhibit in my mental museum of celebrity contacts. Through the generosity of an English couple that served as a host family for me, I was taken to a number of social events at which dukes, duchesses, and other royal whatnots were present. I'm not sure if I was qualified to be at these events (well, I probably was qualified to serve the gravy), but I tried to fit in by concentrating on memories of my mother's voice saying, "Don't wipe your mouth with your sleeve." I think I mostly managed to obey that admonition, but I can't promise that I had a one hundred percent compliance rate. As it turns out, when in the distracting presence of certain royals, I'm not sure anyone would have noticed a quick swipe with my sleeve (across my own mouth, I mean; I don't mean to imply that I could have gotten away with patting some princess on the behind or anything like that).

When I took a tour of a grand country estate owned by the Duke of Something-Or-Other, my tour group was fortunate to find that Lady Something-Or-Other would be giving the tour. Basically her job seemed to be to hang around waiting for the ancient Duke to pass on to the hereafter so that her title would change from Lady to Duchess when her husband, the ancient Duke's son, became the new Duke. So she lived at the estate with her father-in-law, the Duke, while her husband lived in London with his young girlfriend. Yes, with his girlfriend! I found it a bit shocking that people spoke so matter-of-factly about the extramarital affairs and other problems of the royals. Obviously the royals were much more comparable to Hollywood celebrities in the United States, whose every indiscretion made tabloid headlines, than to American government officials, who tend to work very hard to hide their infidelities. So anyway, this poor woman was left in this big empty house out in the country giving the occasional tour, knowing that everyone in the country was aware of her husband's misbehavior. My first impression indicated that she coped with her awful predicament by (how can I put this delicately) taking her hobby of wine tasting very seriously. To be more blunt, the booze on her breath almost knocked me over when I came in the door. Amid the empathy I felt for the pain of her personal situation, I must acknowledge that she gave a most interesting and entertaining tour.

Since I was the lone visiting American in a tour group of British people, she insisted that I accompany her at the front of the line. In fact, half the time that she was describing breathtaking rooms and priceless artifacts, she was only talking to me and no one else in the group could hear her. When we came upon a suit of armor that she described as being from the reign of King Somebody-Or-Other the Third (Fourth?? Who knows??), she noted that the spear that went along with the armor was quite heavy. In order to prove her point, she picked up the spear and, struggling to gain control of it with two hands, thrust it into my arms. It was heavy indeed, and I nodded gravely to show that I was suitably impressed. Apparently, she felt so gratified by my mock-serious response to handling the spear, that she decided I would earn her undying gratitude if I was able to touch and hold various other objects from around the grand estate house. I wish she would have warned me first, however. As I was trying to carefully lean the spear back up against the armor, unsure about how it was supposed to go, she walked ahead and then turned suddenly to toss a couple of heavy brass candlesticks in my direction from about six feet away. Luckily, I let go of the spear and turned just in time to catch both candlesticks. Although I was momentarily stunned, I instantly had a nightmarish vision of what was about to happen as she reached for a large crystal dish. She was about ten feet away from me so I leaped over to the fireplace mantel to re-deposit the candlesticks and try to move closer to her as she tossed the crystal dish toward me from…oh, I probably had gotten back within four feet of her by that time. And so it continued in each room of the house. She wandered, babbled, and tossed objects in my direction. Meanwhile, I scrambled to keep up with her, desperately trying to replace objects before the next one came flying in my direction. The elderly people on the tour group oohed and ahhed with each spectacular catch, as I jumped about like a baseball catcher trying to keep up with the unpredictable offerings of a knuckleball pitcher. The other people on the tour seemed remarkably unconcerned about the possibility that I might actually miss or drop some priceless object. They seemed to be much more impressed, and indeed envious, that I had so quickly managed to establish such a "personal" relationship with a soon-to-be Duchess and that I was actually permitted to handle artifacts that are normally supposed to be viewed but not touched by visiting tourists. The silk pillows were relatively easy to handle, but some of the other objects were quite challenging (and indeed, heart-stopping when one realized their financial worth). The highlight (or lowlight) of the tour was a diving grab of a centuries-old Ming vase from about fifteen feet away, made all the more difficult by the fact that the English don't know how to throw properly (since they are obsessed with soccer, tennis, and rugby, sports that don't exactly develop one's pitching skills).

By the end of the tour, our royal tour guide seemed exhilarated by her discovery of a new and more exciting way to spice up the tours. I was exhausted and desperate to get away from her. The other tourists were buzzing about the memorable event. And thus we departed from our unforgettable tour, only to be reminded of it one week later when the newspaper reported that a priceless Ming vase had been broken at the estate in unspecified circumstances during a public tour. The next week's tour brought news reports about a smashed crystal bowl. The following week, it was damage to a valuable oil painting. As I eagerly looked forward to subsequent news reports about catastrophic occurrences during the weekly tours, I found myself filled with admiration for my hostess. In my view, she really had discovered an effective way to exact her revenge on her husband. By the time he became Duke, the place was going to look like an empty Holiday Inn.

*   *   *

I encountered the soon-to-be Duchess again at a fundraising social event held at the home of the Duchess of Windwillow (or Wallhaven or Westinghouse or something like that). When I was reintroduced to her, she greeted me warmly, as if we were old friends, even though I am quite sure she could not remember me (or much of anything else). As she spoke to me, a small bit of saliva flew from her lips and landed on my cheek. This was a paralyzing moment. Instinctively, I wanted to reach up to brush the spittle away. However, it was an awkward situation because I was standing in a small conversational circle with a soon-to-be Duchess and three proper English socialites. If I reached up, it would call attention to the fact that a royal had accidently spit on me. So the most reasonable course of action, in order to avoid embarrassment for everyone present, was for me to endure this small drip oozing down my cheek as everyone in the group pretended that they never saw it happen. However, the soon-to-be Duchess saved the day, demonstrating that many royals are not merely refreshingly open, but downright uninhibited since they don't really have to worry about what other people think of them.

She cocked her head to the side and said, "Now what do you say when you spit on someone? I've always wondered about that." She didn't seem in any hurry to do anything about the spit. She appeared more interested in philosophizing about a seemingly taboo subject.

Unsure of what to say, I continued to fight my instinct to wipe my cheek by keeping my arms pinned to my sides as I shrugged my shoulders. The others standing in our group simply murmured awkwardly, "Gee, I don't know." Then the soon-to-be Duchess just reached over and started to smear the spittle around on my cheek while saying, "I'm really sorry about that." Our companions, as if choreographed in unison, quickly reached for their pocket handkerchiefs and said, "Permit me to do that." But they were too late. No drip remained after she smeared it around my face. As she fluttered off to talk to other people, I noticed that the English socialites seemed keenly disappointed. They all gave me looks that indicated that they were jealous that I, the undeserving spawn of a rebellious colony, was the lucky one permitted to carry away the souvenir sample of royal gastric juices. As our group disbanded to circulate individually elsewhere throughout the social event, I actually heard one of my conversation companions mutter, "I wish she had spit on me." Personally, I was more concerned about the possibility that my blood alcohol level would rise through skin absorption. I can clearly claim, however, that I have had intimate physical contact with a British royal (as germ-laden and distasteful as it may have been under those circumstances).

The other highlight of this particular social event was when the Duchess of Windwillow (Wallhaven, Westinghouse, whatever) came around herself to collect the paper plates from which we had been eating snacks (that's right, paper plates!). It didn't seem as if she felt her guests weren't worthy enough to eat off the good china. She actually seemed to be an informal person who did not get worked up about formal ceremonies. I think many of the English socialites are more excited than some of the royals about pomp and circumstance. When the Duchess asked me if I was through eating and took my plate from me, I realized how far I had come in an incredibly short period of time. Only a few years earlier, I was the one serving and collecting dishes from the American royalty (Kennedys and others) in the dining hall at Harvard. Now I had British royalty serving me. I was still a dirt-poor graduate student surviving on a one-year fellowship award, but from a celebrity-contact perspective, my life had made a major move forward. As I pondered this turnabout in my life, the Duchess accidently dumped the castoff crumbs and other unwanted contents from various plates onto my lap. But I didn't mind. Notwithstanding a lap full of potato chips and dip, I was now connected (for a fleeting moment anyway) with fame and prominence in an entirely new way.

*   *   *

The highlight of my celebrity experience in England was my encounter with the royal family. I was invited to attend the annual horse races at Ascot. *The* social event of the season. I also was granted entry into the "Royal Enclosure" where I could wander about with the royal family. This was a really, really big deal, although I didn't appreciate it at the time. The entire royal family attends Ascot and they come riding down the track in open carriages while the crowd waves and cheers. Moreover, only royals and English socialites of sufficient standing are granted access to the "Royal Enclosure," the viewing area in which Queen Elizabeth and her family mingle with the select crowd. The scene is all the more striking because within the "Royal Enclosure" all men must wear top hats and morning coats with tails. The women must wear fancy hats with their fashionable, fancy, and presumably designer dresses. It looks like something out of *My Fair Lady* and indeed is presumably the basis for the racetrack scene in that play. Meanwhile, there are some regular people cordoned off in a separate section of the track where they can observe from a distance and bet on the horse races.

It is nearly impossible for a British subject to gain access to the "Royal Enclosure." Unless you are of royal birth, it takes many years of social climbing and financial success to earn the status required for a scarce ticket to this social occasion. Interestingly, however, "Royal Enclosure" members can sponsor foreign guests who can gain access, in the company of their British hosts, merely by getting a letter of approval from their country's ambassador to Britain. I wrote to the American embassy in London requesting such a letter and they promptly sent one on my behalf. A background check might have been in order, but then again, why should the American embassy care about who goes into the "Royal Enclosure?" Thus I found myself renting formal attire, including a top hat, and preparing to meet the royal family.

My expectations about meeting the royal family soon diminished. I happened to mention very casually to my host family that if Prince Charles walked past me in the "Royal Enclosure," I was looking forward to introducing myself.

"*No!*," my host said in a panic-stricken voice, "You must not do that. It isn't permitted. You can only speak to them if they speak to you first. And you certainly cannot touch them. If they offer to shake your hand, then you can shake. But you must never extend your hand first."

I was puzzled. What was the big deal about shaking hands? I had already had one of their distant kin spit on me. I was at least owed a handshake by someone in return. The vigorous and emotional tone of my host's voice started to make me worry that I could easily commit a major *faux pas*. Perhaps even cause an international incident. What if I accidently spit on the Queen? Would I be arrested if I reached out to brush off her cheek? As an American, the whole concept of strict social rules was incomprehensible. People are people. We are all officially equal. If I want to shake hands with someone, why not? I wasn't sure what would happen at Ascot, but I began to reduce my expectations about actually having contact with the highest level of royal celebrities, the Queen and her family.

As it happened, there was special excitement about Ascot that year because Prince Charles was supposed to bring Lady Diana, the woman whom he would marry a few short months later. And, indeed, I got to see the entire royal family. Although my mental celebrity scorecard was rapidly gaining entries, I was a little less excited than I anticipated because all of the British subjects around me were so overly excited. When people around you are overreacting in an extreme manner, I think you cool your own excitement level just to disassociate and detach yourself from the surrounding mania. Thus I wandered about in my top hat feeling as if I was simultaneously watching and appearing in a period-setting film about the English aristocracy in the nineteenth century.

As I walked along, I suddenly noticed just ahead of me that the crowd was parting, not unlike Moses and the Red Sea, and top hats were flying off men's heads like dominoes set to fall consecutively in rapid motion. One after another, men swept off their hats and bowed low to the ground. Women dropped low in formal curtsies. Attracted by the odd sight, I moved toward the scene of over-dressed socialites suddenly moving out of the way and freezing into subservient statues. Sure enough, the Queen herself was walking through the crowd. The Queen ambled slowly through the path opened by the parting crowd. Well before she reached the spot where a particular socialite was standing, that person would bow or curtsy and stare at the ground. Thus they all looked down at the moment when the Queen passed by. No one actually looked at the Queen up close, no one except me anyway.

As the Queen approached where I stood, I lifted my top hat off my head and held it awkwardly in my hand, not really sure what to do with it. I also did not know how to bow. I suppose I could have emulated all of the men around me, but the whole idea of bowing was so foreign to my thinking and experience (spawn of that rebellious American colony that I am) that I really didn't think about doing it. Instead, my thoughts were preoccupied with anticipating my impending brush with a major world figure-type celebrity. If celebrity encounters were like bird watching, in which true aficionados keep a record book of all of the different species of birds that they have personally viewed during their lifetimes, standing next to the Queen of England was probably almost as monumental as viewing an extinct dodo bird. Who could anticipate that it would happen to a kid from Kalamazoo? How could one expect that it would ever happen again? Thus, hat in hand, I stared intently at the approaching Queen.

In retrospect, I feel bad for Queen Elizabeth. Here she was walking along with all of her subjects (as usual, I suppose) dropping low to the ground; bowing, curtsying, and staring at their shoes. All of a sudden, here is this tall blond young man, with longish hair no less, standing straight amid the prostrate crowd and staring the Queen directly in the face. I couldn't help it. As I looked her, I was struck with an inescapable and powerful thought, "She's really, really short!" She looked much taller on television. Just as American politicians somehow disguise or exploit their fat heads on television, the magic of television conveys the impression that the Queen is taller than she really is. So here I was. Looking down at the Queen of England who, from three feet away, is looking directly back at me and appearing surprised that I was still standing upright. And then she looked away. *She* looked at the ground. Now I really feel bad about this. It was obvious that I made her uncomfortable by behaving in such an unexpected, and probably improper, manner. She seemed like a nice enough lady, and here I went and made her feel uncomfortable. In retrospect, I'm probably lucky that she didn't yell, "Off with his head," because she had such reverential and maniacal support among the people in the "Royal Enclosure" that they probably would have done the job right there on the spot with a nail file that someone had handy in a purse. Anyway, I have never taken the opportunity before, so let me do it now. *Hey, Queen Elizabeth. Sorry about that. I didn't mean anything by it. I'm just an uncultured American who never learned how to bow.* (Not really. We have our own culture, defined primarily by pizza, beer, and sports on television, but I'm just saying this to try to make amends).

*　　　　*　　　　*

After my (continuing) lifetime effort of building my mental museum of celebrity encounters, I am happy to report that I have been treated as a celebrity (of sorts) on a couple of occasions. After having written a few not-too-notable books in the academic realm, it happens every now and then that I bump into someone who has heard of me. Once a professor asked me if I had ever read a good book called *Courts and the Poor.* I smugly hesitated before responding, "Why yes. In fact, I wrote it." I didn't really mean to embarrass him. But what could I say? I wandered around for weeks afterward enjoying a delusional feeling of fame and importance. On another occasion, a graduate student was talking to me when he suddenly stopped in mid-sentence and said, "Are you *the* Christopher Smith?" He visibly shrank back, not quite sinking to his knees, as he related that he had used one of my "wonderful" books in a class at another university.

I am quite pleased by these occasional moments that seem to convey that I have attained some measure of renown. However, I also worry. If I only have fifteen minutes of fame promised to me, I don't want to use it all up on the wrong occasions. If the split basketball shorts counted as a couple of minutes, and then there are the incidents with people who've read my books…well, that's a few more minutes. If things keep going in this way, I may have only a minute or so remaining at the end of my life to win a Nobel Prize, Academy Award, or whatever else it is that I was truly meant to accomplish. I mean, I was meant to accomplish one of those things, wasn't I? (Please??)

Chapter Five

Looking for Love

Looking for love in all the wrong places.

Seems like the story of my youth. Much of time, of course, it's not actually love that we talk about. Instead we are preoccupied with relationships and, especially, potential relationships. I spent an incredible amount of time as a teenager (and afterwards) feeling attracted to a particular member of the opposite sex and plotting strategies for becoming acquainted. Often my strategies were quite bold. Buy a dozen red roses, deliver them to her door, and announce, "These were going to be from a secret admirer but my feelings for you are so strong that I decided I had to make myself and my feelings known to you." There was one major problem with such bold strategies. I never actually had the nerve to carry them out. In fact, looking back on my life, it's hard for me to claim that I ever had any nerve at all. The overwhelming reluctance to confront the risk of rejection and embarrassment far outweighed my perpetual desire to actually test the waters of someone else's potential interest in me. I'm happy with my life and my wife so I'm not going to be too crushed if a former cheerleader approaches me at my fiftieth high school reunion and confesses that she always wished that I had asked her out. I'll probably berate myself for being too timid, but on the other hand maybe fate will have spared me from some traumatic event that would have developed in the course of that relationship. Heaven knows, I experienced plenty of trauma in the moments when fate led me to act on my romantic attractions.

*   *   *

When I was a junior in high school, I somehow found myself in a conversation in the school library with a senior acquaintance (female and a very attractive redhead, no less) about a best-selling novel that everyone seemed to be reading at that time. It might have been *The Godfather* or *Jaws* or some other popular entertainment literature of the early 1970s. As was characteristic of such popular entertainment books, this novel (whatever it was) contained some steamy scenes. Our conversation eventually touched upon something about the steamy parts of the book.

"I'm sure certain parts of that book were too embarrassing for you to read," she said kiddingly, with a touch of sarcasm.

"There's nothing in any book that I can't handle," came my reply with mock bravado.

"Or perhaps those were the parts of the books that you didn't understand," she countered.

"I understand far more than people around here realize."

She looked at me skeptically. "You mean you've looked at the pictures in *National Geographic*?"

"Ha," I pretended to laugh. "You have no idea, do you?"

"I have certain assumptions about someone who doesn't seem to have a social life," she said, alluding to the fact that I was never visible at parties, at popular date venues, or in any other way in the company of a girl, including just walking with someone down the hallways of the school. Her observations reflected the fact that I thought about members of the opposite sex quite a bit, but never really had the nerve to ask for a date. At that moment, however, I would have preferred excruciating torture in a medieval dungeon to the prospect of honestly acknowledging the reality of my barren social life.

"You're just limited in your knowledge because you only know kids from this high school," I responded, somewhat haughtily. "No one knows about what I do with girls from other high schools. I know a lot more people around town than anybody realizes." This was a complete fabrication, but I couldn't see how she would know that I was lying.

Suddenly, her expression changed. She looked at me quizzically, as if she wanted to detect from my eyes whether or not I was lying. At the same time, however, she also appeared to be intrigued. It was as if my lie had suddenly made her look at me in an entirely different light.

"Is that so?," she said warily.

"Hey, just because I don't go around talking about myself all the time doesn't mean that I'm not out there staying active."

"So this stuff in the book is no big deal to you."

"No big deal. That's a good way to put it," I said with a wink.

"You are really surprising me, you know," she said, shaking her head.

"There are a lot of things about me that would surprise you a lot more." I was now relishing the fact that she seemed to have this new-found curiosity about me, and even hints of increased respect for me.

"So you think you could surprise me?," she said in a mysterious way.

"Did the book surprise you?," I asked, trying to challenge her.

"I read the book," she said, "and I won't claim to know about everything. But I am curious about what you're claiming to know."

"I know a lot," I declared, trying to sound bold.

She looked at me for a long moment and then shook her head. "I don't believe you," she said, suddenly backing away as if trying to persuade herself that I was attempting to fool her.

I felt my credibility fading so I upped the ante. "If you really want to know what I know, just tell me, and I'll show you."

She laughed. "You're not that bold."

I shrugged my shoulders. "Suit yourself. You're the one questioning my truthfulness. Don't question me unless you're bold enough to find out for yourself."

"Okay," she said. "You think you're so experienced. Let's just see. I don't believe you really know anything about that stuff in the book; nothing more than what you read in some other book anyway."

"I can prove you wrong," I said, half hoping she'd say "okay" and half-hoping that she wouldn't call my bluff.

"Okay. Come over to my house and let's see."

"Your house?" I was jolted by her response. Were we talking about what I thought we were talking about? What if I was talking about one thing and she was talking about something else?

"Sure. My parents go out for the evening every Friday. C'mon over and bring more than your big talk with you." She looked at me closely as if she expected me to concede that I was joking.

Uh oh. She said that like a dare. Inside my brain, I heard a voice telling me to start making up excuses about why Fridays are bad for me. I wasn't sure what to do. Just as I started to speak (still unsure if my voice was going to back out by making excuses or continue bluffing by agreeing to her dare) another student called to her from across the library. She quickly gathered her books and headed away, turning back to me just momentarily to say, "Don't forget. We'll just see about your big talk." She laughed with a weird sparkle in her eyes and then she was gone.

What to do? What to do? I spent every waking minute trying to sort out the situation. I wasn't even sure if we had been talking about the same thing. The more I thought about it, I wasn't even sure what I had been talking about. I went back and read the novel again. Those steamy scenes were. . . steamy! There was much that was modestly explicit and a certain amount left to the imagination, but fundamentally there was no doubt about what those scenes were about. I had to face up to it. My conversation with her was about some serious, well, steam. But what did this mean I was supposed to do? I could set it aside and see if she ever mentioned it again. If she did, then I would know that, in some way, she was really interested in me (to what end, I was not sure). On the other hand, if I just showed up at her house on a Friday, maybe I would be calling her bluff, and she would back away—leaving my newly-cultivated suave image intact. But, what if I showed up at her house and she was really expecting some…steam. Then what would I do? A part of me wanted to go to her house to do something, but the rest of me knew that I didn't know anything about doing that something.

Friday came and went. My parents asked me to stay home with my little brother so they saved me from making any decisions. Throughout the next week of school, I passed the red-headed object of my curiosity in the hallways as often as possible. We never had a conversation, but when our eyes met, she seemed to give me a funny look. There was that sparkle again. Or was it? Maybe I was just reading too much into this. Maybe it had all been a joke. As it happened, the Wednesday edition of the local newspaper carried an Ann Landers syndicated advice column containing a test for rating how "experienced" you are in love and sex. I think it was some scoring system sent in by a reader. There were various point totals for having ever done specific acts. Two points for a kiss and increasing upward from there. All day Thursday at school, students talked about their point totals, with everyone trying to claim that they had many, many points and to avoid admitting that they had fewer than five points. I could never admit that I, in fact, rated a zero. As I tried to avoid being drawn into these conversations, since my evasiveness would inevitably be interpreted (accurately) to mean that I really was not experienced at all, I decided that I would actually show up at a certain house on Friday evening. I would call her bluff. And if she was looking for some…steam, whatever that happened to be (and frankly I had no idea, but then again, she was an eighteen-year-old senior, after all), then I would shoot right up the Ann Landers scoring chart in time to really participate in some conversations the following week.

On Friday night, I found her house and rang the doorbell. To my surprise, her mother answered the door. Her mother recognized me from church. I didn't really know her parents, but apparently they knew who I was.

"Oh," she said with a tinge of surprise. "I didn't know that you were coming over." Before I could say anything, she ushered me into the living room and offered me a seat on the sofa. "Wait right here," she said with a warm smile. Then she walked out of the room and I could hear her call up the stairs, "Dear, you have a date waiting for you."

My mind was in turmoil. Obviously, her parents did not go out on this particular Friday. Now what would I do? I mentally tried to remember if I had any money in my wallet. Did I have enough to take her to a movie as an alternative plan of action? I wasn't sure, but I couldn't take my wallet out of my pocket because I didn't want to get caught looking if anyone came back into the room. As my mind muddled about in confusion about what to do next, she came into the living room, looking absolutely beautiful, I might add. Her hair looked more fixed up than I had ever seen it and she was dressed in a most flattering sweater. Her father followed her into the room, quickly passing her by as he came directly to the sofa to shake my hand and say, "Nice to see you, young man." I was so focused on shaking the father's hand that I didn't initially notice the look of utter shock that marred the visage of the otherwise-most-attractive young woman that I had ever seen. Her father left as quickly as he entered, and I stood staring at my, well, date. I was mesmerized by her beauty and I congratulated myself on having the nerve to actually show up.

She rushed to my side, grabbed my forearm in a tight grip and whispered in my ear, "What the hell are you doing here?" The sparkle was gone from her eyes. In fact, they were blazing with anger.

Now I was feeling a little bit stunned. I whispered back, "Don't you remember? You said to come over on Friday because your parents always go out."

She stepped back and gave me the most bewildered glare. "What are you talking about?" she demanded.

"Remember? In the library? We were talking about the novel...and those scenes...."

She closed her eyes and pressed both of her hands against her forehead. Shaking her head from side to side, she said, "That wasn't a serious conversation. Oh no."

"It wasn't a serious conversation?," I said, repeating her phrase.

Just then the doorbell rang. At its sound, she looked absolutely stricken. She looked over at the door and quickly said to me, "C'mon. You've got to get out of here." The doorbell rang again as she grabbed me by the arm and began to drag me across the living room. As we reached the doorway, we ran smack into her mother who was headed for the front door.

"Aren't you going to answer the door, dear?," her mother said as she reached for the door knob. We now stood frozen at the doorway to the living room as the door swung open and there stood the captain of our high school football team. He looked at me with a puzzled expression as a sense of recognition and a feeling of doom swelled over me like a cloud. It was obvious that she was expecting a date, and just as obvious that she wasn't expecting me.

The mother continued in her friendly mode. "Why Bill, how nice to see you. What are you doing here?"

He started to respond, eyes still fixed on me (a mere acquaintance in the class behind him at school) with his expression slowly changing from puzzlement to a glare, "I thought I had a...." Before he could get the word "date" out of his mouth, the object of my desire, that red-headed vision of loveliness, was pushing me out the door with the strength and speed of Hulk Hogan. As she shoved me past her real date and onto the porch, she summoned a big smile and said loudly, "If you ever need help with that kind of class assignment again, just let me know. Thanks for stopping by." As I watched the door shut and stood on the porch alone, I couldn't help asking myself: Was it possible that I could avoid her in school every day from now until her graduation? I didn't know the answer to that question, but I knew that I would have to pursue it with the utmost dedication.

*   *   *

As a member of the high school basketball team, I became quite friendly with my African-American teammates. Through them, I met a number of my female African-American classmates. Because African-American and white students generally lived on different sides of town, there was limited social interaction between kids who were mostly unfamiliar with each other except as fellow students in particular classes. In contrast to most of my white classmates, I found myself invited to a few parties and other social settings where I was the only or one of the only white people. As I became acquainted with this wider array of classmates, the universe of my objects-of-desire began to span the color line. As with white girls, I still didn't have enough nerve to ask anyone out. However, my mind thought just as seriously about possibilities when I found myself attracted to one of my new acquaintances.

One of my African-American friends from the basketball team continually encouraged me to date a particular girl from his neighborhood whom he said had a crush on me. The problem for me, aside from a lack of nerve about the opposite sex in general, was that I was not attracted to her. In fact, I was most attracted to my friend's girlfriend. One time my friend confided in me that his girlfriend had kissed a white guy at the high school out of curiosity about what it would be like to kiss someone white. He seemed disappointed in her, but was fundamentally understanding about the power curiosity (which was appropriate since I also knew all about the other girls, white and black, that he was curious about). When he told me this about his girlfriend, I did my best to play the role of friend by being supportive, but in reality I was actually thinking, "Man, why didn't she kiss me if she wanted to kiss someone white?" In retrospect, however, such a kiss would not have been beneficial for maintaining the friendships I had developed.

In college, I became good friends with students from various backgrounds, black, white, rich, poor, male, female, whatever. Living in the dorm together and eating together in the dining hall tended to eliminate some of the barriers imposed by the residential segregation that impeded social interactions between students from differing races and social classes back in my hometown. The college setting alleviated the need to get up the nerve to ask someone on a date. People tended to go to parties and movies together in large, mixed groups of men and women. In this social setting, you could just start talking to someone and, if things started to click, it would evolve gradually into a relationship in which you began to go to meals, movies, parties, etc. together as a couple. Within this setting, in which even a coward like me could develop a social life, on several occasions my interactions with friends evolved into the functional equivalent of dating African-American women.

Interracial dating can be a controversial subject. Virtually every television talk show periodically runs stories about problems and challenges for interracial couples. While any two individuals in a romantic relationship (or perhaps that's *every* two people in a romantic relationship) face challenges in relating to each other, interracial couples face extra risks posed by the prospect of external hostility. I only had my life threatened on a few occasions when I was in the company of an African-American woman. More commonly, you can hear people yelling behind you on the street or in a subway station, "Guess who's coming to dinner?! Guess who's coming to dinner?!" Fortunately, many of these moments, like the frequent stares from passers by, are more annoying than troublesome.

During one spring break, I traveled to a major city to visit an African-American woman I was dating. At the end of my visit, she drove me back downtown to the bus station. I bought my ticket for home and we decided to walk around downtown while we waited for my bus's departure time. One block away from the bus station, we passed five men standing outside a liquor store guzzling drinks from bottles wrapped in paperbags. They were poorly dressed and dirty. I saw them only out of the corner of my eye, so I couldn't even tell if they were black or white. We sensed that they were staring at us so we quickened our pace as we walked by. Then one of them yelled, "Hey, you!" Although I normally would pretend not hear comments made by strangers, I instinctively turned my head to look. Three of the men began waving their arms while one yelled, "C'mere. We want to talk to you."

This was not attractive moment for doubling back to engage in a conversation with strangers. As an interracial couple, we had a heightened awareness of the risk of hostility from both African-Americans and whites who disagree with interracial dating. Moreover, it appeared that these strangers had been drinking alcohol, which was usually not an asset for enhancing the quality of intellectual discourse with strangers. Without exchanging a word between us, we both quickened our pace even more. We had the unspoken, shared desire to get away from these men whom we perceived to be potentially threatening while we pretended that we were not actually fleeing. Suddenly, I heard footsteps on the sidewalk behind us. I glanced back and saw that the men were running after us. And I mean *running*! They were gaining ground quickly and now they shouted, "Come back here. We want to teach you some sociology!" Like a pair of trotters who simultaneously break stride, we quickly went from a walk to a gallop. We heard the continued cries of "Come back here. We want to teach you some sociology!" fading farther behind us so we knew that our pursuers' stamina was probably waning. As we reached the entrance to a large department store (which we assumed would be an effective sanctuary), we stopped and looked back to see the five men now walking rather than running in our direction. They were still yelling about teaching us some sociology, but they were pursuing us with much less vigor. I held the door for my companion and just before entering the store, I glanced down the sidewalk one last time. The men were still moving closer and now I could hear a jumble of voices shouting "Robert Park's theory of the race cycle....Talcott Parsons...structural functionalism...phenomenology...." I blocked out the voices, joined my friend in the store, and worriedly planned a walking route back to the bus station that would avoid both the front of the department store and the liquor store.

It was only in thinking about it later that I realized the men really were shouting things about sociology. You always hear about people with Ph.D.'s who end up driving cabs for lack of academic jobs. I had no idea that there was such a glut of sociologists that they stand on street corners rehearsing their lectures. Perhaps their liquid refreshment, which I assumed would be detrimental to reasoned discussions, actually helped them gain new insights about scholarly theories. Maybe my life would have been different if I had just stopped to see what exactly it was about sociology that they wanted to teach me. Ultimately, the immediate perception that our status as an interracial couple had generated the hostility of these strangers placed extra pressure on a relationship that did not have much longer to survive. It wasn't enough that I usually managed to sabotage my potential relationships myself. Now I was letting outsiders impede my romantic progress. Maybe I should have read some of that Talcott Parsons stuff to see if it would have enhanced my love life any.

*   *   **

During college, a female classmate and I decided to take the train from Boston to New York City in order to spend a few days checking out the Big Apple. Despite the fact that she defined us as "just friends," I hoped that our travels together would spark something more substantial and interesting in the romance department. Because of our limited finances, we spent several evenings in Harvard Square bookstores perusing various versions of books on the theme of "New York on $15 Per Day." I identified a YMCA down around 32nd or 34th Street that supposedly had been recently renovated and catered to visiting students. When I departed for New York early Tuesday, I was responsible for investigating the YMCA before her arrival later in the day.

After reaching Penn Station, I walked to the YMCA. I wasn't thrilled by what I found. There was a long row of idle, poorly dressed young men lounging along the outside wall of the YMCA building. They were listening to radios, smoking cigarettes, arguing, and hassling the passing female pedestrians. Things weren't much different inside the lobby. This was supposed to be a co-ed YMCA with separate floors for men and women, but I didn't see any women at all. Feeling overwhelmed by my first taste of the city (I felt like a little ant scurrying at the bottom of giant canyons formed by the skyscrapers) and having no where else to go, I checked in. Upon leaving the elevator at my assigned floor, I hesitated before entering the barely lit, dark hallway. When I entered my small, hot room, I noticed that both the deadbolt and the chain on the door were broken. There was a lock on the door knob, but that didn't seem to offer much security. With some trepidation about the safety of my belongings, I left my suitcase in the room and decided to find the more expensive YMCA up near Central Park that had also been listed in several guide books.

Walking thirty blocks in New York City can be both fascinating and intimidating if you're a simple lad from the Midwest whose only exposure to big cities came from the occasional visit to Chicago and Detroit as well as a few semesters as a college student hanging out in Boston. My senses were overloaded by the noise, traffic, and dirt. In addition, the crowds were never ending. Constant action. A million unusual people and unique sights on virtually every block. But also an uneasy sense of threat; someone could grab your wallet in the chaos and you might never know it. When I reached the other YMCA, it was like traveling from day to night or vice versa in comparison to the downtown "Y." It was on a quiet street. No one was loitering outside the building. The lobby was beautiful. The people inside looked orderly and well-groomed. This was definitely where we should stay. There was no way my friend would feel comfortable at the other "Y."

When I met her train at Penn Station, I immediately told her that I didn't feel comfortable about the less expensive YMCA. I insisted that she stay at the uptown "Y" despite the fact that rooms cost nearly twice as much. She seemed impressed with my perceptions so we headed uptown to her lodgings. The plan was for me to move to the new "Y" for the second night of our stay. After she checked in, we went to dinner and then she said she would like to rest before beginning our day of sightseeing the next morning. As we approached the YMCA, she asked if I might like to come up for a while to talk. I was thrilled to receive the invitation. Unfortunately, the security guard at the elevator was less excited about our plans. He barred me from the elevator because I was not a resident at the "Y." Thus we headed back out to talk for a while at a bar before she returned to the "Y." Afterwards, I walked briskly and nervously through the chilly nighttime air all the way back to my room thirty blocks away. It would have made more sense to take the subway but I wasn't ready for that yet.

I barely slept that night. I kept thinking that someone was trying to break through the flimsy lock on my door. When sunlight came through the window in the morning, I was still dead tired. I needed to check out as soon as possible so I quickly showered with dozens of strangers in the locker room-style bathroom on my floor. It had all of the ambience of the stereotypical shower scene in a prison movie, although actually everyone completely ignored everyone else. There was absolutely no talking. Then I headed for my new residence. I carried my bag all the way uptown. This was a big mistake because I was so drenched with sweat that I was in desperate need of a shower by the time I arrived. Unfortunately it was too early to check in at the uptown "Y" so my friend put my suitcase in her room. We went to a few museums and then came back to make sure I could get a room. We were in luck. A room was available for the night two floors above her fourth floor room. After checking in, we saw more sights and then went out for dinner.

As we headed back to the "Y" that night, she again invited me to stop by her room for a while to talk. I had to suppress a cheer because I really thought my potential relationship was developing nicely. When we got to the elevator, the security guard remembered me from the night before and stuck his hand in my chest as he said, "Didn't you hear what I said last night?"

I waved my room key at him. "It's okay. I'm staying here now."

He looked suspiciously at me and my companion and then said, "You know that no men are allowed on women's floors."

Actually, neither of us knew that, but we nodded our heads as if we had known that all along. In the elevator, I frowned and stared at the floor. I had come so close to capping off the evening by becoming better acquainted. As the elevator stopped on the fourth floor, my friend said to me, "Why don't you come over right now anyway? Just for a little while. It won't do any harm."

It goes against my nature to intentionally violate clear-cut rules. Throughout my entire life, I was always afraid of being caught and punished for some misdeed. Indeed, my primary motivation in life often seems to be the avoidance of embarrassment for myself and others. This time, however, I really, really wanted to sit and chat in informal surroundings, so I agreed. When we got off the elevator, we both looked carefully in every direction before proceeding quickly to her room. At her small room, I sat on the floor and leaned against the bed. We chatted for a few minutes about our day and then she said,

"Stay here for a few more minutes. I'll be right back. I'm going to get my pajamas on." With that, she took some clothing and her toothbrush and headed down the hall to the bathroom. "Pajamas?," I thought, as I resisted the temptation to imagine that she would come back wearing something revealing and provocative.

The next thing I knew my friend was tapping me on the cheek very softly and whispering, "Wake up. Wake up. You have to get out of here."

I rolled over on the floor and tried to open my eyes. Bright light streamed through the window. "What time is it?," I mumbled sleepily.

"It's almost eight-thirty," she whispered.

"In the morning?," I asked, still not fully awake.

"Yes, in the morning." As she spoke, I became aware of the sound of a vacuum cleaner in the hallway outside her door. She whispered again. "The cleaning ladies are already here. They'll be knocking on doors to straighten up the rooms very soon."

"What happened? Why am I here?," I inquired as I climbed to my feet.

"I went to the bathroom to change into my pajamas last night. When I came back, you were fast asleep on the floor. I didn't have the heart to wake you. Then I overslept this morning. I knew you needed to get back to your floor before now. What should we do?"

"I guess I'll just have to find my way out of here," I replied with a shrug.

After the sound of the vacuum cleaner had moved far down the hall, I carefully opened the door and peeked out in the corridor. No one was in sight. The vacuum cleaner had moved down around the corner and I had a clear shot to the elevator. As I whispered, "Wish me luck," over my shoulder, I crept into the hallway. My heart was racing. I felt as if I were committing a crime. As I tiptoed quickly down the hallway toward the elevator, I was struck by the similarity between my situation and the plots in James Bond movies. I was in a tight spot, but with a bit of ingenuity and a bit of luck, I would heroically escape unseen and unscathed. I quickly pushed the "up" button for the elevator and nervously glanced around as I waited. Just as I heard the elevator draw closer, I heard footsteps and voices in the hallway. They were headed in my direction. The elevator door was about to open but I couldn't wait for it. I sprinted down a side hallway and went through a doorway marked "Fire Exit." Lucky for me it was an interior staircase and not some perilous fire escape ladder on the side of the building. I breathed a huge sigh of relief. I had pulled it off. Walking quickly, I headed up the stairs toward my room on the sixth floor. I could hardly wait to take a shower and change clothes after spending the night on the floor in the clothes I had worn the previous day. Moreover, my clothes still carried the unpleasant residue and lingering aroma of sweat from lugging my suitcase for thirty blocks through the hot city yesterday morning. At the sixth floor, I grasped the door handle, still anticipating my shower, when I was shocked to discover that it would not turn. The door was locked. There was no way back onto the hallway from the fire exit stairway. I jogged down to the fifth floor. Also locked. Now what was I going to do? If I pounded on the door and someone opened it, I would probably get in trouble, and perhaps expelled from the building and maybe even arrested for going down the fire exit stairway without permission.

I walked down the staircase and tried to think about what I do. My best hope seemed to be to go down to the first floor, pound on the door, and then claim that I thought this was an accessible staircase rather than a fire escape. That excuse would seem pretty lame considering all of the doors were clearly marked "Fire Exit," but I didn't have many other options. I walked down and checked the door at each floor.

To my surprise, the door was unlocked on the second floor, so I opened it and walked through. Suddenly I found myself in the middle of an elementary school. Apparently the second floor of the "Y" building was occupied by a private school. There were kids walking everywhere at the start of the school day. In an effort to look inconspicuous, I tried to crouch low as I walked down the corridor. Unfortunately for me, few twenty-year-olds can pass for ten-year-olds, especially in a school where all of the teachers recognize all of the students.

"Hey you!"

I tried to ignore whoever was calling me as I walked more quickly down the corridor looking for a way out.

"Hey! Where are you going?"

I didn't look back because I didn't really want to know who was following me. I moved more quickly and nearly broke into a run. In front of me, I saw a stairway leading to the lobby of the YMCA. I scampered down and ran over to the elevator. Unfortunately, my "friend" the security guard awaited me as I reached for the "Up" button.

"Where do you think you're going?"

"I just need to go up to my room to get a few things."

"You can't go up now. They're cleaning each floor. Everybody has to be out during the day. You can go back up after three o'clock."

"Can't I just go up for a minute?," I pleaded. I desperately wanted to take a shower and change clothes.

"No way. That's the rules," he said firmly.

As I tried to plead my case, the elevator door opened and out walked my friend, looking fresh and ready for a new day. "Let's get going," she said. "There are some more museums that I want to see."

I shrugged my shoulders in resignation and subtly lifted my sleeve up near my nose so I could catch a whiff of myself. Whew! I really needed a shower. If it wasn't bad enough wearing these clothes the day before, now matters were even worse because I generated so much nervous perspiration during my James Bond adventure on the fire exit staircase. She grabbed my arm and pulled me toward the door, talking rapidly about the day's agenda. Just before she reached the door, she turned and looked me. Then she crinkled up her nose in a ghastly look of horror. "Didn't you even take a shower today?"

I tried to explain, but she just shook her head and marched off ahead of me, no longer interested in talking to me or even being within six feet of me. Thus ended my prospects for a relationship. She even began to avoid me when we got back to Harvard. It was as if her only memory associated with me was the aroma of my clothing that morning in the lobby of the "Y." I started out thinking of myself as a cool James Bond, saving us both from discovery by the YMCA staff. I ended up in her olfactory memory banks as another entertainment character, Pepe LePew, and that's a difficult image to overcome. If only I had purchased some cologne that morning, maybe things would have turned out differently.

*　　　　　　*　　　　　　*

When I studied in England at the University of Bristol, my prospects for developing a relationship looked dim. There were a number of women who indicated an interest in me, but British university students seemed, well, socially retarded compared to American students. So many British students went to single-sex schools through high school (and worse yet, many were boarding schools) that they weren't accustomed to being around and interacting with members of the opposite sex. Thus their interactions and giggling conversations were (to American ears) not unlike those that occurred in a junior high school in the United States. I initially resigned myself to postponing my pursuit of a romantic relationship until after I returned to the United States at the end of year.

During one of our university basketball games, I landed on an opposing player's foot while taking a shot and twisted my ankle. I fell to the floor and rolled around, writhing in pain. My teammates helped me to the bench because I could barely walk.

The next day, the ankle was very swollen and covered with a large dark bruise. I went to the University's Student Health Center and a doctor concluded that it was merely a sprain. No bones were broken. After the doctor announced the diagnosis and offered me a pair of crutches, a woman in a blue nurse's uniform came into the examining room and instructed me to lie back down on the table. She looked at my chart. "So you're an American? From Harvard, no less?"

I nodded.

"Are you here for the entire academic year?"

"Yes. I'll be here until late summer working on my master's degree."

"You have a very nice voice," she said with a smile. "I really love your American accent. It's just like those actors in the Hollywood movies."

I smiled in embarrassment. "Thank you...I guess."

"Let me take a look at that ankle." She peered closely at the bruise and then began stroking my ankle, actually caressing it and moving her hands slowly and lightly back and forth. This didn't seem to be doing much for the ankle. In fact, it seemed almost...(I thought for the moment for the right concept)...sensual. As the word "sensual" came into my mind, I lifted my head up with a start to see what she was doing. She had her eyes closed and she was rubbing slowly, lightly, and, well, *sensually* back and forth in a manner that didn't appear to have a medicinal purpose. As my heart picked up speed and my brain quickly tried to analyze this unexpected situation, I took a closer look at the nurse. She was an attractive, buxom blonde with a warm smile. In fact, her nurse's dress was so tight she was almost bursting out of it. She was only in her early twenties so she was just about my age. Her eyes were still closed and she had a slight smile on face, as if she was enjoying this more than I was. I looked at her left hand. No rings. Hmmmmm. This was interesting. I decided to lay back and enjoy it.

After several long minutes, she stopped and looked at me with her warm smile. "I want you to come back every day so that I can give you a therapeutic massage."

I nodded my head and tried not to blush about the lustful thoughts that were beginning to enter my mind. Thus I began to return on a daily basis for my rendezvous with her sensual touch. Although I still could not discern any therapeutic effect on my ankle, she continued to show great enthusiasm for each massage session. I would almost say that she seemed to derive a certain amount of pleasure from stroking my ankle. Each day, she closed her eyes, rolled back her head, and quietly said, "hmmmmm" as she slowly stroked, caressed, and massaged each inch of my ankle and foot.

I started to believe that she was practically begging me to ask her out, and perhaps seek even more of her attention. However, I still retained the same problem of lacking the nerve to actually ask a woman for a date. Thus I set about working up to the request through a gradual series of conversations.

One day, when she had just finished the massage, I said to her, "So, do you go out much to pubs and restaurants and places like that?"

She shook her head and smiled that disarming smile. "The nature of my life is such that I don't really go out."

"So you don't have any recommendations for places that an American ought to visit?"

"Oh, I could make some suggestions if that's what you really want. Is that what you *really* want?" As she asked the question, she looked deeply into my eyes. It was somewhat unnerving since I did not really want information. I wanted a date and chance to see where this sensual massage might lead.

I was on the verge of responding by asking her out on a date when the doctor stuck his head in the room and said to her, "I need you in examining room number two, please."

She smiled again. "Sorry I have to go. I'll see you again tomorrow." As she turned to go, she ran her hand slowly along my lower leg one last time. I took that as a signal if ever there was one. I would definitely ask her out tomorrow. Actually, a small, aggressive voice in my brain was encouraging me to be even bolder. "Go ahead and proposition her," it said. But I wasn't confident enough to do something like that. Or was I? That last caress of my leg practically sent an electrical surge through my body. I was suddenly looking forward to the next day with great eagerness.

That evening at basketball practice I must have had a smile on my face. One of my English teammates asked, "What are you so happy about?"

"Oh, I don't know. Maybe it's just that my ankle feels so much better."

"What have you been doing for it?"

"Actually, I've been going to the health center every day and the nurse gives my ankle a therapeutic massage."

"Is she the blonde?"

I turned toward him suddenly with great curiosity. "Yes. Why? Do you know her?"

"Oh, sure. I've seen her when I've gone to the health center. That sister is very nice."

"Sister?," I asked. "Whose sister is she?"

He shrugged his shoulders. "I don't know if she's anybody's sister. All I know…I mean what I was saying is that she *is* a sister. That's what I meant."

I was taken aback. This statement was so shocking to me that I involuntarily clutched my chest with my right hand as my eyes got as wide as the moon. I had been getting a sensual massage from a *nun*? And I had been enjoying it?! I felt overwhelmed with guilt and shame. How could I have thought that she was making a play for me? I must have misinterpreted everything. No. This couldn't be true. I grabbed my teammate by the shirt and said directly into his surprised face, "Tell me. Would a sister wear a blue dress like that?"

He slowly pushed my hand away. "Take it easy, mate. What's the matter?"

"Just tell me. Would a sister where a blue dress like that?"

"Sure," he said. "That's what sisters wear in Britain. Don't they dress like that in the States?"

"No," I said, looking away. "No, they don't." I sat frozen in one spot as he shrugged his shoulders and walked away. Suddenly I was filled with such horror that I felt scarcely able to breathe. So that's why she said her life didn't permit her to go out much. It flashed through my mind that I had come within a single breath of *propositioning a nun*! Thank heavens the doctor came by when he did. It was like divine intervention. I had been saved from making the most awful, horrible mistake of my entire life. I had this strong feeling that I ought to go to confession in order to ask forgiveness for having lustful feelings about a nun. However, since I wasn't Catholic, I didn't really know how to do that. Still, since she was Catholic, maybe I should go anyway. I sat for a few minutes in a state of shock before I was able to drag myself onto the basketball court.

When I got back to my room that night, I said a little prayer asking for forgiveness from the Catholic god and any other church's god that was offended by my thoughts and actions. I firmly vowed never to go to the health center again. It didn't matter how sick I ever became, I couldn't bear the thought that I would see her again, since seeing her would undoubtedly fill me with guilt about the horrible misdeed that I almost did. And thus I never set foot in the health center again and I never saw the nun in the blue dress again.

Many months later, as I was preparing to leave for the United States, I had a conversation about hospitals in Britain. I noticed that my British conversation partner kept referring to nurses as "sisters." Finally, I said to him, "Am I correct in assuming that all nurses in Britain are nuns?"

"Why do you ask that?"

"Because everybody always refers to them as 'sisters.' You know, the term used for nuns, the women who take vows to become members of Catholic religious orders."

He laughed. "No, no, no. They're not members of any religious order. Well, there are probably some in Catholic hospitals. No, we use the term 'sister' the same way that you use the term 'nurse.' In our country, we simply call nurses 'sisters' There is nothing religious about it." His words hit me like a blow to the stomach. Here I had spent all this time dealing with agonizing guilt for having lustful feelings about a supposed nun, and now it turns out she wasn't a nun at all. She was just a regular woman who happened to be a nurse sending out the strongest signals possible that she was interested in a relationship with me. My record with women remained intact. Somehow I had blown it yet again.

*   *   *

During law school, I noticed a striking woman with long, silky black hair. Her name was Carla and she was slender and shapely. In addition, she was always impeccably dressed. She introduced herself to me briefly at the meeting of some student organization and that introduction, in effect, granted me a license to say hello to her whenever I saw her. And believe me, I saw her as much as I could. I felt as if I was back in junior high school and pursuing a secret crush on a pretty girl. I figured out her class schedule and her patterns for going to her locker to retrieve her books. As much as possible, I planned my day so that my path would cross hers and I could say hello. We never had a conversation, and I'm not sure that she even remembered my name, but I had vivid imaginary scenes projected across my brain in which I would ask her out and we would develop an enduring romantic relationship.

The first day of Labor Law class during my second year of law school I was pleasantly surprised to see Carla sitting with one of her female friends. I went over and took the seat directly behind her. Throughout the entire class period, I stared at her beautiful hair and smelled the fragrant perfume that I always associated with her presence. I finally had a class to look forward to, but I was worried that I would be caught daydreaming about Carla if the professor ever surprised me with a question.

The next day, my life got even better. I arrived at the class before Carla and sat in my same seat. Since law students are generally expected to sit in the same seat for every class (to make it easier for the professor to identify students in order to call on them), I anticipated that Carla would sit in front of me once again. To my surprise, when she entered the room, she came straight over and sat right next to me.

"How are you doing?," she asked, with a quick flash of her perfect smile. "I didn't realize that you were in this class, Chris."

I almost fell out of my chair. Not only did she know who I was; she actually chose to sit next to me. Her friend followed along and sat on Carla's other side. It quickly developed, however, that Carla seemed most interested in talking to me. Every day we talked about various things, including classes, hobbies, travel, etc. We also whispered humorous comments to each other whenever something interesting happened in class. In effect, Labor Law served as the perfect context for us to become well-acquainted without me having to take any bold initiative (the very thing of which I was so incapable when it came to dealing with women).

During a telephone conversation, I told my older brother about her. "Ask her out! Ask her out!," he insisted. "Don't you see? She is giving you every possible encouraging signal. She sought you out in the class. She initiates conversations with you every day. Women aren't that friendly unless they want to be asked out." With my brother exhorting me like a coach yelling from the sidelines, I began to plot when and how I would pop the question. The major impediment seemed to be that she was so frequently in the company of other people, especially the woman who followed her around in Labor Law. Still, she was sometimes alone at her locker or in the hallway. Thus I knew my opportunity would arrive very shortly.

Each year the law students' association sponsored a dance to let students chase away the mid-year blahs. In Labor Law, Carla asked me if I was planning to go to the dance. I figured that was a signal that she wanted me to go. When I responded affirmatively, she looked very pleased and said "See you there."

Hundreds of students attended the dance. Probably almost every student at the law school was there. I wandered through the crowded dance floor looking for Carla. Maybe this was my opportunity to ask her out. When I saw her, she was talking intently with a guy I recognized from one of my courses. I waved at her and she waved back (again flashing her perfect smile) but she kept talking to him rather than heading over to talk to me. I had a couple of glasses of alcohol-based fruit punch and I tried to watch her without making it appear that I was staring. A few women asked me to dance, so I even looped around the dance floor a few times, always checking regularly to see if Carla had disengaged herself from that guy. They didn't appear to be a couple. I never saw them dance together. They just seemed to be hanging around together talking.

As the night wore on, I started to feel impatient. Soon my impatience turned to mild depression. Maybe she didn't really like me after all. Maybe I had fooled myself into thinking that I had a chance with her. As I grumbled to myself, I kept drinking the punch, which turned out to be much more powerful than I realized. The next thing I knew, the room was completely empty. I didn't remember the party ending, but then again I was having trouble even standing up. There were a half-dozen students cleaning up and putting away chairs, and Carla and her friend were among them. Although my memories are quite hazy, I believe that I drunkenly followed Carla and her friend about the room saying over and over again, "You know, I really wanted to dance with you." In my mind's eye, I have a picture of them being exceedingly polite to me as I repeated my drunken (albeit truthful) ramblings dozens of times. I just followed and stumbled and rambled. When the room was cleaned up, Carla said to me, "Let us give you a ride home."

I didn't like the "us" in that sentence so I waved them away me. "No, no. I live close by. I can walk."

She gave me a look of sincere concern. "I really think we should give you a ride."

"No, no. Never you mind," I said as I turned and stumbled out the door. When I got outside, I felt more keenly disappointed than I had felt in many years. I had wanted to dance with Carla and ask her out, but something had gone wrong. Was that guy her boyfriend? It didn't seem likely because I only saw her talk to him occasionally at school. They never danced together or held hands. They just seemed like friends. But what happened to the attention that she gave me in Labor Law? What happened to those signals? I was confused, disappointed, and depressed.

I noticed that it had started raining so I tried to jog the three blocks to the house in which I rented a room. Suddenly I stumbled on the slippery pavement. I fell forward and barely managed to get my hands out in front of me to break the fall just as my head grazed the sidewalk. I lay there, face down on the wet pavement, feeling the cool rain fall on top of me. I didn't feel like getting up, but I knew I should.

As it turned out, my vision was so blurry from drunkenness that I couldn't read the street signs or house numbers. I knew my house was nearby, but I just couldn't find it. I wandered the streets aimlessly for a long time and then lay down in someone's front yard to rest. I was awakened by a dog standing next to my head barking and by the feel of a steady, cold rain hitting my face. Struggling to my feet, I glanced at my watch and realized that I had been lost for several hours. Now, however, my vision was clearing and I managed to walk straight to my house. When I dragged my hungover body out of bed the next morning, I noticed that I scraped my forehead when I fell and there was a fair amount of blood on my face and shirt. Later that day, I went to the student health center. They examined and cleaned my abrasion and then taped a large gauze bandage to my head. It was not a pretty sight. In fact, the huge bandage made my injury look much worse than it really was.

Although my physical condition was okay by Monday, I was in a panic about what to say to Carla. I couldn't even remember all of the lunatic, drunken ravings to which I had subjected her. I dreaded the thought of seeing her in Labor Law. What if she hates me now? What if we sit in uncomfortable silence? What if I had blown my chance to develop a relationship with her? I decided that my only hope was to find her before class in order to "break the ice" and renew at least a comfortable conversational relationship. I undertook a systematic, room-by-room search of the law school, desperately hoping to find her before the start of Labor Law. Luck was with me because I eventually found her studying amid the stacks on the third floor of the library. I summoned whatever courage I possessed and approached her with an opening line that I hoped would defuse any tension.

Walking up behind her, I said very quietly, "You know, if you ever see me start drinking potent punch like that again, you really should stop me before I kill myself or worse yet, make a fool of myself in your eyes."

She turned in my direction and registered an endearing look of concern when she caught sight of the huge bandage taped to my head. "Oh my goodness, are you all right?" She reached out to touch my arm. Instantly I felt as if I had managed to put that night behind me. It seemed as if her warmth and interest had returned.

"It's nothing really. I just slipped and fell in the rain on my way home the other night."

"I knew we should have taken you home. I was giving Scott a ride and I could easily have dropped you off right after I left him at his apartment. His girlfriend had to work that night so he was pretty down about having to attend the dance alone."

Her words lifted me to an elated state. She still showed concern about me and, more importantly, that guy was just some friend who wasn't involved with her at all. I felt like shouting "Hallelujah!" but I figured I had done enough foolish things in her presence lately so that I better be more low key for the time being. The thought of asking her out on a date immediately reentered my head. I was determined to take that step and to take it soon. I thought about making the bold request right then, but as I hesitated her female friend arrived to escort her to Labor Law. So off we went to Labor Law. I walked down the hallway with a new bounce in my step, oblivious to the stares of everyone who was seeing me with my bandage for the very first time that day.

A few days later, I was determined to be bold for once in my life. I knew when she went to her locker alone to pick up her books and I would be waiting there for her in order to pop the question. Although I was virtually penniless that year, I figured that I could go without groceries for a few weeks in order to take her to a nice restaurant and a movie. When she saw me waiting at her locker, which was right next to an exterior exit door, she looked very happy. Grabbing my arm and pulling me toward her, she said excitedly, "You should have seen me in Advanced Criminal Procedure. For once in my life, I knew the answers to every single question that the professor posed to the class. I felt as if I was the expert on today's subject. I really feel good about how I'm going to do on the final exam."

"That's great," I said with a broad smile. As I stared into her smiling face, just a few short inches from mine, I was so tempted to kiss her that I could barely restrain myself. She had a bright, expectant look in her eyes that almost seemed to invite me to press my lips against hers. I held myself back and focused my senses on the incredible warmth that seemed to flow from her hand to my arm. Although I was nervous, everything about this warm, excited moment seemed to tell me that the time had come. I was going to ask her out.

As I started to speak, the exterior door opened and in walked a student I recognized from several of my classes. He greeted Carla with a big smile and a wave of his hand. I felt momentarily annoyed. One moment we were virtually alone in this corner of the locker area and now an interloper had thrust himself into our conversation.

"Hello, Bill. How are you?," she greeted him warmly. "Do you know Chris?"

Bill and I nodded politely at each other. He might have actually nodded in a friendly way, but I was too annoyed at him to notice. I shifted my thoughts back to popping the question and hoped that Bill would get on about his business and leave us alone as soon as possible. Things didn't look promising, however, because Bill dropped his backpack to the floor and leaned up against Carla's locker as if he was settling in for an extended conversation.

"So what's new with you, Bill?," Carla asked while showing that endearing smile that radiated warmth and interest.

"Funny, you should ask," replied Bill. "But I just got invited to interview with your husband's law firm."

At the word "husband," all of the blood rushed from my brain and headed toward my feet. I felt as if I would faint. Husband! She's married?! I was stunned beyond belief. Bill continued to jabber about something but his words only sounded like an incomprehensible buzz. I thought I saw Carla flinch (it was barely perceptible) at the mention of the word "husband." Her expression did not change and she did not look at me, but I almost felt as if she didn't intend for me to know that she was married. I kept looking at Bill, as if I was listening to the conversation, but I couldn't help watching Carla out of the corner of my eyes. With her silky hair and distinctive perfume, she remained as alluring as ever, but without warning she had suddenly become untouchable.

I couldn't believe that I had misread all of those signals. She came to sit next to *me*. She initiated conversations with *me*. She leaned over to whisper to *me*. She gave *me* her radiant smile and the warm touch of her hand on my arm. Did I read too much into these things? Where did I go wrong?

Still looking at Bill's mouth move, but unable to discern his words, I visualized the ring on Carla's left hand. It was a thick, curvy gold ring that appeared to have jade and several jewels (perhaps diamonds?)

imbedded in the center. It didn't look like any wedding ring I had ever seen, but it could easily have been designed by her (or her husband) as a unique ring. Come to think of it, it did appear to be very expensive. Maybe I simply looked at the wrong signals. If I had looked at the ring, perhaps I would have realized sooner.

When Bill finally stopped talking, I interjected before Carla could respond to Bill. "Hey, I've really got to go now. See you later."

"Aren't you going to Labor Law?," she said to me with a strange (was it wistful?) look in her eyes.

"Naw, I don't think I'll go today." And out the door I went vowing to find a new law school that would accept me as a transfer student for next year. It would be too painful and embarrassing to face her again, day after day for another entire year. Although I felt embarrassed and shattered, especially when I recalled following her around at the dance saying all kinds of things that undoubtedly revealed the attraction I felt, I also felt a lingering curiosity about what it all meant. Perhaps if I had asked her out, she would have said yes. But then I would have been in a really fine mess.

It almost seemed as if "Looking for Love in the All the Wrong Places" had been tattooed onto my soul. No matter what I did, something always went wrong. When I met and married my wife in the eighteen months following the Carla incident, I almost blew it once again when I was too hung over to get to my feet on my wedding day. I actually hadn't had a drink since the disastrous law school party more than a year earlier, but just as before, I was too preoccupied with various thoughts (this time celebratory) to pay attention to the strength of the drinks being served. Fortunately fate intervened on my behalf (for once) by scheduling the ceremony for seven o'clock in the evening rather than earlier in the day and by lifting me from my paralyzed, prone position on the living room carpet with a couple of hours to spare. If not for these fortuitous developments, I might still be looking hither and yon as love's unlucky loser.

Chapter Six

Working to Avoid the Devil

Idle hands are the devil's workshop.

Now there's an inspiring sentiment. Inspiration by fear, anyway. A slogan that is undoubtedly part of the socialization process to become a hard-working American making positive contributions to society. I can't say that I ever really wanted to work. I can think of many things that I would much rather do. On the other hand, I never wanted to end up associating with or, worse yet, under the control of the devil, so I always knew that I'd have to find some type of career. As a child, I progressed through a succession of intended careers: soldier, artist, forest ranger, gym teacher, astronaut. Unfortunately, nothing seemed to stick. As soon as I learned about one potential career, I'd discover something else that appeared to be more fun. The next step was experimenting with different kinds of jobs. I tried out being a barber by giving my little brother a haircut. Armed only with scissors, I cut a bit here and bit there before focusing my attention on the left side of his head. As I was making significant progress in reducing the length of his hair, he suddenly started to cry and demanded that I stop. He wouldn't listen to my explanation that his hair looked terrible merely because the job was only half done. Instead, my mother took him to a licensed barber (I say "licensed barber" rather than "real barber" because I was a real barber. I was cutting hair wasn't I? How much more real did I need to be?). I'll never know if I would have made a great barber. I wasn't given the opportunity to finish my first project. Now that my brother's thinning hairline has made his forehead grow upward part way across the top of his head, I'll never be able to complete my artistic masterpiece. There simply isn't enough hair there to work on. I guess I was meant to try out other careers instead.

*   *   *

One of my first jobs was as a bus boy at a restaurant that aspired to be classy. Every evening I scurried about removing dirty dishes, placing silverware on tables, and delivering our specialty blueberry muffins to each table. On Sunday, I filled in for the dishwasher on his day off. By working at the restaurant, I learned many tricks of the food service trade. For example, keep the lights down low. That way it's harder for customers to see any hardened food residue stuck to the silverware or tables. At my restaurant, there was a significant drawback to this tactic, however. The restaurant seating area was two steps down from the bar area and entrance. The restaurant was so dark, especially for people entering from the bright outdoors, that time and again customers tumbled down the steps and lay sprawling at the hostess's feet. This was decades ago, before people worried about being sued for everything, so we mostly laughed when we saw or heard customers crashing down those stairs. The only time it wasn't funny was when they actually tumbled into the salad bar directly behind the hostess's station. Then we had to waste a lot of time picking hair out of the lettuce, which was more annoying than humorous. Fortunately, none of these customer collisions ever brought to light the colony of roach-like critters that was later discovered living under the bowls of lettuce and vegetables in the salad bar (So that must be why other restaurants periodically remove the ice and clean the bottom portion of the salad bar. Why didn't we think of that?). I don't think the county health department would have recognized the humor in that situation.

There was tremendous camaraderie among the employees. We were unified in our commitment; not to making the restaurant a success, but to helping each other avoid getting into trouble with the boss. Because the restaurant had a bar, waitresses (they were all female) and busboys (they were all male) helped themselves to drinks and hid their glasses in various places around the restaurant [Note: The drinking age was only 18 in 1976 so we were all of legal drinking age. Young people, don't try this at home.] It was not unusual to find a gin and tonic or a tequila sunrise sitting in the cupboard with the blueberry muffins. The boss never looked in there. Employees would take a drink, hand an order in to the kitchen, take another drink, serve food to customers, and so on. By the end of each evening, the quality of the service had deteriorated but the serving staff was incredibly happy and friendly. We were especially happy when a customer had a birthday. We would serve the birthday guest a free slice of Pepperidge Farm cake and then stand as a group in the walk-in freezer consuming the rest of the cake ourselves, often with our bare hands.

One Sunday I arrived before the restaurant opened in order to wash pots and pans left over from the previous day's closing. I found a mountain of pots and pans lying on the stainless steel counter next to the industrial-sized sink and dishwasher machine. Mixed among the usual pots and pans were several unfamiliar large trays containing bony slabs with greasy fat and meat residue. I wasn't sure what this was, but I knew better than to ask the cook. She was always yelling, "Don't you know anything!" and she never invited questions. I looked closely at the trays and concluded that these were the bony pieces left over when the prime parts of beef had been cut away in preparation for cooking. These pieces were not recognizable to me, and I had worked at the restaurant for months at that point. They sure didn't look edible to me. I was proud that I had taken the time to sort things out for myself without bothering the cook. Thus I took the trays outside, dumped their contents in the dumpster, and brought the trays back inside to be washed.

Ten minutes later, the cook walked past the dishwasher station. She was a large woman with a booming voice and a fiery temper. She appeared puzzled when she went into the kitchen. A moment later she returned and asked me, "Have you seen my prime rib?"

"Nope. Sorry," I replied as I kept washing pots and pans.

"Well, what happened to the trays that I left lying right here?," she asked, pointing to the spot on the dishwasher counter where I had discovered the greasy trays of unidentifiable meat remnants.

My heart froze. I stopped washing and looked straight ahead at the brick wall. I didn't have the nerve to look at her. "The trays of greasy bones?"

"There was some bone in there because it's prime rib," she said impatiently. "Now where did it go?"

I paused for a long time before replying, "I threw it all in the dumpster." Every muscle and fiber in my body tightened in anticipation of the impending torrent of anger and obscenities. I had seen her tear people down like a Marine drill sergeant dismantling a young recruit. Now my time had come. Strangely, however, she didn't yell. I didn't hear anything. So I turned slowly to look at her out of the corner of my eye. Her eyes were wide open, as if she were in shock. Her lips were moving, but she had lost her voice. I could barely hear her whisper, over and over, "You threw out my prime rib? You threw out my prime rib? You threw out my prime rib?...." I turned toward her and began to babble apologetically, "I'm really sorry. I didn't know. I thought it was some stuff that you cut off of the prime rib. It didn't look at all familiar...." I offered to climb into the dumpster to retrieve it, but (fortunately for me and the day's customers) she just shook her head slowly from side to side. As I babbled, she turned and walked into the kitchen, as if in a trance, still repeating over and over her uncomprehending query about what I had done.

I was certain that I would be fired, especially since prime rib was our widely-advertised Sunday special. And now we had none. I have no idea how many hundreds of dollars worth of meat I blithely tossed into the cloud of flies buzzing around the trash dumpster. I know it was a lot. Far more than I could pay for even if they withheld all of my pay for a month. As it turned out, the manager was merciful and the cook seemed to forgive me (eventually). But I clearly got the message that I had no business working in the food service industry.

*　　　　　*　　　　　*

I tried serving as a telephone customer service representative in several settings. With United Parcel Service, my undoing came when I kept telling people that they could send packages from the mainland to Hawaii by truck. It wasn't that I actually thought a truck could go from the mainland to Hawaii. It's just that when you answer the same questions over and over again, your eyes (and brain) cloud over and you cease to hear the precise details of customers' questions. I think UPS should simply stop shipping to Hawaii. Then the service reps, with their brains flying on autopilot, would not be forced to try to shift gears whenever somebody wanted to send packages via ground transportation to the state that happens to be surrounded by water.

When the Internal Revenue Service selected me to answer tax questions on the telephone, I received extensive training about tax laws and typical tax problems. Unfortunately it was too much information for my training class to absorb. It turned out that the agency was not able to choose new employees based on the planned test over tax law. So many people flunked the arithmetic portion of the exam that they had to keep everyone who could add and subtract just to fill positions. Thus they had to hire people like me who had almost no comprehension of tax laws. The main thing I knew about taxes was that it was not a good idea to fill out your 1040 form after drinking a bottle of wine. I tried that as a college freshman and it didn't work well. In fact, the IRS sent the form back and told me to do it over again. I think that they said something about not signing your name in crayon but I don't really remember.

Along the way, I learned quite a bit about income taxes just by answering people's questions, and I did not hesitate to make up a response when I didn't really know the answer. Hey, with millions and millions of tax forms, how many of these people were likely to get audited anyway? In addition, some of the calls were quite interesting and memorable.

"Good afternoon. This is the IRS Customer Service Center. How can I help you?" My introduction was always flawless. It was after this point that things usually went downhill.

"I need to ask some questions about taxes."

"Please go ahead. I'm happy to help."

"I need to know if I am supposed to pay taxes."

"Did you earn income in the past year?"

"Yes."

"Then you really are supposed to pay taxes just like everyone else."

"Am I supposed to have some particular forms?"

"Your employer is supposed to give you a W-2 form showing your wages and the taxes withheld. You send a copy of that in with the 1040 form that you use to calculate if you must pay additional taxes or if you get a refund. Did your employer send you a W-2 form at the end of January?"

"No. I'm self-employed."

"Oh. Then you need to use your own records of income and taxes. And you might have to get the form for self-employment taxes, too."

"I don't really keep good records."

"Oh. Then do the best you can. Be as honest as possible."

"I'm a patriotic citizen and I want to pay my fair share of taxes. That's why I'm calling."

"Well, that's certainly good to hear. Maybe there is a small business association in your line of work that could provide you with some advice or assistance in preparing your taxes."

"I doubt it. I'm in a specialized personal services business."

"There really are trade associations for almost everything these days. Just look in the phone book."

"Believe me, honey, I know lots of people in this business and none of us are in the phone book. Most of us don't even have an address."

"Whatever you say. Just do the best you can. Do you have any other questions?"

"Yeah, can you tell me about the oil depletion allowance?"

I cringed when I heard that phrase. I had heard the phrase along way before but I had no idea what it was. I faked it as best I could. "Could you tell me something more specific about your situation? That may help me answer the question in a more specific way."

"Sure. I basically wanted to know if the cost of massage oil could be deducted or something like that under this oil depletion allowance thing?"

I thought momentarily and then shrugged my shoulders. "Of course. It's oil isn't it." But then I thought for another moment. "But, on second thought, I think it only applies when it's related to the production of income, like in the oil business."

"I'm not in the oil business but I use massage oil for my business."

"I think you're all set then." She seemed like a nice enough person. I had a bad feeling that she might get audited, but then I realized that since she didn't have a phone number or address they might never find her.

Unfortunately, it turned out that I was the one being audited at that moment because this was one of the calls to which my supervisors were listening. To my surprise, they said that massage oil was not relevant to anything unless this taxpayer happened to be a masseuse or something. I argued that this caller was obviously at least an "or something" if not an actual masseuse. My supervisors disagreed. In fact, they seemed to believe that this citizen was engaged in some kind of illegal activity, and they blamed me for not getting more information. It has always been my strong belief that criticism of employees tends to create a hostile work environment, so I strolled right out the door and instantly became an ex-IRS employee. In a very odd coincidence, the IRS audited my tax filing that year. During the audit, I added to my knowledge about taxes. I already knew not to drink a bottle of wine before completing my 1040 form. Now I learned how useful it was to save the wine and bring two bottles for sharing during the meeting with the auditor. We had a great time. I don't know why other people always complain about audits. I'm thinking of claiming 43 dependents this year just to see if they'll send the same guy back for another audit party.

*   *   *

After drifting between jobs, I was happy to discover the concept of the internship. I could learn about a job and sometimes even get paid without having to make any commitments. Once I discovered this concept, it was just a matter of identifying the types of jobs that I wanted to learn about. By this time, I was a student at Harvard, so potential employers were interested in me sight unseen. In fact, I usually fared much better when they looked only at the Harvard label on my resume. Things didn't always go quite so well when they actually had to meet me.

First, I decided that I wanted to work in city government. I could grapple with pressing urban problems such as crime, education, economic development, and housing, and thereby help to improve the lives of my fellow citizens. During Christmas, I wrote to the city manager of a mid-size city. He was so enthusiastic about my Harvard label that he immediately promised me a paid summer position. He told me about an elaborate internship program he was developing so that outstanding students from the very best schools could rotate through the city departments acquiring management experience and making substantial contributions to city projects. I planned to commute to the job from my parents' house so I even managed to minimize my living expenses. As I moved back home for the summer, I fantasized about all of the money I would be able to save for school.

I called the city manager's office to inquire about when I should begin. His secretary told me that he would get back to me as soon as possible. Hearing nothing, I waited a few days and called again. The next week I called again. Two weeks later, my mother got tired of seeing me around the house (and she was annoyed at the city manager, too) so she made me tell the secretary that I would be sitting in the city manager's office at 8 a.m. on Monday morning and every day thereafter until he followed through on his commitment to me. When the city manager arrived at 8:30 a.m. on Monday and saw meet sitting in the waiting area, he said, "So you're Smith? Where have you been? Are you ready to start?" A little voice in my head (this one was probably my father rather than my mother) told me to punch the guy in the mouth. But I didn't really have any other job options that summer. In my eyes, Burger King wasn't an option. It was more like a punitive sentence. So I kept my mouth shut, smiled, and followed the city manager into his office.

It became immediately apparent that the grand internship plan had never materialized. Thus the city manager said, "Things didn't quite work out as I wanted. But I'm going to keep my word about giving you some experience in city government. Today I'll put you in the highest paying available opening on the city payroll and then in the next week or so I'll be able to move you over to my office in city hall." That sounded pretty good when he said it. Some of the luster diminished when I found myself sent to the city bus garage north of downtown to become a part-time temporary bus dispatcher. To make matters worse, no one told the transit system managers who I was. As far as they knew,

I was some spy sent over from city hall. Suffice to say, my welcome was wary rather than warm.

A few hours later, I found myself, with my eyes barely open from lack of sleep, standing in the dispatcher's office at 4 a.m. watching the chaos that is called getting the buses out in the morning. The dispatcher had to assign buses according to which buses were actually operable, the order in which they were parked in the garage, and the timing of each route's first run. The process was complicated by a particularly tense moment in union-management relations in which drivers demonstrated their dissatisfaction with contract negotiations by waiting until the last possible moment to punch in on the time clock and then arguing about the nature of amenities available on their assigned bus (e.g., windows that open, air conditioning, etc.). The process was a blur. Then drivers started to radio in reports about problems such as mechanical failures and uncooperative passengers. The dispatcher had to memorize which bus was being driven by which driver and where they were on their respective routes at given moments during the day. The scene was utterly incomprehensible. I watched for eight hours and retained only one bit of information: the obvious fact that the dispatcher had absorbed an incredible amount of knowledge about the transit system from doing the job for over twenty years.

I had no idea how the bus system worked. I didn't know the location of bus stops. I didn't know what rules and regulations applied to the bus drivers. I also didn't know if I should bother learning very much since the city manager was going to bring me back over to city hall any day now. Thus I basically tried to absorb the ambience of the scene. In the eyes of the transit system managers, however, I was extra set of hands available for their use for an unknown but finite period of time. Therefore they decided to seize this opportunity to permit the dispatcher to go on vacation. On my third day in city government, the city bus system was under my control.

I had only been in charge of the dispatcher's office for an hour when the phones were ringing off the hook about buses not showing up for their routes and thereby making people late for work. The callers who informed me about this situation were not actually telling me anything new. I could see the drivers standing right there in their lounge area drinking coffee and taking their sweet time about getting to work. Since I didn't understand how to read the reports about which buses were inoperable, I kept assigning drivers to broken down buses. Then they would tardily saunter back to the dispatch window to tell me about the problems. Drivers who had operable buses would stroll back in to tell me that they weren't supposed to leave until some other route left ahead of them, otherwise it would goof up the coordination of bus transfers. I was frantically assigning and reassigning buses and listening to screaming bus passengers on the phone. Eventually, I got all of the buses on the road and they were only about two hours late.

Before I could relax for a second, the radio calls began to come in from the drivers. A bus broke down on West Main Street. I called out to the maintenance shop to see if someone would take the service truck out to fix it. The mechanics responded quickly. Whew! Then another bus had mechanical problems. Unfortunately, the service truck was busy across town. Now I was supposed to find a relief driver to take a different bus out to that route. Of course, I didn't know about this procedure since this situation did not arise the previous day during my hours spent observing the dispatcher. To this day, I don't know what happened to the passengers on that disabled bus. Maybe they walked. I hope they're not still waiting.

The radio crackled again and again with questions and problems. I was virtually useless and the drivers knew it. But they seemed to enjoy putting me on the spot. They perceived me as representing management, especially since they heard that I had come over from city hall. Thus I was an unwitting (and undeserving) target of their enmity. A call came over the radio from a bus that was looping through the downtown business district.

"Hey, dispatch. This is bus 104. I've got an unruly passenger here. He's bothering everyone else on the bus. I think he's drunk."

"Okay, bus 104," I said, not knowing what to do.

"Dispatch, this is 104 again. What are you going to do about this situation? I'm going to have to pull over and stop until this gets solved."

"Okay, 104." I was paralyzed with uncertainty.

"Dispatch, do you still read me?"

The driver's question gave me an idea. "Sorry, 104. I can barely hear you. There must be something wrong with the radio."

The driver laughed. "There ain't nothing wrong with that radio. I can hear you just fine. Now what are you going to do?"

I paused for several long seconds. Then I had no choice but to ask, "Um, 104, what exactly am I supposed to do?"

Another laugh came over radio. "They didn't teach you much at city hall, did they? You're supposed to call the supervisors in the mobile units."

I had met the supervisors the day before. Two older gentleman who seemed particularly comfortable sitting around drinking coffee, chatting, and eating donuts. Unfortunately, they had both called in sick at the start of the work day. Now I was really stuck. I was tempted to call one of the managers from the front office. On the other hand, I didn't want to look helpless or incompetent. As I thought about the situation, I realized that I could always ask a manager for help later, so I might as well see if there was another option to use first.

I hit my "call" button. "Bus 104, come in. This is dispatch."

"I'm still here, dispatch. This is 104."

"Okay, 104. Can you turn up your radio?"

"What?"

"Can you turn up your radio?"

"Look, dispatch. If I turn up the radio, then everyone on the bus will hear everything you say."

"That's okay, 104. Please just turn it up."

"If you say so, dispatch. There you go."

I took a long breath and then yelled into the microphone with the deepest voice I could muster, "HEY, YOU. TROUBLEMAKER. YES, YOU. YOU DRUNKEN SLOB." From the driver's microphone, I could hear my own voice echoing through the bus. "THIS IS GOD. I'M WATCHING EVERYTHING THAT YOU'RE DOING. YOU'VE GONE TOO FAR THIS TIME AND NOW YOU'RE GOING TO PAY. YOU EITHER GET OFF THIS BUS RIGHT NOW OR A BOLT OF LIGHTNING IS GOING TO COME THROUGH THE WINDOW AND KNOCK YOUR BUTT OUT INTO THE STREETS."

Holding my breath, I listened closely for a response. After a moment of silence (stunned silence I hoped), there were suddenly loud peals of laughter. Many people (I couldn't tell how many) were cracking up with laughter. The laughter continued, long and sustained for more than a minute. Then the driver, who could barely speak because he was laughing so hard, came back on the radio. "Hey, dispatch. It worked. Sort of. The guy was laughing so hard that he almost wet himself so he got off the bus. That's the good part. The bad part is that we're about two blocks from the transit center and he said he's walking over to where you're at to find this dude who thinks he's God and then kick *his* butt out into the street. Good luck, dispatch. Bus 104 out."

One problem solved and one new problem created. That felt like my motto as bus dispatcher. Fortunately, the transit department was accustomed to irate customers so the building was securely locked and there was bullet-proof glass protecting the receptionist. When I heard later about some "nut" who came through the door and beat on the glass while demanding to "have a meeting with God," I acted as if I didn't know anything about it.

Because of the front page newspaper article about the day's problems with the transit system, my career as a dispatcher ended quickly. On day four in city government, I was sent to work in the bus maintenance department. Fortunately, they knew better than to have me repair buses. Instead, I sorted invoices and then built some wooden shelves to hold surplus bus seats. After the mechanics saw the shelves, it was clear that they regretted permitting me to use their good lumber. (Hey, if they offered woodworking at Harvard, I probably would have done a better job.) Near the end of the day, one of the maintenance supervisors came into the office where I was sorting invoices. He sprawled lazily in the chair and smiled at me. I nodded in his direction, watched him carefully out of the corner of my eye, and continued to sort the invoices.

"You're having kind of a rough time here, aren't you?," he said in a friendly way.

"You might say that," I replied warily. "But it's still a learning experience."

He paused for a few seconds and then asked, "Have you ever driven a bus?"

"A bus?"

"Yes. A bus." He laughed. "That's what we have around here, you know."

"Nope. Never had the opportunity."

"Wanna go for a drive?"

A part of me immediately recognized a big warning buzzer silently sounding within my brain. Unfortunately, the rest of me was so bored that I said, "Sure, why not?"

The next thing I knew, I was behind the wheel of a city transit bus with an "Out of Service" message in large letters where the route number was usually posted. I received about thirty seconds worth of cursory instructions and then I was wheeling that Sherman tank out of the bus garage. In retrospect, it probably would have been best for the supervisor to drive me to an empty parking lot to practice first. Instead, I found myself out in downtown traffic trying to handle a monster vehicle whose unfamiliar dimensions I had no hope of gauging. As I drove down the street with the distinct feeling that I was about to sideswipe each nearby vehicle, the supervisor kept screaming, "Get away from the street signs! You're too close to the side of the road!" Screaming is not an effective method of instruction when attempting to teach me new skills. It merely made me nervous and prone to swerving back and forth within my lane. Glancing at the supervisor, I could tell that he was having regrets about this opportunity or practical joke or whatever it was intended to be.

I quickly discovered that, like lumbering elephants, buses do not stop on a dime. This discovery made me grip the wheel more tightly and pray that no pedestrians crossed my path. In light of the panicked look on the face of my host, I decided that I should just loop around downtown and then head back to the garage. We were doing well from a physical damage perspective, but not from the perspective of our nervousness and fear. Then I hit a telephone pole while rounding my final turn to head back toward the garage. I didn't really hit the pole. I cleared it with the front of the bus when I turned. Somehow, however, the pole must have moved slightly as I passed by because it reached out and snapped the outside mirror off the bus. My host and I started to realize that this was probably a crime since I had neither official authorization nor a chauffeur's license. He put his face into the palms of his hands and cried out, "Oh no!" I really wanted to do the same thing, but my hands were clutching the steering wheel so tightly that I was unable to bury my face anywhere (I might have been able to bash my head against the steering wheel, but I was too busy at that moment to consider whether that or some other form of suicide would have been preferable to having the transit department hold me responsible for the damage to the bus).

Back at the garage, the supervisor said, "Don't tell anyone about this."

"What about the mirror?," I asked.

"I'll take care of it," he replied wearily. Then he looked at me sternly. "Just promise me that you'll stay away from my buses."

"Whatever you say, chief," I said with a weak, forced smile.

The next day they moved me to the front office of the transit department and anointed me as the new "Transit Planner." I got the impression that word had gotten out about my little excursion behind the wheel. I didn't know what a transit planner was supposed to do, because I spent the rest of the summer just reading reports about various policies in the transit department. I never saw the city manager again and it was clear that the reports that he received about me from the transit department did not encourage him to bring my Midas touch over to city hall. I'm sure he tossed and turned in his sleep just thinking about the carnage that might result if he let me help out at the police department or worse yet, the sewage treatment plant. ("Who opened the sluice gates and sent that river of sewage into the city's drinking water reservoir?" "It was that new kid sent over from the city manager's office." Oh, happy day!).

At the end of the summer, the city manager sent me a note thanking me for my service to the city (which was pretty inexpensive since they paid me as a part-time temporary bus dispatcher for the entire time). The note also included a brochure about careers in banking. Thus my career in city government ended. It wasn't for me anyway. Too many problems. Too little nap time.

*   *   *

My next internship provided me with an exceptionally unique experience. I got a job giving away money. Now this was something even I could handle. Because of my Harvard label (again), I was given a summer position at a major foundation. I had no idea what I was going to do when I arrived for my first day, but I figured they didn't do too much heavy lifting. During a Christmas vacation interview, I had met one of the vice presidents. When I reported to his office my first day during the summer, he sent me down the hall to work for a program officer responsible for selecting educational projects for funding. The program officer greeted me with a hearty handshake and friendly smile. I instantly liked this work environment. No one seemed to be under any stress. Everyone seemed very happy. I guess that's understandable when you already have the money that other enterprises in society are trying to gather and accumulate. The program officer sent me to a conference room where he said I could attend a meeting with a grant applicant who was visiting from Washington, D.C. He headed off to the restroom with a final instruction. "If they get there before I do, just tell them I'll be along in a few minutes."

When I walked into the conference room, I was shocked to see George Romney, the former governor of Michigan, former Secretary of the U.S. Department of Housing and Urban Development, and former presidential candidate, waiting to greet me. Romney was accompanying the director of a public service agency for which he served as president of the board of directors. Despite his advanced age, Romney looked exceptionally fit and trim. He jumped to his feet and introduced himself and the agency director. "Are you Mr. Schultz?," he asked.

I shook my head. "No. Sorry. He'll be along in a few minutes. I'm Chris Smith."

"Well, Mr. Smith, or may I call you Chris?" He smiled when I nodded my head affirmatively. "It's awfully nice of you to take the time to meet with us."

I just smiled and nodded my head again. I had no idea what to say.

"We're here to tell you about our programs," he announced as he launched into a speech about the value of this public service agency. I tried to interrupt to tell him that he should wait for Mr. Schultz, but as he kept talking, I really couldn't bring myself to interject any comment. So I sat and listened. What I heard was a most impassioned and persuasive presentation. In the short span of less than five minutes, he had sold me on the importance of his organization and the value that could be derived from additional foundation funding. At the end of the talk, he looked into my eyes with this glowing warmth that reflected the power possessed by truly effective politicians to draw listeners into the perception that they had made a direct personal connection with someone prominent and powerful. "Be honest. Tell me what you really think? Do we deserve funding from this foundation?" The sincerity he projected was utterly disarming.

"Well, I don't know. We really should...." Before I could finish rambling, he cut me off (in a nice way, of course).

"I know that you don't like to make snap decisions. No one does. I just want to know what you honestly *think*. I have given you the essential information. Now what do you think about the funding issue? Don't you have some kind of opinion that you can share with us? We've come all the way from Washington and if what we have to say lacks impact, then we need to know it."

I nodded in agreement and said, "In all honesty, I think you should get every penny that you're asking for. Perhaps even more so that the value of your contributions to society can be increased."

Instantly, Romney jumped up and grabbed my hand, pumping it vigorously. "Thank you. Thank you. You have no idea how much good this will do out there in American society." He wheeled around and threw his arms around the agency director who, although silent throughout the brief meeting, was now on his feet saying "Thank you. Thank you. Thank you." As their gratitude poured forth in cascading "thank yous," Schultz entered the room, observed the happy scene, and remarked. "Wow, I'm really glad to see that everyone hit if off so well." As Schultz shook hands with Romney, he said to me, "Chris, can you go down the hall and get us some coffee? Then I need you to run a little errand. They forgot to deliver our bagels so you need to run across the street to the deli. Just pick up the bag with my name on it. They're waiting for you."

Our visitors' happy smiles slowly melted away into puzzled frowns. They stared at me as I headed toward the door. Behind me, I could hear

Schultz telling them that I was a student intern spending my first day observing activities at the office. At the door, I glanced back and saw that Romney looked utterly deflated and forlorn. I felt bad about his misjudgment concerning my status and authority. He wanted me to be honest, so I gave him what he asked for. While I felt bad for Romney and his partner, I left the office with a spring in my step. "Unbelievable," I thought to myself. "It's only my first day in the office and I already have a former governor treating me like a big shot and asking me for money."

"What will happen tomorrow?," I wondered. "Some former president, hat in hand, pleading with me for a few dollars?" In reality, the next day wasn't very exciting but former President Jimmy Carter did turn up a few weeks later to ask for money. Fortunately for Carter (and for me), I was introduced as an intern at the start of the meeting so he didn't fall victim to Romney's unfortunate misunderstanding.

Although I enjoyed wandering around to various meetings and project sites and watching people throw themselves at my feet, I discovered that I didn't have much of a chance to develop a career in the foundation world. The program officers all had Ph.D.s in some policy area. If I really wanted to work at a foundation, I had many more years of schooling ahead of me. Since I had yet to decide whether I would go to graduate school, I set aside the foundation idea and never managed to return to it again.

*　　　*　　　*

During law school, I explored another career option. I became a part-time teacher inside a prison. I thought I might enjoy teaching, but where else could someone get hired without any teaching experience or demonstration of expertise? I just hoped that I had a friendly audience for my experimental attempt at becoming an educator.

I applied to teach a Spring semester course, but I was told that the positions were all filled. Suddenly, the day Spring semester was scheduled to begin, I received a frantic call from the prison's education coordinator. He asked if I could start teaching a law class that very evening. Although I had not made any preparations, I said "Sure." I drove out to the prison at the appointed time, stopped my car at a microphone stand to identify myself to the guard tower, and then parked in the front parking lot. The maximum-security prison was a massive fortress-type structure. Gun-turret towers dotted the tall brick walls. When I rang the doorbell of the massive iron door at the front of the prison, the situation seemed very similar to all of those horror movies in which strangers lost in the countryside on a stormy night knock on the gigantic front door of a huge haunted mansion. The similarities were eerie. Standing alone before a huge iron door. A cold wind pelting my face. The distant sounds of yelling from behind the door. I found myself apprehensively hoping that my experiences inside these walls would not be as nightmarish as those of the poor victims who enter the movies' haunted houses.

When the door opened, I was pointed toward the visitors' room where I had to pass through a metal detector and fill out a form absolving the prison of liability if I were to be injured or killed during my visit. Not a very happy document to contemplate and sign. I hadn't known what to wear so I just wore jeans and a flannel shirt. I didn't want to impose too much social distance between myself and my students by dressing in an excessively formal manner. I figured I'd get better cooperation if they saw me as a "hip" graduate student.

When the education director poked his head into the room, he seemed annoyed. "All of the other teachers are waiting. We need to enter as a group. Didn't I tell you that you need to be here thirty minutes early?"

"No. I don't think so."

"Well, you do. Come along." He acted as if he did not believe my response. He led me through another massive iron door which was buzzed open by a corrections officer sitting in a glass-enclosed booth. Inside this door, I found four middle-aged men dressed in sport coats and ties standing in front of a wall of iron bars with a small barred gate. Behind the bars, I could see prisoners milling about staring at us. I was surprised to see that they weren't wearing any uniforms. Some of them wore denim jackets and white tee-shirts which were apparently prison-issued because they were identical. Others wore work pants, jeans, and whatever else they wanted. It didn't fit my image of what a prison would look like. To the left on our side of the bars was a desk with a corrections officer standing and talking on the phone. To the right was another glass enclosed booth. This one contained three officers as well as racks of rifles and shotguns. The prisoners were very noisy as their voices bounced off the concrete walls and created an echo chamber effect. My four colleagues looked very nervous.

I whispered to one of them, "Have you been inside before?"

He shook his head. "This is the first class of the semester for us. What about you?"

"I'm totally new," I replied.

He nodded. "I didn't remember seeing you at orientation."

I started to ask, "What orientation?," but the education director began to speak loudly to the desk-bound guard. "Can you open the gate? We're behind schedule already."

The guard continued to talk on the phone but held up his index finger as if to say, "Just a minute."

The education director did not like that response. "Look. We have to get in there."

The guard held up his finger again, now with his own look of annoyance. However, the education director would not accept anything except obedience. "I'm not kidding around here. Open the gate. Now!"

The guard's face flashed with anger. He moved the telephone receiver away from his mouth and bellowed toward the prisoners, "Get away from the bars! Visitors coming in!" The prisoners loitering in the vicinity generally moved back two steps, dropped their voices, and stared at us. The education director was already gripping the barred gate when the guard pressed the electronic lock which permitted the director to pull the gate open. "Get through quickly," he commanded. We practically jumped through the gate behind him and then huddled in a group as he shut the gate. As the bars of the gate were reunited with the rest of the barred wall, we heard the loud "click" of the lock which had now effectively trapped us inside with the desperados. It was hard not to have a Daniel-esque feeling of being face to face and helpless in the lair of the lions. I stood up straight to try to look physically stronger, yet at the same time I felt my face fix itself into an inane smile which practically cried out, "I'm a total weakling. Please don't hurt me."

The education director began to lead the four well-dressed teachers toward the corridor on the left. When I started to follow, he turned around and instructed, "You don't come with us. You're with them." He pointed to three muscular African-American inmates who stood nearby staring at me in (what I perceived to be) a menacing manner. I must have looked completely bewildered so the education director lectured me with impatience. "Didn't I tell you? The other courses are presented by the community college but you're teaching the law program sponsored by the Black Prisoners' Caucus. We'll be down in the education wing while you'll be teaching in the prisoner organization office wing. I have to oversee the college program so I can't be in two places at once. Don't worry. The Black Prisoners' Caucus is responsible for your safety." With that, he briskly pushed my colleagues around the corner and out of sight. Standing in one spot, I looked at my three hosts and they looked at me. Then one of them took a step forward and announced with great formality, "We're your sergeants-at-arms. C'mon." As they turned to walk up the central corridor, I glanced at the barely visible officers sitting behind the darkened glass in the booth only a few feet away. I was tempted to mouth the words "Help me!" but I didn't have the courage to do anything which might upset my hosts. When I began to follow the prisoners, one of them dropped back to walk behind me.

As we walked up the corridor, with nary a corrections officer in sight, I experienced a deja vu-type flashback. This place reminded me of my junior high school! The concrete and brick walls painted in a depressingly-neutral, institutional shade of an unidentifiable color. The corridor was filled with young men engaging in what I would label as adolescent play behavior. They took swings at each other in mock fights. They insulted each other. The exuded bluster and bravado. There was one big difference from a junior high, however, (in addition to the absence of women, except for a few female corrections officers) quite a few of these guys had actually killed somebody and only a couple of people at my junior high ever did that.

I tried not to stare at anyone but my heart was starting to race and I desperately wanted to swing my head in all directions to make sure that no one was running up to attack me from behind. If someone had attempted an attack, I don't know what I could have done to prevent it but at least I would get a glimpse of my attacker before I breathed my last breath. I could tell that many men were eyeing me as I passed. In such a closed environment, it would be difficult not to notice an unfamiliar face. I set my face in a serious expression, stood tall, and tried to walk with an air of confidence, just like I did to deter predators back in junior high school. In retrospect, my junior high school, with its occasional race riot and stabbing, provided far better training for this moment than all of my experiences at Harvard and law school. Such moments make you think about precisely which contexts and experiences in life actually provide useful educational experiences.

When we turned toward a short corridor of offices, we were greeted by a half-dozen additional prisoners. These were the officers of the Black Prisoners' Caucus and I was pleased to see that they seemed quite grateful for my presence. They were only allowed to sponsor one "outside" program and they had great difficulty recruiting any lawyer or law student to make the long drive to the prison. Whenever they thought someone had signed on, the person would back out when he or she discovered that it was to be taught separately from the community college program and in a part of the prison that was removed from the well-guarded education wing.

I chatted with the Caucus officers as they sized me up. The sergeants-at-arms stood by silently except for one who made a point of walking over to a flowerpot, reaching into the dirt, and pulling out a razor blade with which he cut off the filter from his cigarette. He was so dramatic in his actions that it was quite clear that he wanted me to know about the razor blade. I was uncertain whether this was supposed to threaten me, make me feel unsettled, or what. In retrospect, I think he intended the gesture to reassure me that the Black Prisoners' Caucus was well-armed and prepared to guarantee my safety. My mother called me up a few weeks later and said, "You are with guards all of the time, aren't you?," while trying unsuccessfully to mask the sound of concern in her voice. Based on what I had learned by that time after several visits to the prison, I said "No. I don't want to be associated with corrections officers. If trouble breaks out, I'm going to be a lot safer under the protection of the Black Prisoners' Caucus." My mother, like many other people, had the misperception that officers within prisons are armed. In fact, they are completely unarmed and it must be so since they tend to be outnumbered twenty-to-one (or worse) by the prisoners. If they carried weapons, the weapons would be taken away by the prisoners during a disturbance. Weapons are locked up in accessible areas at the front of the prison, but they would not help corrections officers in the corridors and tiers of cells during an uprising. As I observed the black prisoners' commitment to maintaining their program, I came to realize that I was relatively safe, or so I told myself anyway.

My first class went well. A mix of black, white, and Asian prisoners attended. They were, not surprisingly, very interested in learning about law. They were also interested in trying to get me to help them with their cases. Because penniless offenders are not entitled to be provided with attorneys in the later stages of post-conviction legal processes and in preparing civil rights lawsuits, many of them hoped that I would provide free legal assistance. By the close of class, I figured out that I needed to avoid making any commitments. I would be friendly but I would maintain social distance. Because I had left my watch in the locker with my wallet and car keys in the visitor's entrance, I kept asking prisoners in the class about the time. It turned out that I was relying on slow watches.

As we completed our class discussion and I fended off individual requests for legal assistance, one of the Caucus officers burst into the room and said, "You were supposed to be back at the gate twenty minutes ago. I promised the education director we'd have you back by eight-thirty so he could talk to you before he leaves early tonight. I think we probably missed him." The sergeants-at-arms and this Caucus officer surrounded me and accompanied me down the corridor at a rapid pace. As we got within sight of the gate in the central corridor, the Caucus officer patted me on the back, thanked me for coming, and said he looked forward to seeing me again the following week. He dropped out of the convoy and disappeared down another corridor. When we reached the large loitering area in front of the gate, I turned to thank my escorts for their assistance. They took my expression of gratitude as the signal that they were dismissed from their official duties for the evening and they disappeared up the corridor again. As I approached the gate, I could see that a different officer was manning the desk. I walked up to the gate, waved my hand to get his attention, and said, "I'm ready to go now."

He looked at me and laughed. "Like everybody here doesn't feel the same way."

I thought this was an odd response so I repeated more emphatically, "Really. I'm supposed to go now."

The officer looked annoyed. "Get back from the bars."

I stepped back and waited for the sound of the electronic lock, but the officer just turned away and began writing something. "Excuse me, officer," I called, noting a slight tremor in my own voice. "I'm the new law teacher. This is my first night. The class is over now. I need to drive back to town. Just ask the education director."

"He just left ten minutes ago with four guys in suits. Cut the crap. Get back from the bars and start heading toward your cell."

I was filled with a sense of panic more powerful than anything that had ever seized possession of my body. The officer thought I was a prisoner. Because I was wearing jeans and a flannel shirt, I was dressed in a style identical to that of many other prisoners. Looking back over my shoulder, I could see assorted loiterers watching me and listening to the conversation. A few of them were suppressing laughs. Others were just staring at me impassively. To my eye, they looked like leopards who had spotted their quarry and were lying motionless in the moment before they pounce. It might have been my imagination, but in that instant it was difficult not to feel like a mouse who had wandered into a cats' convention. Reflexively, my two hands interlocked in a prayerful position. I shook them in front of me very deliberately as I called out again and unsuccessfully sought to disguise the note of pleading in my voice. "Officer, please. I'm serious. Just call somebody and find out."

The officer placed his left hand against his temple and closed his eyes as if I was giving him a headache. With a sarcastic tone, he said, "Okay, put your hand under the light." I had noticed this small fluorescent-looking lamp just on the other side of the bars. It was too far to reach but close enough to shine light on objects stuck between the bars. I thrust my hand through the bars in the direction of the light. He glanced at my hand and yelled, "Now get the hell away from the bars!" Unbeknownst to me, since I was not at the orientation, all visitors who enter the prison beyond the visiting area are stamped on the hand with invisible ink that is only visible through the special ultra-violet lamp. In order to be released through the gate, you must have the stamp. Unfortunately, I not only did not have the stamp, I didn't even know enough about the stamp process to argue with the officer about why I did not have the stamp. In retrospect, I must have missed getting stamped in the chaos at the gate when the education director was yelling at the desk officer.

My mind wanted to race with a burst of adrenaline to think of a solution to my increasingly desperate situation. Unfortunately, I was filled with a paralyzing fear that seemed to switch my mental processes into slow-motion. Suddenly, I was startled to hear the short burst of an alarm bell. At the sound of the bell, prisoners began to shuffle slowly down the corridors toward their tiers of cells. Several of them continued to stare (glare?) at me as they walked slowly away. I stood in one spot still trying to think. The desk officer glanced up and saw me still standing there. "If I have to tell you one more time to leave the area, you're getting a ticket." When he said the word "ticket" my mind filled in the additional words "to freedom" and I suddenly saw how I might gain my release. I grabbed the bars and started climbing, while simultaneously yelling, "Go ahead and give me a ticket. Give me ten tickets." I managed to shin my way up about four feet off the ground by the time he yelled, "Get off the bars" and simultaneously called some code number into a radio. Within seconds, three corrections officers forcibly removed me from the bars and gave me a less-than-gentle landing on the concrete floor. My body went limp and I smiled happily as they dragged me down the corridor toward some unknown destination. Sometimes it pays to get into trouble.

By the time I left the prison two hours later, I had met an assistant warden, chatted with a couple of captains, and been introduced to belly chains and leg irons. When there was no trace of me in prison records and no prisoners missing from their cells at evening count, the bureaucratic wheels began to turn in a favorable direction. Although the officers of the Black Prisoners' Caucus reportedly vouched for me when questioned in their cells by a captain, I did not win over my captors until I persuaded them to get my wallet from the locker in the visiting area. The assistant warden apologized about the misunderstanding, but I didn't really care. I was just happy to breathe freedom's air once again in the prison parking lot. Naturally, the education director subsequently blamed me for failing to follow his directions, but I had figured out by then that I would stay as far away from him as possible.

*   *   *

My search for a suitable career began with an effort to avoid having my idleness condemn me to the "devil's workshop" (whatever that is). The search ended as I stood literally locked within the setting which many people undoubtedly regard as the worldly equivalent of the devil's contemporary hangout. I found nothing attractive about the threatening, depressing environment of prison. However, the experience of teaching a class opened my eyes to the attractions of this new career possibility. It was challenging to prepare presentations that would both inform people and hold their attention. It was also nice to be in charge. No bosses in the room telling you what to do. By the end of the semester, I was headed in a new career direction. As I surveyed my work experiences, including food service, telephones, city transit, philanthropy, and prisons, I was left with one lingering question: what new disasters awaited me in my pursuit of an academic career? If I had known the answer to that question, I probably would have become a dermatologist. At least I would have known how to examine my own moles. Instead, I entered a peculiar form of self-imprisonment, locking myself for hours at a time into rooms in which I am outnumbered ninety-to-one by grungy-looking people who stare at me impassively, occasionally with a touch of menace or stifled laughter. The only things missing are belly chains and leg irons. But in my professional world, mortgages, car payments, and kids' orthodontic bills serve the same confining function by dragging us back into lion's den of lecture halls week after week, semester after semester, and year after year.

Chapter Seven

Those That Can't Do

Those that can't do, teach.

I have always objected to that oft-heard expression. However, I eventually found myself headed for a teaching career because of what I couldn't do: namely, work at a regular job. I needed more autonomy. I needed a setting in which I could be my own boss. I needed the sense of status from standing before a lecture hall with two hundred eyes and ears focused on me. More honestly, I needed a few more years of graduate school just to give myself time to see if I could decide what I really wanted to do. Even if I never figured out a career that suited my abilities (whatever those unidentifiable attributes turned out to be), my prison experience told me that I found sufficient motivation and enjoyment in teaching to prefer that activity over any other job I had experienced thus far.

* * *

Applying to doctoral programs turned out to be a problem. I got married after law school and committed myself to finding a job so that my wife could finish her degree. It only seemed right that I should support the family. I had spent eight years in college already (Harvard, England, and law school), so it wouldn't be fair for me to keep going to school when my wife had never had the opportunity to be a full-time student. Thus I planned to get a job in Washington, D.C., where I had worked for two summers along the way and still presumed I had valuable contacts, while my wife would go to college full time to finish her final two years' worth of credit. I didn't take any bar exams so I wasn't qualified to practice law, but I assumed that I could find some kind of administrative position in government. Within thirty-six hours after the wedding, we were in Washington looking for an apartment. Unfortunately, we collided with a powerful Catch-22. We couldn't find jobs without having an address and we couldn't get an address without proving to landlords that we had jobs. After one day in Washington, I awoke my new bride early in the morning and asked her, "Where would you rather live, Seattle or Boston?" Because she had never traveled farther east from Michigan than Ohio nor farther west than Chicago, this was rather like asking a lifelong vegetarian if she preferred porkchops or rump roast. Her only response was to give me a wide-eyed look of horror that clearly conveyed the message "I think I've cast my lot with a mercurial nut." She was literally speechless about my decision to discard so quickly our months of planning (and telling family and friends) that we would reside in Washington. I took her speechlessness as a "no preference" vote and before sunrise we were headed north toward New England. Imagine my father-in-law's surprise when I flew to Michigan to get our possessions and I rented a truck to go to Boston rather than to Washington, D.C.

In Boston, I had friends with whom we could stay and whose address we could use while we found jobs. My wife found a job first and then we got an apartment. Unfortunately, it was one with rent so steep that it consumed eighty percent of her take-home pay. That was okay (or so we thought) because I was going to find a "good job." As it turned out, I was incapable of getting a job that would pay enough to permit her to become a full-time student. I had the chance to work in commercial lending at a large bank, but I just couldn't see myself putting on a suit every morning (or in the case of my limited wardrobe, the same suit every morning) and talking on the phone all day while sitting in a cubicle in a glass tower. I had an opportunity to handle regulatory affairs for business consultants who were trying to set up medical centers around the country. However, I couldn't escape the feeling that they really didn't know or care much about medicine. They had simply figured out how to provide services that would permit them to tap into Medicare payments. I also was offered a legal position with a consumer protection organization, but the salary would have barely covered the rent. The more I looked at jobs, the more I became convinced that I needed to get back on track and move toward something more suited to my interests (and general ineptitude).

By the time I figured out that I needed to push ahead to graduate school, I had already missed the application deadlines to nearly every major university in the country. To top it off, my wife had decided that since her belongings had moved all the way to New England, she preferred not to force them to move back to the Midwest or elsewhere (were her suitcases really having that much fun?). So I looked around New England and found one university, and only one, where I had not clearly missed the deadline: the University of Connecticut at Storrs. Since it was March already, it appeared that I had missed Connecticut's deadline but their application date was not stated as if it was a final deadline. When I called Connecticut's Political Science Department and mentioned my Harvard degree (there's that magical label again), I received a very welcoming and encouraging response.

In light of this response, we decided to visit the campus. One Sunday afternoon, we headed down I-84 from Boston to Connecticut. We could see that we needed to leave the highway and travel on two-lane roads in order to find the University. On the map, we carefully circled the spot where two country roads, Route 32 and Route 44, met at a little dot labeled "Storrs." We exited I-84 and followed Route 32 south as instructed by the map. When we arrived at the intersection of

Route 44 we found…nothing. We were in the middle of country fields. We could see a few old buildings comprising the small campus of a state school for the handicapped off in the distance. There was, however, no university. We sat and stared at the map and then stared at the fields around us. My wife was the first to react.

"We aren't moving here."

"What do you mean?"

"If you can't find a major university, then you have no business aspiring to attend it."

"I'm sure it's around here somewhere," I said, trying to calm her increasingly agitated state.

"How can there be a major university around here? Not only are there no university buildings, there are no people, no stores, no nothing. Just country." She frowned and pursed her lips.

"Why don't we just look around a little bit?," I replied. "I'm sure we can find it."

She crossed her arms and looked defiant. "There is no town. There is no university. We are staying in Boston."

Well, she was right about one of those statements. There was no town. The town of Storrs is the figment of a mapmaker's imagination. We eventually found the university in the middle of the country on a parallel country road. But there was no town. Only a post office, a gas station, a grocery store, and…that's about it. Not an auspicious beginning to my new career. But she was good a sport about it. Since I managed to find the University, she permitted us to move there.

✳   ✳   ✳

As I enrolled in the doctoral program, my wife managed to get a scholarship to permit her to (finally) become a full-time student, too. Now I was faced with reliving one of the low points of my Harvard career: research methods and statistics. This time, however, it wasn't so bad. The professor was nicer. He didn't call on us. I was also among several similarly situated colleagues who shared my apprehension about confronting all those numbers and equations. For a few weeks, I almost thought I was keeping up with the class. However, when the professor began to write equations on the board that contained Greek letters, I knew that I had been left behind, probably for good. I concentrated on keeping my eyes open (a major challenge at times) and looking straight ahead in order to give the appearance of attentiveness. Focusing on my posture and appearance also helped to mask my true feelings which could be summarized in two words: utter panic.

Our grade for the course was to be based on a final project that we would complete with one of our classmates. My partner was someone who spoke out frequently in class, so I felt relieved that I could ride his back to the finish line. When we met together to discuss our project, he was more loquacious than ever.

"Do you understand any of this stuff?," he asked.

"Not really. That's why I was so happy to be paired with you."

He laughed. "I don't know any of this stuff. I just talk in class to get good grades. Make them think that you know what they're talking about, you know," he winked at me with a big smile.

"You mean…."

"I'm just trying to get some good grades in grad school so that I can apply to law school. I'm going into corporate law and I'm going to rake in a pile of money. I didn't really work very hard as a undergrad. But, boy, did I party! Of course, I'm not working too hard right now either. But I've gotten a lot better at playing the game. And what a game it is. These professors have no idea what's really going on."

I found all of this talk extremely disconcerting. My face probably revealed my feelings.

"Hey, man, don't worry about a thing. I'll figure it all out," he said, brimming with confidence as he punched me lightly on the shoulder. We divided up the project and I volunteered to compute chi-squares and some other simple statistics that I had managed to figure out from the formulas in the textbook. (Personal computers and software packages were not yet widely available to handle these chores for students). My partner assured me that he would add "some pizzazz" to his half of the presentation, but he couldn't tell me what that would be. I gritted my teeth and prayed that any mistakes he made would not be held against me when grades were assigned.

A few days before the project was due, my partner told me to leave my part of the project in his mailbox because he would take charge of putting the entire presentation together. I hated to trust him, but I knew so little about how a statistical presentation should look that I had no choice but to hope that he really could put our presentation together with "some pizzazz." He also told me that he would handle presenting our project to the class because he enjoyed getting practice for his future career as a lawyer. "Schmoozing the audience" was the phrase I believe he used to describe the talent he was developing.

On the night of our presentation, I was troubled when my partner did not arrive at class on time. I waited and waited by the door, but he never showed up. The professor said to me, "Didn't he tell you? He had a family emergency and he had to leave town for a few days. Fortunately, he handed in your final version and he told me that you need this copy in order to make the presentation." My heart sank, my stomach ached, and pretty much every other internal organ simultaneously rebelled to fill me with physical discomfort and mental distress. As I watched the other groups make their presentations, I noticed that the clock seemed to be working in my favor. This was the last class meeting, but fortunately my verbose future-professor classmates were well on their way to using up the entire class period. With ten minutes to go in the class, the professor cut off another group because, as he put it, "I want to leave time to hear about the most interesting aspect of the project that Mr. Smith is going to present."

At that point, I had only flipped through the final report. I assumed that I would only talk about the portion that I had written, so I wasn't worried about describing what my partner had done (whatever that was). As I walked to the front of the room and began to describe the various calculations that I had made, the professor interrupted. "Yes, yes, that's all fine and, frankly, pretty much the same as what everyone else did. Since we don't have much time, why don't you talk about the time-series analysis in the other part of the paper?"

"Time-series analysis?"

"Yes, the graphs in the back. I was so pleased and impressed that you showed such initiative in tackling advanced techniques that we didn't study this semester; so advanced that they're not even in our book. You set quite a good example."

I turned to the back of the report and found several graphs labeled "Time-Series Analysis." Each graph contained a series of jagged squiggles going up and down, with a vertical axis containing escalating numbers and a horizontal axis with points labeled for each month over a ten-year period. Not knowing anything about the graphs, I simply began reading the accompanying paragraphs in the report about how the graphs illustrated patterns of change in voting rates over the period of a decade. As I read aloud in a wooden monotone (probably from being in a state of shock), the other students began to put on their coats and leave when the clock reached the end of the class period. The professor seemed distracted answering questions from other students so I departed as quickly as possible before he could ask me any questions about our project.

A few days later, I saw my partner in the hallway. He smiled broadly as he approached me. "I hear you did really well on the presentation. In fact, did you know that we're getting an A minus for our grade?"

I was barely listening to him because I was annoyed that he had failed to appear for class. "Where were you anyway?"

"Oh, I went to New York. I got offered tickets to this great rock concert at Madison Square Garden and it was too good to pass up."

"You left me stranded so that you could go to a rock concert?"

"I knew that you could handle it. See, everything worked out."

"Where did you learn about that time-series analysis stuff?"

Again, the familiar laugh came forth. "That professor. What a dupe? I don't know a time-series analysis from a World Series analysis."

"But where did those graphs come from?"

"Graphs!," he laughed again. "Those weren't graphs. That was somebody's EKG."

"EKG?"

"Yeah, electrocardiogram. You know, like one of those earthquake charts of somebody's heartbeat." I must have looked utterly bewildered, because he continued quickly. "I have a friend who works in a doctor's office. He got me some old EKGs. I just cut them up and labeled them from something that they looked like in some statistics book. It worked out rather neatly, don't you think?"

At this point, I was trying not to think, especially about the prospect of being expelled from the university for fraud. I spent a few days trying to decide if I should turn him in for academic misconduct, but then he solved my dilemma for me by getting caught tearing pages out of books at the library. I went to the professor to explain that we had each written separate sections of the paper. But before I could explain what I knew, he cut me off. "Don't worry. We'll just make you the sole recipient, instead of the joint recipient, of this year's Outstanding Graduate Student Paper Award." The professor was too busy to continue our conversation and he never listened when I tried to raise the subject again. Thus I became condemned to a life of constant fear about the possibility that potential employers would actually believe this professor's subsequent letter of recommendation on my behalf which described me as "highly proficient in quantitative methods and statistics." Hey, I was still the guy who once drank a bottle of wine before botching the completion of my IRS tax forms. Thus my ability to complete quantitative calculations might bear some relationship to the word "highly" but I was as far removed as one could be from the appellation "proficient."

                 *   *   *

After a couple of years at Connecticut, I neared the completion of my doctorate. Now it was time to apply for teaching positions. Fortunately, I was selected as a finalist for several positions at various universities around the country. Thus I had to spend several months periodically traveling to interviews.

One of the problems with traveling for interviews is the prospect of having other people control the scheduling of your flights. Let's say, for example, that you're not terribly fond of a particular airline or aircraft or a particular seat location. When you are a job applicant, especially one who has spent so many years in college and graduate school that your student loan debt has been included in the formulas for the country's national deficit and Gross National Product, you are too desperate for opportunities to raise picky questions about travel arrangements. For some reason, I had such disconcerting experiences during these trips that I began to think that fate was sending me a message. Of course, I couldn't figure out what that message might be. Perhaps it was "Don't seek a teaching career." Alternatively, it might have been "Keep your feet on the ground."

On one of my first flights, which went from New York to Texas, I was on a DC-10 (or similarly large aircraft). During the take-off, the pilot decided to give the passengers a special treat: we got to watch the take-off from the pilot's perspective. As the plane headed down the runway, the pilot switched on a video camera stationed behind his shoulder that broadcast live pictures of the runway ahead. Personally, I've never wanted to have a pilot's eye view of take-off. During take-off, I generally concentrate on pretending that I'm sitting in the living room reading a magazine. It keeps my mind off the fact that I'm about to become a lawbreaker. I'm very much in favor of obeying rules, so I always have some residual discomfort about violating the law, especially the law of gravity. I mean, if it's a law, then it probably wasn't meant to be broken, was it? Unfortunately, on this occasion, I was seated directly in front of the rear passenger compartment movie screen. This made it a little bit difficult to concentrate on the magazine and pretend that I was just sitting at home when a few feet from my face was a gigantic projection of the landscape rushing toward us at hundreds of miles per hour. I could not avoid peeking up at the sight. Within moments, we were airborne. I could hear all of the creaking joints of the aircraft as I felt myself tilted backward in the plane's struggle to break free from the earth. All of these sensations are normal for any flight, but the abnormal aspect was looking ahead and seeing nothing but blue sky on the screen. Were we were going *straight up*? Were we flipping over in a 360-degree loop? When the horizon is not available as a reference point (and I was too far from any window to see the earth), you can't tell what the plane is doing (or how it is doing it). For people who are prone to panic attacks, this is not reassuring. It is also not helpful when such people must get off the plane and immediately interview for a job.

On later flights to other interviews, I was on one plane which stopped in the middle of taxiing down the runway because a decision was made to replace the tires. On another flight, smoke began pouring through an air vent in the cabin as the plane cruised high in the air. The flight attendant told me reassuringly with a faux smile "Don't worry. It's just steam," but frankly, even if that was true, it was not very reassuring. Didn't the stewards on the Titanic offer that same smile and say, "Don't worry. It's just an iceberg?" Is there supposed to be steam rushing into the cabin of an airliner? I don't think so. I know they offer kosher meals and hot towels, but I never heard of the option of an in-flight steam bath. Fortunately, we were approaching our destination so (except for the excited screams of a few of my fellow passengers; also not good for the panic attack-prone flyer) we landed quickly and never had the opportunity to learn what was really going on.

On my final interview flight, we had reached take-off speed, become airborne, heard the creaking joints, and tilted backward in our collective fight against gravity, when the plane's engines suddenly lost power. We jerked downward and bounced back onto the runway. It was not a soft landing. As we rolled down the runway, decelerating rapidly, the pilot nonchalantly spoke over the intercom.

"We just lost all of the oil in engine number 2. So we'll just have it checked out. I'm sure it won't take too long. Sorry for the inconvenience."

Hey, don't apologize. I was just happy the oil didn't disappear about twenty seconds higher up into the clouds. However, I was faced with a dilemma. I knew that I did not want to ride on this airplane. If something is wrong with the engine, how do I know that they'll actually fix the problem properly when they're in a hurry to keep their flight schedule? On the other hand, someone was waiting at the airport in Cleveland to pick me up and take me to my job interview. I needed this job because I was striking out all over with my other ill-fated trips. But who wants to stand up and say, "I want to get off this plane." That would be sort of like announcing, "Ladies and gentlemen. I am a chicken. The yellow streak down my spine is speaking to me more loudly than the call of my intended destination. Therefore, HELP!! PLEASE LET ME OFF THIS PLANE!" Apparently, (and I presume this must have applied to at least some other people on that crowded aircraft), my aversion to public embarrassment was stronger than my impulse to save my own life. Does anyone get rewarded for this sort of martyrdom? ("We are honoring Mr. Smith with the Congressional Medal of Illusory Courage for his incredibly convincing performance as an airline passenger who, knowing that he was about head skyward on a defective aircraft, remained seated and silent, and thereby avoided embarrassment to himself and others. Awarded posthumously, of course").

When the plane came to a halt on a distant runway strip far from the terminal, the passengers sat is silence for five long minutes. Then, suddenly, my life and sanity were saved by a nearby passenger who stood up and announced quite loudly, "I need to get off the plane in order to make a phone call." Suddenly, people were leaping up all over the cabin, sort of like a jack-in-the-box convention in which all of the toys' springs trip at once, announcing, "I have to make a call, too." "Me, too." "I have to call my office." I didn't need much additional encouragement to join the burgeoning crowd. Fortunately, this occurred at a time before there were phones available for passengers on airplanes and no one yet carried a cell phone in a purse or pocket. The flight attendants gave us disgusted looks but then went forward to discuss the situation with the captain. In a few minutes, the captain announced, "For those of you who want to leave the aircraft at this time, there is a bus coming to take you back to the terminal. I must warn you, however, that if you depart, you will not be permitted back on board. As soon as everything is squared away, we will be leaving." This message, which seemed to be delivered like a threat, was not the least bit persuasive. In fact, the threatening tone with which the flight attendants badgered us with reiterations of the warning, "Once you step off, we will leave without you," served only to reconfirm the decision made the escapees. It seemed clear to me that there must be something *really* wrong with the aircraft for them to get so nasty about discouraging us from leaving. I thought I might be surrendering my shot at a job, but my now (finally) declining heart rate and blood pressure reinforced my decision to abandon ship.

When my two dozen comrades joined me in exiting the plane and boarding the bus, we avoided making eye contact with our fellow passengers. It was as if we were getting in lifeboats and they were continuing with a misguided belief in the travel-worthiness of their sinking vessel. On board the bus, we could see what none of the people on the plane could see. Larry, Darrell, and his other brother Darrell had removed an engine from the plane, dismantled it into a million little pieces-parts, and had it strewn across canvas tarps laid on the tarmac. They weren't actually fixing anything. Instead, they just stood in a group, staring at the engine parts, and scratching their heads (literally!). I've never felt more confident about a decision.

Of course, the defective plane did eventually fly to Cleveland. It arrived well ahead of my later flight. This caused various complications when my irritated host, anticipating the end of an extended waiting period at the airport, was disappointed to discover that I was not actually aboard the very late flight that I was supposed to be on. When I arrived an hour later, I was not greeted with the usual happiness and warmth. Despite the rocky start, things went well with the interview, except for my anticipation of boarding the (predictably) defective aircraft that would be waiting to take me back to Connecticut. Because my luck with airplanes seemed to be getting worse and worse, I decided that I would find an alternative means to get myself from Cleveland to Connecticut. Of course, as a poor graduate student, I wasn't blessed with many financial resources with which to secure alternate modes of transportation. I had a credit card, but there was some question about whether it had any more value at that moment then a run-of-the-mill piece of plastic such as a wrapper from a package of cheese. Fortunately, there was just enough credit available to permit me to decide whether to share my cloud of misfortune with Amtrak or Greyhound. I chose Amtrak (and I notice that their profits have been declining ever since).

I soon learned that one of life's great challenges is to convince other people that you are utilizing air travel when, in fact, you are using alternative means to go from place to place. After the interview, I was driven back to the Cleveland airport about an hour before my four o'clock flight. It took significant persuasive efforts on my part to convince my host that he did not need to wait at the airport with me until I boarded the aircraft. After all, if he was waiting, then I might actually be forced to board. Once having rid myself of my escort, I called Amtrak and heard the unhappy news that the only train headed east would reach the downtown station at 2 a.m, unless, of course, it was several hours late as usual. Thus I discovered another difficulty of pretending to fly. You get stranded at airports far from where you really want (and need) to be. This can be a major problem when: 1) you are unfamiliar with the city; and 2) you have little or no money. But life's an adventure, I had visited Cleveland before, and I had a few dollars with which to ride the subway (or "rapid transit") system. And thus I spent nearly eight hours riding back and forth between downtown and the airport, seeing the same slice of Cleveland (mostly interior subway tunnels) pass by the window over and over and over again. By the time I got back to Connecticut many hours later, worrying the entire time that someone from the job interview would call prior to my arrival to provide some additional information about the university or to ask a question, I felt as if I had earned that job. I thought that there must be some reward for involuntarily spending so much time wandering around Cleveland, and the fates agreed. I got the job. Perhaps if I could have gotten myself stranded in an even less desirable location, such as Amarillo or Punxsutawney, the fates would have rewarded me with a higher salary. Oh well, I was happy just to have the opportunity to call myself a professor.

✳   ✳   ✳

Teaching is a challenge. When lecturing about the same topics semester after semester, you must work hard to maintain your enthusiasm and interest when all of those around you are, well, sleeping. Occasionally, the students' interest will be aroused and their attention will be grabbed when, for example, one of their sleeping colleagues falls out of a chair. However, except for such amusing disruptions, there is always great uncertainty about how well the students are absorbing material that is being forced upon them. When the students write papers or essay exams, it becomes clear how much (or how little) the teachers' efforts are paying off. Herewith are some examples of students' written work in my courses on courts and law:

"For the trial, they bring the accused into the courtroom." (One can just imagine the judge saying, "Stand up, you *&%$#$@#$%*&%$*#&%!").

"The first amen meant something about free speech." (So do all of those "amens" in church have anything to do with constitutional rights?).

"The judge hits the table with the gravel." (But she undoubtedly made someone else sweep it up later).

"The judge set the bale on the defendant." (And if it was big, they might have needed a pitchfork to dig him out).

"As an entire nation, we must sacrifice to pay the bill of rights." (Yes, but will we get a receipt?).

"When the United States was founded by Thomas Jefferson, some people were not even aware what had been lost." (That's because it wasn't lost; it was losted).

"Lawyers are in charge of lintigation." (And whether they use a whisk broom or pick out each piece by hand, their clothes always look much better afterward).

"These *lawyers no wear lawsuits* are to be filed." (But hopefully they also "no" enough to wear some kind of clothing when they go to court).

"A jury of peers peeks secretly through the courtroom window but a regular jury sits in the jury box." (So those are the people hiding behind the curtains at the courthouse).

"Congress created a statue and covered the entire nation with it." (And since it was made of bronze, the entire population was crushed like little bugs).

Oh well. Perhaps students were placed on the earth to amuse their teachers. However, this is actually a disconcerting thought, since students grow up to become people who hold jobs. Thus when I am about to undergo surgery, I am tempted to ask the doctor if she was once a student. I'm not sure I want to hear the answer. I prefer to think that she was born a doctor. (And please don't tell me otherwise).

*   *   *

There are certain aspects of a teaching career that no one warns you about. For example, no one told me about the bats. We probably envision the ivory towers in which professors work as being relatively safe, clean, and boring environments. In reality, because academics are so inept with basic life skills, like pest removal, these ivory towers are magnets for pests of every imaginable stripe (including school administrators and inattentive students). For example, my office on the top floor of a five story building was built in the spot of the not-so-mythical fly graveyard. Just as elephants go to a certain spot when it's time to die, most of the flies in Michigan come to my office to meet their demise. It's not because I kill them. Quite the contrary. They enter the room, affix themselves to the ceiling, and calmly meet their maker. Most of them manage to anchor themselves securely, but sometimes their dusty cadavers fall like weightless raindrops into my coffee cup, students' hair, and other unwanted locations.

I have learned to live with flies. It's apparently part of my job to work respectfully within their cemetery. And since I have an umbrella attached to my chair and another protecting my desk, it's not such a big problem. The bats, however, are another story. I had never actually seen a bat up close and in the daylight until several of them began to fly laps around the hallway of my floor. Now I know to leave the little furry lumps alone with they attach themselves to the walls and ceiling. They're basically a live-and-let-live sort of creature (as long as you're not an edible bug), but they don't seem to like having their naptime disturbed. Thus whenever I enter the hallway, I look in both directions for the tell-tale signs of bat activity, typically screams and scurrying students. When I see them flying laps, with the characteristic quick, smooth flap of the wings, I know that I will avoid trouble by crawling down the hall to the photocopier. Only rookies and the unwary don't know that bats fly chest high in hallway races. I had always wondered why professors so often wore corduroy pants and had leather elbow patches on their tweed jackets. Now I know. It is to move down the hallway while crawling close to the ground in order to live in harmony with the bats that share our ivory towers.

I have also learned that bats don't like elevators. Perhaps they suffer from claustrophobia or something. Anyway, one of my little airborne mammalian friends joined me in the elevator one day just as the elevator doors were closing. Apparently, he took a wrong turn while flying laps in the hallway because he was not a happy camper. I dropped to the floor while he flew around in wild circles within the confined space. He began to make some disconcerting sounds that I perceived to mean, "Let me out of here." However, since my facility in the bat language is limited, I decided to lie perfectly still just in case he was really saying, "I'm so mad that I'm going to bite the next thing that moves."

At first, I didn't appreciate the bats and I wished they could be removed from building. This is apparently impossible since they can squeeze through the smallest of spaces and thus always find their way back "home." Eventually, however, I came to appreciate the bats for their deterrent effects on other annoying pests. For example, on the day after a term paper is due (the day when millions of procrastinating students rush to your office to give you five million lame excuses), I just take a pencil and poke a couple of little furry balls hanging on the wall and, lo and behold, the student traffic quickly decreases as the bats take flight for their daily exercise. They work even better with administrators. I used to be burdened with dozens of requests to serve on committees throughout the university. However, ever since a bat flew out of my briefcase when I was in the administration building for a meeting, the powers-that-be have decided that it's best to keep me isolated in certain buildings on campus. Except for those moments when I'm crawling down the hallway trying to carry both a briefcase and a coffee cup (try it at home; it ain't easy), I sometimes think that I've never had more useful friends.

*   *   *

The most pressurized aspect of academic life is the burden of "publish or perish." If you don't do research and get that research published as books and articles, you can lose your job (early in your career) or have your salary frozen (once you've written enough to get job security). The ever-present threat of these sanctions can lead to creative contortions in trying to gain credit for various forms of writing. When you look at someone's publication record, you're not always sure what you're seeing. And sometimes new professors out looking for jobs aren't sophisticated enough to put the necessary gloss on their achievements. For example, I interviewed one job candidate who was refreshingly open, but hopelessly doomed (I believed) to the unemployment line.

"I see on your publication record that you were a 'secondary contributor' to this book on the U.S. Supreme Court. How much of the book did you actually write?"

"Oh, I didn't write any of it," came the eager reply.

"Then what does it mean to be a 'secondary contributor'?"

"I just ran over to the library a lot to photocopy articles that the authors needed in order to write the book."

"That makes you a 'secondary contributor' to the book?," I asked in an incredulous voice.

"Sure. The preface to the book says, 'Secondarily, [my] contributions to the book were invaluable.' I think it's legitimate to let people know that I deserve credit for my contributions."

"What about this academic paper entitled, 'Brief Contribution to Geographic Judicial Knowledge.'"

"I'm pleased to say that I wrote that entire thing myself."

"But it says that it was only one page long? What was it about?"

"I was at this academic conference at a big hotel and this famous judge came up to me and asked if I knew where he could find the men's room. The hotel was so big that I had to draw him a map on a cocktail napkin."

"And that's it."

"Yep. I enhanced the judge's geographic knowledge and it was in writing."

"Let me ask you something. On your other interviews, has anyone ever asked you about these publications listed on your record?"

"Nope. You're the first person to ask."

"Well, I hate to ask this question, but have you ever actually written anything that was published as a book or as an article in a scholarly journal."

"No. And I don't ever expect to either. I'm just not any good at writing that sort of stuff."

"But it says here that you once taught an upper-level course called 'Writing Research Reports and Scholarly Publications.' Did you teach the course or not?"

"Yes. Yes. I taught the course. In fact, I think it's the best course I ever taught."

"But how could you teach it if you say that you can't write?"

"Easy. I've been well-trained in the philosophy of 'Those that can't do, teach.'"

"Have you gotten any job offers thus far?"

"I'm close. I'm a finalist in two places to become an instructor specializing in courses on research and writing."

"Doesn't anyone ever ask you about the details of your experience with research and writing?"

"No. They just look at my record and when they see what's listed there, they congratulate me on my fine work."

I was a little bit surprised that his approach to a teaching career was working so well. Maybe that's why I had such a hard time getting hired for my first job. I didn't think that I had written anything when, in actuality, if I had thought about it more, I probably had made notes on a cocktail napkin or something like that somewhere along the way. After the candidate left my office, I made a mental note to go to the library to check the list of salaries for all university employees. I had a feeling that salaries were much higher in the Department of Neuroscience. Although I knew nothing about the biology or chemistry of the brain, it now appeared that I had overlooked many different fields in which my lack of expertise would permit me to start an entirely new teaching career and make more money while doing it. Maybe if I just drew a picture of a really big head on a napkin, I could call it "Limited Dimensional Imagery of a Cranial Representation." That might be good enough to become a distinguished professor some place.

Chapter Eight

A Slave to the Castle

A man's home is his castle.

I always liked that expression. It conveyed a sense of ownership, dominion, and absolute control. And when I finally bought a house, I discovered how true such an expression could be. The problem was that my "castle" had ownership, dominion, and absolute control over me. Not only did it drive me to the threshold of bankruptcy, it constantly tormented me with needed repairs, usually at the most inopportune moments, both financially and personally.

*   *   *

Heading down the path toward home ownership is like a dangerous exploration or adventure. You enter unknown territory and encounter people speaking a foreign language. Mortgage. Points. Down payment. Interest deduction. Equity. Private mortgage insurance. Closing costs. These terms have no meaning to the renter. But to the aspiring homeowner, they function as the moat around the castle. Only by climbing over them successfully can one make the transition from feudal serf (i.e., renter) to king of the castle.

When I became a parent, the pressure began to build to purchase a home and cease paying rent. My aunt told me, "You really must buy a

house so that you can take advantage of the mortgage interest deduction."
I nodded my head sagely in agreement while making a mental note to
check my foreign language (i.e., financial) dictionary to find out what she
was talking about. My parents began to express concern about the
possibility that their grandchild and her future siblings would never live
in their own house. To top it off, my wife began to talk to me as if I were
the impediment to her desire to attain the American Dream of home
ownership. In reality, there were little problems, such as the down
payment and loan qualification, that kept our potential castle's moat too
deep and too broad to cross. However, there is a tendency to put a human
face on blameworthy objects of scorn, and my face was chosen to do that
job with respect to my wife's frustrations.

Eventually, we educated ourselves about the foreign language of
home ownership (although I still don't think we're fluent). We also paid
off debts, saved, prayed, and did whatever else we could to get our
financial house in order. Then we embarked upon the exciting portion
of the journey: visiting houses. When we went to visit our first house, I
intentionally left the checkbook at home because I feared (accurately)
that my wife was so excited about the possibility of buying a house that
she would want to fork over earnest money for the first house we
saw...no matter what it looked like. We didn't know anything about
calling a realtor to guide us as buyers. We just called the realtor who was
selling the house and walked through the door like a couple of rubes
wearing bull's eye clothing in the sights of an experienced marksman.
Immediately, we began to learn about all of the house's "great" features
and how these features fit our needs. For example, I learned about the
concept of the "half basement." It was described to us as a smaller
basement area that was very functional for holding the furnace, washer,
and dryer, yet also was easy to clean and keep uncluttered because of its
small size. When I went down the stairs to look at the half basement,
what I found was a small slab of concrete just big enough for the
furnace right next to the door to a cave. Literally. There was a doorway

leading to a huge dirt crawl space. I was going to ask if we were supposed to rent the space to a family of bears, but I thought I saw glowing eyes in the darkness so it seemed best not to upset the tenants by joking about their home. We had told the realtor that we wanted a house with a fourth bedroom or den to use as an office. Although this was a three-bedroom ranch house, the realtor assured us that there was a space that could be used as the fourth bedroom. When he accurately surmised that I was not amenable to calling the cave-like dirt crawl space an "office," he nimbly shifted directions and led me to the attic. After climbing a precarious ladder, not unlike one leading to the crow's nest on an old sailing ship, I found myself hunched over while standing in a sweltering space with the ceiling only four feet from the floor boards. "Here's your office," the realtor announced with a smile. While it did indeed remind me of an office because there were so many bats hanging from the ceiling, I could not really picture working in this glorified sauna for short people.

Although I had ruled out the house, my wife was eager to make an offer. Fortunately, there was no checkbook handy. Even more fortunately, I was able to convince her to look around a bit more before settling on a house. Eventually we found a four-bedroom house that in size (but not in condition) both fit our aspirations and exceeded our budget within a range that was acceptable to our lender.

I called a house inspector to take me through the house looking for defects before we reached a final agreement on the sale. He seemed to think the house was pretty good. But then again, he wasn't the one who was going to have to worry about paying for the laundry list of small, needed repairs that he was compiling. When we reached the fireplace, I asked him to show me the open and closed positions for the flue mechanism so that I wouldn't fill the house with smoke the first time I started a fire. Crouching with his head inside the fireplace, he reached up and said, "See, you just pull the handle back this way in order to get it in the open position." As he pulled the handle, he suddenly leaped backwards screaming, "Oh my gosh! Oh my gosh!"

I was startled and I immediately began to imagine that he had found a corpse or bats or something else creepy inside the chimney. "What is it? What is it?," I yelled.

"It's raccoons!," he cried. "There are five of them in the chimney right there by the fireplace."

"Well, for heaven's sake, close that thing back up!" I practically pushed him back toward the fireplace. He quickly reached inside and pushed the lever shut.

"You're going to have to get them out of there. Plus you should get a cap for the top of the chimney so they don't keep going in there."

I shook my head. One more expense to add to the list. As it turned out, loud rock music drove the raccoons from the chimney long enough for a cap to be installed. This was the first repair on my new home, but it was far from the last.

Before we could move in, I wanted to paint a few rooms. I started with the kitchen, which had three different types of wallpaper, all of which had been installed with superglue. I used a wallpaper steamer. I used chemicals. I used a knife. I used profanity. Yet nothing seemed to work very well. Many, many days and hours later, the kitchen was wallpaper-free and freshly painted. Up in the office bedroom, I faced similar problems. The teddy bear wallpaper had such powerful adhesion that I tore off pieces of the underlying wallboard in trying to remove it. Because I couldn't paint very effectively over the damaged wallboard, I decided to nail wood paneling over the wallboard instead of painting. Unfortunately, the lumber store did not have enough sheets of any particular pattern of wood paneling to permit me to panel the entire room. Instead, I bought two kinds and figured (wrongly) that no one would notice if there were two different colors, patterns, and wood grains in the wood paneling. The task of fitting the wood paneling in the room was complicated by the fact that I did not have an electric saw. Instead, I was trying to cut wood paneling to precisely measured dimensions using a hand saw. When someone says "Don't try this at home," they aren't necessarily referring to the dangerousness of a particular activity. They could be talking about avoiding unsightly, ugly home repair results. Thus I can say from experience: don't try to cut wood paneling with a hand saw. I think my wife could make the case even more forcefully. For some reason, her aesthetic sense was deeply offended by the presence of a crazy-quilt jigsaw pattern of wood paneling in one room of her house. Maybe that's why the door to that room was always kept shut. And sometimes when I was working inside the room, she would lock the door, too.

*   *   *

As a homeowner, I have an especially difficult time trying to understand my neighbors who keep their lawns in such immaculate condition. In part, this may be because I have trouble relating to grass, trees, and bushes. They're plants. I'm an animal. Why should I care if they have enough nutrients and regular haircuts? We aren't even remotely related from a species perspective. In addition, I grew up in a house in which we took a decidedly different view of lawncare; decidedly different than the neighbors anyway. Everyone else in the neighborhood would carefully fertilize, water, and otherwise tend their lawns to keep them green and gorgeous. Once each year, however, our lawn would become the center of neighborhood attention. That was always the week in which our dandelions were in full bloom. The entire lawn would be covered with those beautiful yellow flowers. It was only much later in life that someone told me that dandelions are not actually flowers. Because yellow is one of my favorite colors, I have trouble accepting the fact that some people label dandelions as "weeds." I still think they're beautiful and underappreciated. My neighbors (then and now) took a different view, especially the week following bloom time when the springtime white "snow" (i.e., dandelion seeds) covered the yard and, with each gentle breeze, spread its joy and beauty throughout the neighborhood.

After we bought a house, I succumbed to my wife's expressions of enmity toward dandelions and agreed to put a weed killer-type fertilizer on the lawn. I bought a drop spreader at Sears and assembled it myself. It wasn't too hard to assemble, although I couldn't figure out how I ended up with extra metal pieces and screws when I completed the job. I poured my bag of fertilizer into the spreader and this time, for once in my life, I even purchased the name-brand expensive stuff. I carefully read the directions on the bag about what setting to use on the drop spreader. Then I started with a long row along the lawn at the edge of my neighbor's property. I made one long pass and then came back again. When I looked at the spreader, I was shocked to discover that half of the fertilizer was gone. This was perplexing since the bag of fertilizer was supposed to cover the square footage of the entire yard and then some. It was obvious that my spreader was dropping too much fertilizer despite the care I had taken in following the directions. It occurred to me that perhaps the spreader wasn't assembled absolutely correctly (there were those extra pieces after all). It seemed more likely, however, that this was a message from fate telling me that my lawn didn't really need much fertilizer. So instead of continuing with rows moving in from my neighbor's property, I just pushed the spreader while running hurriedly around the yard in circles to hit the most noticeable dandelion patches. Thus my wife couldn't say that I didn't try to satisfy her expectations about a flower-free, I mean, weed-free lawn. I thought about buying another bag of fertilizer to finish the yard, but the stuff was too expensive and I wasn't sufficiently committed to the task. So I finished off the bag here and there in the yard and then went into the house to announce the success of the operation.

Two weeks and a couple of rainfalls later, the doorbell rang. My neighbor was standing outside with a very apologetic look on his face.

"I'm really sorry," he said. "I had some beer before I fertilized my yard last time, but I must have been drunk or something."

"What are you talking about?," I asked.

He motioned for me to come outside. Pointing to the edge of the property, he said, "Obviously, I came over the property line and poured too much fertilizer along the edge of your yard." I didn't even need to look closely to see that the two spreader strips along the edge of my property were a deep, dark green color that was far different than the color of the grass in the rest of the lawn. The grass looked tall and thick and healthy, unlike most of the rest of the yard.

"Oh, that's my fault," I reassured him. "I was trying to fertilize and something went wrong with the spreader." He looked very relieved as he returned to his house. The experience made me think that I should buy another bag of fertilizer and turn the rest of lawn into that beautiful, luscious green color.

The next day we were awakened early in the morning by the sound of people talking on our front sidewalk. When I looked out the window, I saw several people taking pictures of the lawn. Two vehicles parked in front of the house were from local television stations. I went outside to see what they were doing and I found myself mobbed, as if I were a rock star arriving in town for a concert. Microphones were thrust in my face and questions rained upon me.

"Do you know how these patterns got here?"

"What do these symbols mean?"

"Do you believe that extraterrestrials might have visited your house?"

As I stood in utter puzzlement amid the chaotic hubbub of questions and theories, I began to piece together the situation. A television station's traffic helicopter had flown over the house and noticed the intricate patterns and symbols in the yard. The local news media rushed over out of curiosity about the strange sight. Somehow or other, reporters from certain national tabloids (the kind on sale in supermarket check-out lanes) picked up the story and arrived at the same time. As I tried to explain that the patterns were meaningless and I had merely been running around the yard trying to hit pockets of dandelions before the fertilizer ran out, the local reporters looked disappointed and wandered away. The tabloid people, by contrast, stuck around to take more pictures. Sure enough, my house was featured in two national publications the following week. I wonder if I can put on my resume that I own a house that was visited by aliens. Notwithstanding the true circumstances of the lawn, who's to say it has never happened. In fact, those tabloid people seemed pretty alien to me.

*   *   *

When I moved to a new house, I felt greater pressure to pay attention to my lawn. Most of the people in the neighborhood hired lawncare professionals to spray and cut the grass. Everyone else seemed to make lawn maintenance a personal priority. I was initially happy to have the best crop of dandelions for miles around, but when my wife joined the board of the neighborhood association, I was forced to conform. Recalling my fertilizer experience at the old house, I bought an extra bag and covered the entire lawn. In some spots, I couldn't really see how much fertilizer had fallen onto the grass, so I went back and added extra. The lawn at my old house had turned out so green and beautiful (in certain spots and patterns anyway) from the extra fertilizer that I envisioned my new super-fertilized lawn becoming the envy of the neighborhood.

This time no one needed to come to the door to tell me what had happened to the lawn. I could look out the window and see that the entire lawn turned a dry, yellowish-white color. I killed nearly every blade of grass out there. There were just a few hardy patches of turf that had survived my nuclear-esque chemical onslaught. Not only that, but weeds started to move in. Not beautiful weeds, like dandelions, but all kinds of thick, gnarly plants that spread across the yard like little anchored serpents. Frankly, it was quite embarrassing. I took personal pride in dandelions, despite others' looks of disapproval, because I had a long-standing personal relationship with and appreciation for dandelions. Now I was presiding over a very visible and obvious moment of plant genocide. My wife suggested that it was time to turn to professionals for help. But I refused to admit that I can't handle a lawn. It's just a patch of grass, isn't it? This isn't rocket science (unless, of course, there really are extraterrestrials involved).

I headed for the garden store and checked out my options for planting various kinds of grass seeds. I opted for the kind labeled "Fast-growing." I needed to alleviate the visible embarrassment as quickly as possible. I also purchased (at fairly significant expense) quite a few bags of high-quality topsoil. I didn't trust the quality of the soil in the yard, especially after it had been doused with deadly chemicals. Then I went home and worked the yard with a hoe, inch by inch removing dead sod and replacing it with new topsoil and grass seed. The results were miraculous. Initially anyway. The grass grew very quickly and the image of the dead grass disappeared from my mind (and hopefully from my neighbors' minds, too). However, the grass kept growing and growing. Moreover, it was (when fully thickened) a hideous bright, light green color. It almost looked like fluorescent green. When contrasted with the surviving patches of normal sod, the new grass looked bizarre. It looked even more bizarre when compared to the color of other people's lawns. To top it off, the grass grew so fast that I had to cut it every three days. Even when it didn't rain at all, the grass kept growing and growing. If I let it go for a week, it looked as if we lived in an abandoned house. When I called to order a pizza, the delivery person would just say, "Oh yeah, you're the ones with that strange green lawn." Yep, that's us. We don't need our house number on the mailbox anymore. We could just put the letters "STRANGE GREEN LAWN" on the side of the mailbox and our mail would still get to us.

In an effort to regain some control over my life (or at least seize a few hours of autonomy back from my slavemaster lawn), I suggested to my wife that the front of our house would look truly lovely if it were covered with woodchips and scenic plants (i.e., no grass). I know that she really doesn't want the lawn-free look, but she is starting to face the music about my green thumb (or rather lack thereof). Thus far, I managed to convince her to let me remove the sod in one experimental section and I am fairly confident that one more season with a crop of dandelions and strange fluorescent grass will push her over the edge. Come by in a couple of years and we'll have a maintenance-free pine forest in front of the house. I'm looking forward to it. And so are the neighbors.

*   *   *

The longer you own a house, the bolder you become in undertaking repair projects. One day I decided to replace a truly ugly faucet. I went to the hardware store and bought an attractive install-it-yourself faucet. The package said "easy as 1-2-3." I read the directions carefully, saw that it required only a couple of tools and a few simple steps, and proceeded with confidence in the thought that the job could be completed quickly. Step one said, "Remove old faucet." Well, it turns out that this is the hardest step of all. That faucet had been there since George Washington's presidency and by George it had no intention of leaving its home. I spent hours under the sink tugging at pipes, running to the hardware store to purchase specialized tools, and then tugging unsuccessfully at the pipes once again. It turns out that the old faucet isn't so bad. I decided that I really like it after all; at least that's what I told my wife when she inquired about why I stopped installing the new faucet.

I did learn something from this episode. The next time I was tempted to remove a faucet (this time because of a problem with dripping), I bought a new faucet, gathered all the tools, looked closely at the pipes under the sink, and then…called a plumber. The thought occurred to me, "What if I succeed in removing the pipes and the faucet, but then something goes wrong and the entire house fills with water? Then what would I do?" It suddenly seemed wiser to call a bonded professional whom I could sue if something went wrong.

My proudest moment as a homeowner came when I replaced a sump pump. For those of you who have never experienced the joy of sump pump ownership, this device sits in a hole in the basement floor and automatically pumps out any water that accumulates in or under the basement. When a sump pump ceases to function, water under the house may start to seep through any cracks in the floor. The first time I saw a small spot of water by a crack in the basement floor, I feared that my entire plumbing system was having problems and that it would cost thousands of dollars to bring in a jackhammer to tear apart the basement to find the problem. When I called the plumber, he charged me seventy-five dollars to walk into the basement and shake the pipe connected to the sump pump. When he shook the pipe, the pump came to life and pumped all of the water away. From then on, I shook that pipe every day. Unfortunately, one day the pump refused to kick on, even with vigorous pipe shaking, so I was forced to conclude that the pump had died.

I went to hardware store to look at sump pumps but, as usual, I was reluctant to ask questions because I hated to reveal the depth of my ignorance. When a store employee began chatting with me about sump pumps, it turned out that he was a virtual "Professor of Sumpology." This guy knew everything. Within minutes, I was purchasing the right pipes, valves, and other pieces-parts that are necessary for proper sump pump installation. Before I knew it, I was up to my elbows in rusty, cold sump water in the pump's basement hole. As I worked to remove the old pump and then put in the new pump, as well as new pipes, the water level in the pump hole kept rising and rising. Just as the water level approached the top, I got my entire contraption together and working. It was one of the proudest moments of my life. My report on this accomplishment was not particularly well received in my Harvard class reunion report, but I actually believe it is a more impressive accomplishment than winning election to Congress or becoming a federal judge or that other stuff that my classmates are always bragging about. I did this with my own two hands and there wasn't one campaign contribution involved.

∗   ∗   ∗

Home ownership is a volatile element when combined with marriage. It becomes a constant source of debate and discussion. Which project should be done next? Can we do it ourselves or do we need to call a professional? How much money should we sink into the house? Should we try to buy a better house? I was led to believe that my wife would be happy just by the mere fact of finally owning a house. After all, this is the woman who was eager to make an offer on a house with a cave for a basement and a sauna-like attic office. It turns out that gaining ground on her goals for her house just makes her want even more. This became especially true when some millionaire built an $800,000 house in view of our kitchen window. Now my wife must look out across the backyard every day and see all of the amenities that are beyond her reach. She knows that she can't have an $800,000 house (or even a $200,000 house). To compensate for that disappointment, she has specific plans for how we will renovate and improve each room of the house "when we have some money."

Because I don't want to enhance her disappointment by pointing out that we might never have "some money," I look for inexpensive ways to improve those parts of the house that she finds most objectionable. For example, she really wants a finished basement. One day I surprised her by building a wall in the basement that achieves two of her primary goals. First, it separates the basement into an area for the washer and dryer and an area for the ping pong table and the kids' toys. Second, it prevents people on the staircase or in the toy room from being directly confronted with a view of our mountain of dirty laundry. I used the Berlin Wall as my model in the sense that my wall was also erected virtually overnight and without warning. Rube Goldberg would be proud of the mosaic pattern of crisscrossing two-by-fours that provides the framework for the wall.

If a professional builder looked closely, he or she might be disheartened or even critical about the use of old shoelaces to attach the wall to the vertical columns under the house's support beam. I really don't care, however. Because of the importance of basketball in my life, I am more aware than most people that shoelaces are a multi-functional building material that is unsurpassed in strength and durability. Well, okay, they break sometimes. But I'm sure they can hold up a wall. Can't they? I mean, if you think about a man's home being his castle and then you picture the real castles in Europe, what do you see? You see widespread deterioration. You see walls falling down. You see crumbling towers and piles of collapsing bricks. Now think about the differences in building materials between then and now. They had bricks and mortar. They had wood. They had shingles of various sorts. But the one thing that they didn't have was…yes, you guessed it, shoelaces. Look at the feet of any suit of armor from those old castle days. There is absolutely no evidence that shoelaces had been invented yet. Thus when I want the improvements and repairs on my home to endure in the way that a castle was meant to endure, I put my faith in modern developments. The shoelace: a building material for the ages.

Chapter Nine

The Birds and the Bees

Wow, the world has really changed.

When I was a kid, you never heard anything about sex on the radio and you never saw anything about sex on television. Remember the old *Dick Van Dyke Show* on television? The married couple, Rob and Laura, wore long pajamas and slept in separate single beds. There were no references to sex, not even any innuendo. In the old days, the most interesting thing about lunchtime was spelling out words in your Alphabet Soup. Now soap operas give you midday simulated sex between unmarried couples, wriggling and writhing between satin sheets. No wonder kids today can't spell.

At least with television you can turn the channel to get away from the bombardment of sexual imagery. It's much tougher today with the radio. You're driving down the street with your kids in the car just listening to the music, and suddenly a commercial comes on. A chorus of deep male voices singing jauntily, "TROJAN MAN. TROJAN MAN. TROJAN MAN." The first time I heard it, I didn't initially realize that it was a commercial for condoms. Some of the scripts are actually somewhat amusing…if the kids aren't in the car. The AIDS crisis of today has made us all aware of the connection between sex and death, but nobody seems to realize that sex may be a major cause of automobile accidents, too. I know this first-hand since I practically swerve off the road leaping for the tuner button to change channels before one of my kids asks me what the "Trojan Man" commercial is about.

*   *   *

Once upon a time, like other adolescents, I had great curiosity about sex. I did not lack for information, but it seemed pretty clear that the technical descriptions and diagrams contained in sex education classes and health education books did not capture the essence of sex. There wasn't very much that was attractive about cut-away anatomical drawings of internal tubes and organs. Looking at those diagrams, I found myself repelled rather than attracted to something (and I wasn't really sure what it was yet) that seemed to fascinate so many other people. There must be more to it. Where was the intrigue and excitement, or whatever the elements of sex were that drove discussions about the subject into secretive, whispered conversations at the back of the classroom?

I stumbled upon that "something" about sex in *The Summer of '42*. No I wasn't born yet in 1942. My discovery came in the book, which later became a movie, about a teenage boy whose humorous struggles with sexuality at the dawn of manhood and in a moment of international upheaval and tragedy ultimately culminate in a poignant, momentary encounter with a young war widow. I know that the poignancy and meaning were lost on me because I was preoccupied with emulating the protagonist's successful expedition toward sexual discovery.

I decided that I needed to be ready for my Summer of '42 in case it happened to come along. From my sex education class and health education books I had learned enough to know that being truly prepared for my Summer of '42 meant one thing: obtaining some condoms. I didn't really know where to get any. You certainly never saw them in stores back then. On the other hand, however, I didn't really know what they looked like. I had a description from *The Summer of*

'42 in which the teenager goes into a drug store and asks for them, telling the store owner that he wants to use them as water balloons. However, I couldn't imagine myself walking into a store to ask somebody for them. I didn't have the nerve. Besides, what if they didn't have any. Then I'd look pretty foolish. What alternative item does one purchase if the druggist says that they don't have any condoms? There must be some alternative item, but I wasn't certain what it was and I didn't want to reveal my ignorance by saying, "Well, if you don't have any condoms, then I guess I'll just take the big tube of 'Preparation H' instead." I didn't know what Preparation H was for, but since hemorrhoids seemed to be another "adult" subject, spoken about in whispered, secretive conversations, I figured that had to be about sex, too. But I wasn't quite so confident about my knowledge, since I had never seen any technical drawings on the subject in sex education classes or health books.

In pondering my problem, I noticed a small advertisement in the back of a magazine: "Adult products by mail. Very discrete. Mailed to you in a plain brown wrapper." This was surely a sign from Venus or Cupid or some other god of love that my Summer of '42 might be on the horizon. I sent in my order for condoms. Probably the first order they ever received which was paid for by an envelope full of wrinkled dollar bills and a jangle of quarters, dimes, and nickels.

Then I waited. Every day I checked the mail for that plain brown package addressed to "Chris Smith." Everything was falling into place. I even planned how to respond to my parents' question: "What was in that package addressed to you today?"

"Oh, it's just a science kit that I ordered from the Boy Scout magazine." Sounded perfectly plausible. Perfect. Ingenious. I had anticipated everything. Or so I thought.

It turned out that the adult products company was extraordinarily dedicated to the idea of protecting its customers' privacy. When these people said in their ad that they were "Very discrete," they meant that they were "Very, very, very discrete." Mailed to you in a plain brown wrapper. Obviously *very* discrete. And to protect the customer even more, the return address was just a post office box number in New York City with no company name. Of course. Who would ever suspect what was in the package?

In planning their business, they obviously asked themselves, "What else can we do to protect our customers by being very, very discrete?" Well, it turns out that they came up with one more thing: they only used your first initial in the mailing address. Very, very discrete. "TO: C. Smith." It was almost like writing "Our Valued Customer" in invisible ink right next to the name.

There was only one problem: my mother's name is Carolyn.

What do you do when they mail your box of condoms to your mother?

I would like to see some of the genius contestants on *Jeopardy* tackle this question. I'm not sure there is any easy answer. As a teenage boy, the most promising solution appeared to be scraping together my remaining wrinkled dollars and jangle of quarters, dimes, and nickels to see if I could afford a one-way bus ticket to Montana or at least to the other side town or anywhere other than my house.

I was upstairs in my room when I heard a loud voice from downstairs, "What are these? Condoms? What is this? Whose are these?"

I thought I heard my name called. I still don't know if she actually called for me, but my guilt-ridden mind and racing heart certainly put her voice in my head, ordering me downstairs toward the living room. I actually went down the stairs pretty quickly, although something about my thumping heartbeat made it feel as if I was hitting each step in slow motion. Thump. Thump. Thump. Every footstep seemed to echo a bit as it hit each stair step. There's a picture in my head of feeling like a death-row inmate going down the corridor toward the moment of reckoning.

With each step down the stairs and across the living room toward my waiting, bewildered, and (need I say) upset parents, my brain sifted at turbo-speed through a variety of possible strategies. I had always been blessed with a quick mind, yet when it moved ahead of me at warp speed, it was tough to keep up.

As it turns out, there are a number of useful things that you can say when they mail your condoms to your mother. And I feel lucky for having been able to figure out what they are.

"What are those things, Mom? I've never seen anything like that before."

"Condoms. Oh wow. How did you get yourself on that mailing list, Mom?"

"A sampler pack? And I would have thought that by this time you would know exactly which style and color are best for you."

Unfortunately, these witty gems came to me more than twenty years too late. I feel as if I'm lucky to know what to say in this particular situation, because now I can help other people if they ever find themselves in this predicament. As a teenager standing in that living room, however, my brain was like the Starship Enterprise as it disappeared from the screen at warp speed and even Mr. Sulu couldn't bring it back to me. Thus, at the dawn of manhood, I was forced by circumstances to confront an adult situation by summoning my accumulated years of maturity and committing myself to respond in a calm, straightforward manner. A key moment had arrived in my transition from adolescence to that next stage in life.

When I was asked point-blank, "What do you know about this package of condoms?," I responded reflexively and without hesitation.

"They're for David."

I thereby defused the unwanted conflict and attention by placing the blame on my older brother who was 100 miles away in college, living in a dormitory, and seemingly unreachable by telephone at all hours of the day and night. He was utterly incapable of defending himself or refuting my response.

Eyeball to eyeball with adulthood, I blinked. But hey, sex does funny things to people, especially confused adolescents. At the time, it was as if a nuclear bomb had been dropped on me, yet through great luck, it had failed to detonate. Everything worked out fairly well except that my mother had my condoms and I still wasn't ready for my Summer of '42. Of course, this seemed like a sign that my Summer of '42 was nowhere to be seen on the horizon.

*   *   *

At the time I was in high school, the civil rights movement had pushed the country toward significant changes in people's thoughts and actions about race relations. My generation of students participated in these changes as we rode buses to desegregated schools and interacted with unfamiliar classmates from neighborhoods other than our own. In this atmosphere, at least a few people found their adolescent curiosity about sex mixing with their new experiences and curiosity about people from other races. You could see this curiosity going in both directions. White students were curious about African-Americans and African-American classmates were curious about whites. Interracial dating, however, was not universally approved, in part, no doubt, because of parental fears about interracial sex.

One of my African-American teammates approached me at the conclusion of basketball practice one day. As we walked to the locker room, he said, "I need for you to do me a really big favor."

"Sure, man. What do you need?"

He eyed me carefully, apparently to detect any sign of a negative reaction, as he said cautiously, "Well, there's this white girl that I want to go out with."

"Oh yeah? Who is she? Do you want me to introduce you?"

My helpful and enthusiastic response made him relax as he continued speaking, now more excitedly. "Oh no. We're all set up. It's Susie Johnson. I know she likes me and she wants to go out with me."

I was puzzled. "So why do you need my help?"

"She wants to go out with me, but her parents won't let her go out with any black guys. So I want you to pretend to be her date. Pick her up at her house and then take her home later. How about it?"

"Sure. No problem." My chest puffed up proudly. I was about to become a soldier in the continuing battle for racial equality. My contribution to the cause was going to be modest. My biggest challenge would be finding some clean pants and a not-too-wrinkled shirt for Saturday night. It was not exactly like facing down fire hoses and police dogs on a civil rights march, but it still seemed as if I was going to make my contribution to social progress.

When I arrived at the Johnson house at the appointed hour to pick up Susie, I knew my face was flushed with guilt. I'm really a terrible liar. What if they ask me questions about where we're going? What if my story doesn't match what Susie already told her parents? What if she felt guilty about lying and already told them about this little deception? What if…?

Fortunately, Susie met me at the door and yelled back over her shoulder, "See you later, Mom?"

I heard a voice call from another room, "Have a good time, dear, and don't stay out too late."

I took Susie to her rendezvous and then went home to watch TV. A rather typical Saturday night for me. The evening became less typical later when I heard the car horn honking in my driveway to let me know that I needed to deliver Susie home again.

Over the ensuing weeks, the curious couple quickly became the kissing couple. I know because they kept kissing in front of me whenever I was supposed to take Susie home. One time my friend even went with me to take her home. This made me very nervous. What if her parents suspected something? Fortunately, Susie and her beau had done a good job at school of pretending that they didn't even know each other so no one even suspected.

As it happened, my own social life was picking up. I finally got up the nerve to ask out Jane, a girl who was obviously giving me the eye in math class. For our first date, we were going to the movies. Unfortunately, 1 also had to pick up Susie for my friend that night. However, I had it all planned out. I could pick up Susie, deliver her to the rendezvous, and then pick up my date to go to the movies. All I had to do was get my date home before I had to bring Susie back to her house. Everything looked good on paper, but that should have been my first clue that disaster lurked ahead.

I picked up Susie as usual. I had even become accustomed to chatting with her parents while waiting for her to get her coat. This made me feel a bit guilty about the deception, but I reminded myself that my efforts were a necessary part of my contribution to social progress and racial equality. After I delivered Susie, I picked up Jane and headed for the movie theater. I had carefully selected a film that would give me time afterward to take Jane out for ice cream or something and still get Susie home on time. Moreover, this movie, *Bang the Drum Slowly* was the tragic story of a terminally ill baseball player and his remarkable friendship with another player. Sort of a *Brian's Song* with curve balls and homeruns. The touching story on the screen was supposed to produce off screen results. At least in the script I kept rewriting in my head. The emotional tragedy pushes your date closer against you. As you dry her tears and reassure her, you get your first kiss. Well, I didn't know for sure if that would be part of the night's script, but I was hopeful.

As we waited in the ticket line, I noticed the back of a familiar head farther up in the line. Oh my gosh! It was Susie's father. Susie's parents had come to this movie and they thought I was out somewhere on a date with their daughter. Jane was standing next to me, leaning against my arm and resting her head on my shoulder. Meanwhile, my body was frozen in a total state of panic.

"You know what, Jane. I don't really want to see this movie. Why don't we go get some ice cream and then come back in an hour when the other movie is going to start."

"But I really wanted to see *Bang the Drum Slowly*. I love movies that touch my emotions and make me cry." She looked very disappointed.

My eyes were still fixed on the back of that familiar head as I tried to pull Jane out of line. "Well, I'm sorry about that but I don't really like, um,…baseball movies. They chew tobacco and scratch themselves and it's always so slow moving."

"So what's the other movie?," she asked, trying to look above the other people to see the movie name on the marquee while I pulled her backward through the crowd.

I found myself looking up, too, trying to see the name of the other movie. I was so intent on seeing *Bang the Drum Slowly* that I hadn't paid close attention to the other offering. "It's really supposed to be a great film. I read some reviews that said it was an artistic triumph."

"So what is it?" she asked with annoyance, as I started pulling her around the corner.

I glanced quickly back and tried to reply nonchalantly, "Oh, it's called *Invasion of the Blood Farmers*." [Note: Really! Look it up in a video guidebook.]

"What?!" She looked at me with uncomprehending shock.

It took an entire hour of talking over ice cream sundaes for me to make progress in having her look at me as if I were a normal human being again. At the end of the hour, however, she decided that she would rather go home than see a movie about Druid vampires or whatever, notwithstanding my reassurances that this was an Oscar-caliber film (or so I hoped, as I had told her). Suffice to say, my first kiss did not materialize on her doorstep.

After I took Susie home that night, I wrestled with the difficulty of becoming someone else's permanent chauffeur and thereby limiting the opportunities for my own social life to develop. I decided to tell

Susie and my friend that we could not keep going on this way. They would have to find some other way to maintain their relationship without my help. My dedication to advancing social progress had to give way to my desire to kiss a girl or whatever else might happen in that regard.

The next day at school, my friend grabbed me in the hallway and pulled me into an empty room with a worried look on his face.

"What's the matter?" I asked.

"A problem has come up."

"What kind of problem?" I was really curious since I hadn't even told him yet that I was dropping out of the date scam scheme.

"Susie's parents just found her birth control pills."

My eyes widened in shock. Had they been doing *that*? I responded spontaneously, "Oh man, what are you going to do?"

He gave me an odd look. "Don't worry about me. What are YOU going to do? Susie's dad wants to talk to you about what he thinks you're doing with his daughter."

Then it hit me. They think I'm her boyfriend. Oh no. What else could go wrong?

As I walked down the hallway in a daze, I found out what else could go wrong. Jane came marching up to me and yelled (in a voice that could be heard by everyone within the two neighboring counties) "How dare you ask me out when you're going steady with Susie Johnson? Her mother mentioned you to my mother. How could you even think that you could use me in your two-timing scheme?" She didn't slap me in the face, but she might as well have. My cheeks weren't merely burning; my reputation and entire being felt singed.

I knew I wouldn't be going back to Johnson's house again and I prayed that her parents would not call my house. However, when I arrived home after school, my mother was waiting for me.

"Do you know a Susie Johnson from school?"

My heart sank and I looked at the ground as a soft "yes" escaped from my lips. Why did they have to call my parents? This was big trouble.

"Well, I need for you to run this over to her house right now. These are the publicity flyers for the PTA meeting next week."

"Did Mrs. Johnson call you or something?" I tried to mask the trepidation in my voice.

"No. I talked to her last week. We're on the same committee and I promised her that I would the send the flyers as soon as they came back from the printer."

"Couldn't I just give them to Susie at school?" I held my breath and waited for my mother's reply.

"No. She needs them today."

"I'm kinda busy. You know, lots of homework. I don't think I'll be able to go."

"Listen. I'm very busy. I need you to go, and I need you to go right now. I told her that you would be there this afternoon. So please go now!"

I knew that any further delay would simply arouse my own mother's suspicions. So it seemed best to just face the music from Susie's parents and feel grateful that they had not dragged my parents into this mess. I grabbed the flyers from my mother's hand and jumped into the car. As drove, I gripped the steering wheel tightly and attempted to fend off the suffocating feeling of impending doom.

I walked up the Johnson's front sidewalk like a man headed for the gallows, sweating profusely, and having no idea what I would say. In a few moments, I would be helping to pick out china patterns with both barrels of a shotgun pressed against my neck. Before I could ring the bell, Susie opened the door.

"I'll take the flyers for my Mom," she said. "Thanks for bringing them over."

She seemed completely, well, normal. As if she didn't have a care in the world.

"Um, what about the…well, I heard that there was a situation with your parents and that, you know, they think that I, well, you and me…" I stammered slowly, trying to understand her calm expression.

"Oh, you mean the pills?" She laughed. "That's not a problem. I just told my parents that they belong to my sister Sarah. They believed me." Like my brother, her sister was away at college residing one hundred miles away, living in a dormitory, and virtually unreachable by telephone at any hour of the day or night. Utterly unavailable and incapable of refuting this story. I guess I wasn't the only one who found it convenient to have an absentee sibling with whom to "share" blame.

As I turned to walk back to the car, Susie called me. "Have you talked to your brother lately?" she asked.

"No, actually. I haven't talked to him for a few weeks."

"Well, guess what? Sarah told me that she's dating your brother David. How about that? What a small world?"

I nodded my head in surprise.

She was quick to continue. "One more thing, though. You better warn David to try to avoid my parents until this business about the birth control pills blows over. See ya." And with that cheery farewell, she shut the door.

Warn David about Susie's parents and the birth control pills? He was still bewildered about why Mom kept lecturing him about condoms. I never told him either story.

*   *   *

When I got enough nerve to make another attempt to prepare for my Summer of '42, I scouted around for a drug store that wasn't normally too crowded. I paced back and forth on the sidewalk waiting for a moment when there were no customers in the store. When the moment came, I rushed into the store and then moved nonchalantly up and down a few aisles looking for condoms. I didn't see any boxes that looked like those in the plain package sent to my mother. Since no one was around, I decided to ask the clerk behind the counter.

"Excuse me, ma'am."

She busily moved around behind the counter, utterly oblivious to my presence.

"EXCUSE ME, MA'AM."

"What do you want?"

"Well, I was looking for something and I, well, I couldn't find it."

"What is it?" She looked busy and impatient.

"Well, I was looking for condoms." Even as I said the word "condoms," I knew I was mumbling.

"What did you say?"

"I said I was looking for some condoms."

She looked utterly bewildered, as if I was speaking Ukrainian or something.

I repeated myself, "I'm looking for some CONDOMS."

"Some what?"

"You know, CONDOMS!"

Unfortunately, I had failed to notice that people were coming into the store during my exchange with the clerk. In fact, since it was Senior Discount Day on Wednesday, a van full of seniors from a nearby retirement home had arrived at the store in a group. As I practically yelled the word "CONDOMS!," I noticed a couple of gray-haired ladies standing nearby. Their heads snapped in my direction as I said the word.

"What do you mean?" said the confused clerk.

Now I was stuck. Do I just say "forget it" and all but confess my embarrassment, or do I persist and achieve my objective?

"Ahhh." I cleared my throat and searched for something else to say. "I'm looking for birth control devices. You know prophylactic devices. You know...." My voice trailed off as I noticed everyone in the store staring at me and listening to my every word. Somehow I had managed to recreate an entire scene from *The Summer of '42*; the scene where the kid ordered ice cream and everything else under the sun in a comic effort to buy condoms without attracting too much attention. Now I managed to attract everyone's attention but the clerk still seemed not to know what I was talking about.

I was completely stuck, staring helplessly into the face of the perplexed clerk while feeling many sets of eyes boring into my back and multiple ears straining for the next installment of this bizarre conversation. Then one of the gray-haired ladies standing next to me said matter-of-factly to the clerk, "The kid wants some rubbers, honey."

"Oh." The proverbial lightbulb obviously went on above the clerk's head. Now she nodded with the look of recognition. But then she threw me off balance by asking, "What kind do you want?"

I knew from my prior experience in attempting to order condoms that they came in different colors. However, she didn't seem to be asking about colors. She was asking about "kinds." Thinking quickly and logically, I made a confident reply: "I want adult size medium."

The senior citizens in the store burst out laughing. If the floor had opened up to swallow me at that moment, I would have happily disappeared into oblivion. Obviously I said something very funny and very wrong.

Some old guy behind me said, with a laugh, "Always ask for extra large, sonny. Don't give away any of your secrets." He walked away from the counter still laughing and saying audibly to himself, "medium, ha ha ha, medium. I can't believe it."

"Don't mind him," said the elderly lady next to me. "Just get the red box."

"Not the red box, Hazel," said another lady. "I think the ones in the green box are better."

"Are you thinking of yourself or are you thinking about this young man?" said yet another grandmotherly lady.

"I'm talking about him. What do you think?," came the irritated response.

"Don't get mad at me," said her critic. "I'm just trying to help."

A debate seemed to be erupting around me, so I just shouted out "I'll take the red box." Then I put ten dollars down on the counter and ran out the door. The last thing I heard as I headed out the door was one of my elderly advisors calling after me, "You should have gotten the green box. Get the green box next time."

When I got home, after finally having obtained the elusive objects, I was curious about how they worked. This was at a time before AIDS education. This was at a time when sex education was comprised of confusing anatomical drawings. This was at a time when, well, I'm not sure how people learned to use condoms correctly.

I tore open one small plastic package. Suddenly my fingers were covered with slime or oil or something. The small rubber object squirted right through my fingers and onto the floor. I had no idea what I was getting into by purchasing the lubricated kind. But I was quickly getting the idea that maybe I should have bought the green box.

Over and over I tried to pick up the small rubber object, and it kept jumping out of my slippery hands and scooting across the floor. It was exactly like trying to scoop up a goldfish that had leaped out of your hands while being transferred between tanks. I chased the condom around the floor for a few minutes before trapping it under my hand. It squirmed as if still alive, but it stopped wriggling when I pressed it to the floor. When I pulled my hands away slowly, ready to grab it before it could jump away again, I noticed that it was matted with cat hair and lint. This wasn't going to work.

I washed my hands (again and again and again) but I couldn't get the lubricant off my fingers. Shrugging my shoulders, I resigned myself to a acquiring a new nickname, probably "Butterfingers." I also resigned myself to leaving those slippery fish condoms alone, unless and until I actually needed one.

*   *   *

Then it finally happened. I had my Summer of '42. Okay, so it seemed as if I was nearly 42 years old, but hey, I got there eventually. Arriving at this point (finally) helped to answer many questions that had bedeviled me throughout the years of my obsessive curiosity about sex. For example, I always wondered if men automatically became aroused at the sight of, um,…an undressed woman. If so, it would seem to make married life awkward since presumably the marriage partners get dressed and undressed perpetually in each other's presence. Do they always close their eyes in the morning so that everyone can get to work on time without taking a time out for, um,…whatever arousal may lead to?

Fortunately my Summer of '42 answered that question for me because I got married. The marriage perspective helped me to see how men can view undressed women and not react at all. As a husband, I could see quite clearly all of the daily elements and rituals that suppressed arousal: the scarf on the head at bedtime to hold the hairdo in place while sleeping; the mudpack on the face to keep aging skin pores open and youthful; elastic waistbands to hold a bulging belly in place; hours spent teasing wisps and curls of uncooperative hair; perpetual self-centered preoccupation with detecting gray hairs on the aging head; ragged underwear long overdue for replacement. The list can go on and on, but hey, I spend so much time doing this stuff, that I hardly have a chance to notice when my wife is undressed.

*   *   *

In light of my trials and tribulations in sorting out sex, I am challenged to think about how to teach my children about the subject. Television and radio are no help. The subject comes up again and again in various ways, no matter how quickly I try to change the channel.

Driving down the road once again, only half-listening to the radio, the familiar refrain fills the air, "TROJAN MAN. TROJAN MAN.

TROJAN MAN." Unfortunately, I am just a moment too slow in reacting by changing channels.

"Hey, Dad," says my six-year-old son, "What was that song?"

"What song?" I ask innocently. And before he can answer, I try to change the subject. "Look at those cows over there in that field."

Unfortunately, my son is not easily distracted. "But Dad, what was that song?"

"Song? What song are you talking about?"

"The song on the radio."

"Oh, I think this is an old song by Frank Sinatra."

"Not *this* song, Dad. The one that was on before you switched stations."

"What song are you talking about?"

"You know, that song that's on the radio all the time. It goes 'TROJAN MAN. TROJAN MAN. TROJAN MAN.'"

I cringe as he sings the song, imitating perfectly the timing and tone of the commercial jingle. I think very quickly and try to cut off his singing. "Oh, *that* song. Ummm,…that's the fight song for the University of Southern California. They're called the USC Trojans. Named after ancient warriors from a Greek city, just like Michigan State University has the MSU Spartans. Different Greek city, but same warrior idea."

"Oh," says the precocious lad.

I give myself a silent pat on the back for handling the situation so deftly. I have only a moment to congratulate myself before his curiosity is revived.

"So Dad, do the USC Trojans have a mascot?"

"You mean a dressed up character who leads cheers at the football games?"

"Yeah. You know how some teams on TV have people dressed up like Tigers or other animals. I just wondered how a Trojan mascot would dress up."

The boy is so bright and observant, I thought to myself, he really makes me proud. "Well, as a matter of fact, the Trojan mascot rides around inside the stadium on a horse and waves a sword at the crowd."

"Oh." The boy is obviously thinking, probably visualizing the Trojan warrior on the horse, since at this stage of life his imagination and hours of play are filled with warriors, knights, pirates, and other combatants.

After a moment of silence, the high pitch of my son's six-year-old voice interrupts my train of thought. "There's still something that I don't understand, Dad?"

"What is that, son?"

"How can a guy dressed up as a giant condom ride a horse and wave a sword?"

Wow, the world has really changed.

About the Author

Christopher E. Smith, a professor at Michigan State University, is the author of sixteen books.

9100897R0

Made in the USA
Lexington, KY
28 March 2011